MW01234490

THE BLOW-UP

THE BLOW-UP

JAMES BARRY

BRASH
BOOKS

Paperback ISBN-13: 978-1-954841-33-8

Published by
Brash Books, LLC
PO Box 8212
Calabasas, CA 91372
www.brash-books.com

To Norma, one of the earliest fans of this book.

Lawyers are like priests; people come to them and disburden themselves of their troubles, and get consolation, if they pay well for it; but there is one point in which they don't treat them like priests; they don't confess all their sins.

—Thomas Chandler Haliburton

PART ONE

CHAPTER ONE

This is a hate story.

The kind of hate born of unconscionable betrayal. A hate that burns, and in burning, consumes. That immolates that monthslong soul-ache that had you entertaining fleeting thoughts of ending it. The kind of hate that fuels more hate, replicating itself like runaway cancer cells.

This is a hate story.

Which is to say, a love story gone sideways.

My husband of fifteen mostly happy years died in a house explosion. Naked. Next to a woman who was also naked. Two naked bodies. Even with the force of the gas explosion, which hurled bits and pieces of the woman's right-side-of–Montauk Highway, a short-walk-to-the-beach, twenty-thousand-foot-Peter Cook–designed Hamptons mansion hundreds of yards away—a seismic blast that might be expected to strip clothing from body, leaving it like those naked silhouettes they found plastered to walls in Hiroshima—they were able to determine there wasn't any clothing.

They were naked when the house blew up.

Naked when the EMTs and local police and bomb squad unit picked through the rubble and found them.

My husband and her.

Emma.

I was at the law office at the time. I was preparing a criminal defense case with an irrefutably guilty client who'd embezzled a lot of money. *Hey, it's not like I murdered someone*, you say in an argument about nothing. The kind of argument I used to have with my husband about forgetting to cover the lawn furniture before a looming thunderstorm, back before he died naked in a gas explosion next to a naked woman who also died.

My client was guilty of embezzling more than eight million dollars, but it's not like he'd murdered someone.

Having represented murderers before, this felt less morally reprehensible. I've never been able to reduce criminal defense to a sporting event where the only thing that matters is winning. I can recite verbatim the mantra that *Everyone is entitled to the best defense and it's up to the jury to decide.* I even believe it on occasion. I just can't shake my Catholic girlhood, during which I was spoon-fed guilt instead of oatmeal. I grew up on guilt. It's ingrained in me.

I was preparing this client for cross. Jefrey—with one *f*, he made sure to let me know when he'd first introduced himself. I'd been tempted to ask him if the other *f* had been misplaced, but refrained.

Murderers you don't put on the stand. Embezzlers you do. Especially if they look relatively sympathetic and have a good story. If they can make even one person on the jury believe they were going to pay it back. That it was a loan, really. Not officially, of course, but the *intention* was to pay it back. Absolutely. And the money was simply to get out of the hole so his family, two kids and a wife, wasn't thrown out of their home, a six-bedroom Amagansett monstrosity complete with gunite pool and Har-Tru tennis court he'd help *purchase* with that embezzled money—but that part would be left out. It was the getting-thrown-out-of-their-home part of the story that might engender sympathy. Two kids—eight and eleven—out on the street. My client had done it for them—taken that officially unofficial loan.

"You doctored the company books. Yes or no?" I was playing the prosecutor. I enjoyed playing the prosecutor with guilty clients because it nourished my own guilt. Paid proper homage to it. As if I was speaking with the same voice that used to demand a litany of my most recent sins from the other side of the latticed confessional screen. *I spoke back to my mother, Father. I cheated on a test, Father.* When I played the prosecutor, I was the prosecutor. For those two or three hours, I was.

"I was going to pay back the—"

"Yes or no. Did you doctor the company books?"

"I didn't want anyone suspecting until—"

"Your Honor, I ask the court to remind the defendant to answer yes or no."

"*Yes.*"

"If you were going to pay back the money, why did you doctor the books?"

"I ... because I ..."

"It's a simple question. Why did you doctor the books?"

"I didn't want someone discovering it, you know, before I could pay it back ... "

"You mean you didn't want them noticing because you were *never* going to pay it back."

"No ... I—"

"*Did* you pay back the eight million five hundred thousand dollars?"

"I was in the middle of ... I was accruing—"

"Yes or no. Did you pay back the eight million five hundred thousand dollars or didn't you?"

"Not yet."

"So that's a no. No ... you didn't pay back the eight million five hundred thousand dollars." I enjoyed this nonstop verbal slapping. My client's face was growing increasingly redder, as if he couldn't quite believe the person he was paying to be his advocate—to be on his side—was being entirely the opposite. Was attacking him. And doing it in a highly realistic manner, so realistic that if he didn't know any better, he'd almost think, well, that maybe she meant it. That she really was castigating him. *Humiliating* him, even.

"Can we take a break?" he asked me.

"No."

"Why not? I need a smoke."

"You can't smoke in here."

"I'm paying you five hundred dollars an hour and I can't smoke in here?" He looked indignant, his florid face having almost imperceptibly shifted to anger. Same color—different emotion.

"Right. You can't smoke in here."

"Fine. I'll smoke *outside*."

"No breaks. You won't get any on the stand. When things get difficult, you can't tell the judge, 'Hey, I need a smoke, so how about we take a break.'"

"You're not the judge. You're my lawyer. A lawyer I'm paying through the nose." Jefrey's nose seemed to have a perpetual sniffle. He'd already used two tissues from the box I kept conveniently located within arm's reach on the French Provincial desk *I'd* paid through the nose for. *Cocaine?* Probably—one of the many high-priced things that eight million five hundred thousand can buy you.

"You're paying me to keep you out of prison. It'll help if you don't sound as if you're evading questions by asking for a break every two minutes. So ... shall we?"

He stared at me as if wondering whether he should continue to take it—my bullying, my general brusqueness. Being a master of the universe, he wasn't used to being addressed this way. He was used to people bowing and scraping. Only he was trying to keep his universe from being reduced to a seven-by-eleven-foot cell with a wafer-thin mattress, an open metal toilet, and a roommate named Vinnie.

"Sure," he said begrudgingly. "Shoot."

That's when my assistant knocked on the door.

Right then.

I said, "Yes... what," and she meekly opened it with a face that was the polar opposite of my client's. Deathly white.

And she told me that there'd been an accident.

CHAPTER TWO

I met my husband in law school. That is, I was in law school at Northwestern and he was visiting someone there.

A woman I knew.

Who invited me to lunch, where I was the distinct third wheel.

I think Elinor wasn't sure about him—about Jason—and she wanted my disapproval or my blessing. Or maybe she just wanted my company, in case the lunch proved torturous.

They'd met at a party back in New York, had emailed each other fairly regularly since, and now here he was for an official first date complete with unwilling chaperone. She'd picked Joe's Shanghai, a Chinese hole-in-the-wall popular with law school students on a threadbare budget.

The lunch wasn't torturous.

Let me amend that. It was mildly so—at least for me—since I found myself attracted to him in the peculiarly chemical sense. It wasn't his conversation, which consisted of a lot of hedge-fund talk. That's what he did—he'd started a hedge fund, which to this day I'm not sure I can competently define. Finance isn't my thing.

But I felt an undeniable sexual allure. Which made sitting there witnessing his first date with someone other than me irritating and uncomfortable. I'd been through a dry spell lately—my last serious boyfriend having departed my apartment and the city of Chicago with an admonition that someday I would make someone very unhappy.

It turned out to be an accurate enough prediction.

It's not me, it's you, I said to him when I called it quits. Deliberately turning that overused and trite expression on its head for the sheer pleasure of saying it out loud. I know, kind of bitchy of me. But I needed to wound him because I wanted a clean break—we'd already had two or three *vacations* from each other that always ended with us drifting back together almost by default. I was too busy studying legal statutes to find someone else. He was too enamored.

There's that moment when every cute idiosyncrasy of your significant other turns into a grating annoyance. The things that once made you swoon now make you hurl. The way Alex licked his forefinger before turning the pages of the *Chicago Sun-Times*. The way Alex liked to softly hum to himself when he was contemplating something—uniquely and especially irritating when I was bent over a desk contemplating tort law. Even the way he neatly folded his clothes before sex. No passionately ripping off clothing for Alex—it seemed more like he was packing for a business trip, the eventual destination being somewhere between my legs.

If you think this sounds petty and demanding and even cruel, you wouldn't necessarily be wrong.

Mea culpa.

The heart wants what the heart wants, someone once stated—but by extension the heart *doesn't* want what the heart *doesn't* want. I didn't want Alex. Not anymore.

Jason, on the other hand, was someone I could see wanting. We used to play a game—my college roommate and I—we titled Wouldn't Kick Them Out of Bed. Sitting at a table in the college cafeteria—or buried in the back of a lecture hall where the instructor couldn't hear us—we'd peruse various potential hookups and rate them *would* or *wouldn't*. The game taught me the confounding subjectiveness of sexual attraction. What Kim wouldn't kick out of bed I wouldn't let anywhere near mine, and to be fair, vice versa.

I wondered what Kim would have rated Jason.

He wasn't handsome in the traditional sense, if there even was a traditional handsomeness anymore. He had a strong chin that looked like it could take a good left uppercut—my dad was a boxing enthusiast who'd idolized Muhammad Ali and tried to teach me the intricacies of one-two combinations. We'd shadow-box around the living room—not the usual dad-daughter kind of bonding. In the years A.D.—After Daniel—I'd studiously taken on the duties of substitute son.

Jason had nice eyes. Hazel. I kept thinking those eyes lingered a little more than necessary on me. He was politely including me in the conversation—the way politicians are taught to look left and right on the podium, making sure both sides of the audience are drinking in their mock sincerity. Jason was doing the same thing—Elinor and I were sitting directly across the table from him and he was dutifully going from her and back to me as if his head was on a hinge.

It's just that he seemed to linger longer on me. Maybe I was just wishing for that.

I'd already searched for disqualifying characteristics as a way to tamp down my attraction and make me feel better about not being able to act on it. It's what you do when you meet some-one who's otherwise attached. You search for things you don't like. Is that a pouch by his midsection? Are his teeth off-color? Is he actually stupid?

Hard as I tried—and I tried mightily—I couldn't discern any deal breakers with Jason. Maybe one. He seemed to tilt somewhat Republican. George W had taken his title of com-mander in chief literally and commanded us into Iraq, where an increasing number of servicemen were getting blown to bits and where they were quickly running out of places to find those elusive weapons of mass destruction. W had even done a video where he'd joked about it—searching under the Oval Office couch for them. *No weapons of mass destruction here,* he'd exclaimed in that Texas twang of his. It was supposed to be funny. It wasn't.

But Jason was more or less defending him by reciting all the atrocities of Saddam—gassing the Kurds, jailing his opponents, torturing members of the national soccer team who'd failed to prevent a winning goal. Never mind that we'd entered a war under false pretenses, he was saying—we were getting rid of a bad dude.

I wasn't political. But I still knew a con job when I saw it.

Yes. W-defending was a possible de-qualification, but a pretty poor one given that Jason attested that he hadn't actually *voted* for W—he just saw the justification for him invading a sovereign country for no particular reason.

"What kind of law are you studying?" he asked me. He'd already asked Elinor the same question—*corporate*, she'd stated. She wanted to make a ton of money and retire to a farmhouse in Provence by age forty-five.

"Criminal," I answered.

That piqued his interest. Or maybe it was me that was piquing his interest. I hadn't gone full out for this lunch because I was supposed to be attending as a neutral observer, as opposed to an enemy agent.

I hadn't labored over my makeup, applying and reapplying my eye shadow, tying up and letting down my wavy blond hair—naturally wavy, by the way, and by most accounts my single best feature. I hadn't obsessed about my outfit either. I'd gone for plain-Jane—the kind of clothes that let you recede into the background. Jeans and a simple sweater. No discernable cleavage—which, by most accounts, is my second-best feature. It being late April, Chicago was easing out of its arctic-like windscape and into a hesitant but hopeful spring. I could've worn something plunging. I could've gone short skirt, or even longer skirt but with enough slit to bare some leg. Yes—my third-best feature. It would've been temperature appropriate.

I hadn't. I was going to play wingwoman and the dress code for wingwomen is unprovocative.

Still he seemed interested.

"Prosecute or defend?" he asked me.

"One from column A and one from column B," I replied, thinking I might as well make use of our current setting—a scratched linoleum table with three half-eaten plates of moo goo gai pan. That was the typical route, wasn't it? Starting off in some prosecutor's office where I'd make no money but placate my Catholic guilt just enough to overcome my future sins as a criminal defense attorney. I'd planned it all out.

He'd laughed at my joke, which admittedly wasn't much of one. That's when I thought I might be right after all. That he was feeling what I was, having come to lunch for the entree but falling for the side dish instead.

I think Elinor noticed. I saw a look on her face that bordered on perturbed when Jason asked me some follow-up questions, laughed at another one of my non-jokes, smiled a little bit wider than necessary. You know. Flirted with me.

I had a choice now.

Retreat out of deference to Elinor, which, after all, was what it said in the girl-code manual.

Or go for it.

She hardly knows him, I told myself. One meeting at a party in another state and some back-and-forth emails. It wouldn't be like I was busting up a marriage. Or even a relationship.

Just a friendship.

I smiled back at him. I softened my eyes. When I was relating a lascivious story having to do with one of my law professors and his twenty-two-year-old adjunct, I casually leaned in and grazed his hand. As if I were just making a point instead of making a move.

In the end, after we finished a lunch that had turned noticeably frosty—at least on my side of the table—I got a message from him on Facebook. That's when Facebook was still considered moderately cool as opposed to the place where seventy-year-old grandmothers post pictures of their cats.

Hey Caron, he wrote, *I hope I'm not being forward but thought I'd say hello.*

What took you so long, I wrote back.

And that was that.

Until I picked up the phone that had been answered by my now shell-shocked assistant.

I'm sorry to tell you there's been an accident. I'm sorry to tell you your husband is deceased.

The deceased person my husband was found lying next to wasn't mentioned.

They must've figured one shock was enough.

They were right.

I collapsed.

CHAPTER THREE

This is the procedure for identifying a dead husband.

You go to the morgue at the Suffolk County Medical Examiner's, a nondescript building in a nondescript town called Hauppauge.

They bring you into a small beige room—just big enough for the medical examiner, the police detective, the body, and you.

The body has already been wheeled in. A white sheet covers it.

The medical examiner asks you to take a deep breath. He explains that the explosion did extensive damage to your husband's face. He knows this will be difficult for you. He asks if you're ready to identify the body.

You nod yes.

He lifts the sheet—just enough to uncover the head. The last time you saw this head it was peering into the bathroom mirror this very morning. Now it's lying on a steel gurney covered by a thin white sheet.

The medical examiner was right. The explosion had altered Jason's face. As if it had deliberately sanded down his features. He resembled those plaster corpses in Pompeii Jason and I had marveled over on our long-ago honeymoon to the Amalfi Coast. Those Pompeii casts in the shape of actual people—a cowering woman, a sheltered child, a chained slave—but not actual people. More like half-finished people.

"It's him," I said.

"You're sure?" the ME asked gently.

"Yes."

Jason had been critically searching his face in the mirror this morning, kneading it this way and that, examining it at various angles. As if he wanted to see how it might appear to someone who might be gazing at it later that day. From below, maybe. Or from above looking straight down.

Her.

"I'm sorry," the police detective said. It wasn't the first time he'd said that to me today. The first time was on the phone when he told me my husband had died in a gas explosion.

The second time he told me he was sorry was when he divulged that someone else had died with him.

A woman.

There were two things to be sorry about here. My husband had died. My husband had cheated.

I nodded.

The ME handed me a small bag. Jason's rose-gold wedding ring, the Rolex I'd bought him for our tenth wedding anniversary—the glass face was cracked. Jason had given me a pearl necklace in return. *Pearls before swine.* I don't know why that popped into my head or where I'd heard that expression before. Was it Shakespeare? Something to do with the inability to appreciate beauty. Swine are incapable of it.

My assistant, Jennifer, had driven me to the morgue.

This was after she'd picked me up off the floor.

It had taken my brain a second or two to process things. First the words and then what those words meant. Jennifer later told me I'd calmly placed the office phone back into its cradle before crumpling to the floor. I was aware of the carpet rushing up to meet me, surprised I was caught in this banal cliché of shock but seemingly unable to resist it. I felt both lighter and heavier than air.

I heard my client utter a curse as he shot up out of his chair, heard Jennifer gasp as she kneeled down and tried to lift my head up off the floor. It took the efforts of both of them to finally get me upright. That and a bit of Evian water sprinkled on my face, which I suppose is the modern equivalent of smelling salts.

Jennifer had walked me into the morgue but not into the room itself. She'd waited outside out of deference, or simple fear. When I walked back out, I could tell she was trying to read the signs in my face. *Relief* or *grief*? On the drive over she'd asked if the police were a hundred percent sure that it was *Jason*. Could they have made a terrible mistake?

No, I said. I don't think so. It was his car parked outside the house—a classic red Corvette he generally used only on weekends to save on the wear and tear. They'd run the plates, looked in the glove compartment, and retrieved his registration. His wallet was discovered in the rubble. It was still tucked into his pants. The pants he'd taken off in another part of the house before heading naked downstairs to the fireplace. That's where they'd found them. Lying in front of the fireplace. Two naked people.

Jennifer looked confused. Apparently she couldn't see relief or grief in my face. She had to ask me, just like the ME had.

"Is it him?"

"Yes."

"Caron…I'm so…" She didn't know what to do. Hug me? Pat my hand? Burst into tears? She knew Jason hadn't been found alone because I'd told her. This would be a common problem for friends and acquaintances over the next few days. How to react exactly?

Offer your sympathies to the widow for her husband's death? Or offer your sympathies to the widow for her husband's betrayal? *Sorry* seemed to cover both.

Thank you, I'd reply. A one-size-fits-all response.

There were other duties to perform now.

A funeral. Several of our friends offered to help me plan the arrangements. I was cognizant of the fact that they were *our* friends as opposed to mine, and already mapping the fault lines they'd be sure to split along. Jason had been the glue that held most of our friendships together, the initial draw that bonded us. Of the two of us, he was the natural bon vivant, the socially adept master of ceremonies. He genuinely *liked* other people. I could take them or leave them. Maybe it was my chosen profession, which tends to give you a more jaundiced view of humankind—a misnomer if there ever was one.

Janice—of Janice and Larry—Larry being an erstwhile golfing partner of my husband's, offered to call the funeral home and take care of everything.

"Which funeral home?" I asked her. Did you pick funeral homes the way you do resorts or restaurants? Look up their ratings on Yelp? *Watch out: poor service and ambience that borders on funereal.*

"I used one for my father," she said. "They were very helpful. Swan's Funeral Home in Sagaponack."

Swans. There was an ever-present pair of them in the green-black pond where Montauk Highway bent into East Hampton. I'd always wondered about those swans—visible year after year. Surely they couldn't be the *same* swans. Were they replaced every few years by the town—like Christmas ornaments?

"I think I need to take care of the arrangements myself," I said. It seemed like the thing to do—arrange for your own husband's funeral. A task you weren't allowed to foist onto someone else.

Janice had come over to my house bearing food. She wasn't the only one. Food seemed to be the de rigueur sympathy gift. Baskets from Round Swamp Farm. Spreads from Golden Pear. Feasts from Mary's Marvelous. Enough food to fill a banquet hall. Jason would've immediately gone for the Egyptian dates prominently displayed in Janice's food basket—his goto delicacy. In ancient Egypt they used to stuff food into the pyramids so the dead wouldn't starve in the afterlife. Would it be blasphemous of me to suggest placing a few of those dates into Jason's coffin—an homage to the high priest of Hampton's hobnobbing?

I almost said it out loud. Glad I didn't. I don't think Janice would've appreciated the underlying sarcasm.

"Whatever you *want*, honey," Janice said. I'd noticed people were taking on a kind of caregiver posture with me—both physically and tonally. The way people act around the elderly. Stooping a bit as if trying to meet shrinking seniors halfway and softening their voices as if anything louder would physically harm them.

"Yes. That's what I want," I said, a little more sharply than I'd intended. *Spare me your sympathy.* That's what I felt like telling them. All of them. Janice; my assistant, Jennifer; Larry; Grace; Margaret; my husband's partner, Mathew; my father, widowed ten years ago and slowly wasting away in Urbana, Illinois; my husband's mother, who'd called me from Florida and whispered, *How will we ever survive this, Caron?*

His death, or his fucking someone else while dying? I almost asked her. Which one was she specifically referring to?

There was a game I used to play with Danny when we were kids—Rock, Paper, Scissors, Match, where match vanquished paper, rock vanquished scissors, and paper vanquished rock.

Anger vanquishes sympathy. It eats it for breakfast.

Janice offered to at least accompany me to the funeral home, and I took her up on it. *Moral support*, she promised.

If you've never shopped for coffins, it's a little like picking out furniture for a room you're never going to set foot in. Your husband's study, for example—a room I probably visited three times in my life. The last time surreptitiously sniffing for clues. I'd picked up on things.

Dinner conversations that had become oddly strained. Smiles that seemed awkwardly forced. Sex that had become distinctly mechanical.

No need for Hercule Poirot here.

Just a wife with half a brain and an empirical belief in a human being's limitless capacity to deceive.

The funeral director at Swan's Funeral Home led us to the *showroom*—yes, that's what he called it. As if he were about to offer us a new-model car.

The first question you need to answer: coffin or casket? Apparently they're two different things. A coffin is hexagonal or octagonal, he explained. A casket, rectangular—and often, but not always, with a split lid for viewing purposes.

Given what the gas explosion had done to my husband's face, viewing wouldn't be on the menu.

Then there are the *materials*, the funeral director continued. He spoke in the kind of voice you'd want on one of those apps that help put you to sleep. The voice equivalent of gentle rain or a lapping ocean tide. *Soothing*, you'd call it.

In the premium level: mahogany, walnut, and cherry.

Midlevel: oak, birch, and maple.

Walmart level: pine, poplar, and willow.

The caste distinctions didn't end with the wood. There was the metal to consider—the handles and trim. Standard steel, stainless steel, copper, and bronze. Tin wasn't an option.

This being the Hamptons, there was also a section with environmentally friendly caskets made of wicker, seagrass, and bamboo. So everything *blends* back into a completely natural state, he explained.

This being the Hamptons, I felt compelled to go premium.

I chose a mahogany casket with standard steel handles and a plush inside lining. Jason had been particular about our mattresses—firm enough to lessen the strain on his golf-tortured back but soft enough to deep-sleep on.

I won't tell you the price of the casket.

It was obscene.

Janice dropped me off back home. It felt distinctly different walking in. A place that suddenly reeked of solitude. It had always been too big, the kind of place I was always trying to *inhabit*. There was too much empty air. It felt like the Thanksgiving meal Jason and I consumed during the first year of the pandemic—just the two of us because we had no kids (we'd tried and failed and then grown used to our selfish lifestyle) and because whatever relatives we had were too cautious to chance it. Still, I'd prepared the usual feast—it was habit. A ten-pound turkey, pecan stuffing, mashed potatoes, sweet potato casserole, roasted cauliflower, homemade bread, butternut squash soup, a deep-dish apple pie.

It was enough to feed the Brady Bunch.

We ate perhaps a quarter of it, possibly less. The mostly-still-there turkey, the bulk of the stuffing, potatoes, casserole, and pie remained laid out across our dining room table like a poster for conspicuous consumption. All that waste.

That's how I felt about our house.

We had a condo in the West Village overlooking the Hudson, which was still defined as our main residence on tax returns, but over the years our two homes had more or less reversed themselves. With us hardly noticing, we'd begun slouching toward Babylon.

Now this home felt even larger. All this space and only one person living in it. One of my favorite books as a young girl was *The Haunting of Hill House* by Shirley Jackson. Where a Gothic mansion literally subsumes someone, ingesting her into the very floors and walls, turning her into a kind of ghost who will forever haunt it. I feared that would be me.

I couldn't sleep.

I was trying to remember what I'd said to Jason when he left the house that morning. It would be the last thing I'd say to him.

Have a nice day.

Yes.

CHAPTER FOUR

The funeral was boisterous and dignified. Both.

Boisterous because several of Jason's friends decided on humor as the best salve—that the funeral should be a celebration of Jason's life rather than a mourning of his death. It reminded me of the speeches at our wedding fifteen years ago from Mathew, the best man, and a few other of Jason's various lifelong friends. Filled with vague allusions to his previous carousing, sprinkled with semi-dirty jokes and the kinds of stories that made me wonder if this was the same Jason I was marrying.

What's that they say? *Lovers and other strangers.* You could substitute *husbands* for *lovers* and be equally correct. Trust me on this.

Mathew's eulogy was heartfelt and humorous.

They'd started the hedge fund together. They'd both grown rich from it. Bought similar kinds of toys: classic cars, nice-sized boats, way-too-big houses. Mathew told a golf story—the kind of story probably only golfers would appreciate, but this being the Hamptons, that would've been most of the audience. *Is that what you call the mourners at a funeral?* I wondered. An *audience*? Or is it *congregation*?

The story involved Mathew and Jason on a golf jaunt to Northern California, and Jason hooking a shot so badly that it took down America's national bird. Killed it, apparently. *It's the only* eagle *Jason ever managed*, Mathew said, and the audience laughed appreciatively. Then a misstep—buoyed by the generous response to this deprecating golf story about the newly deceased,

Mathew made the impromptu decision to throw in another. *And sorry, pal*—as he smiled and looked heavenward—*but the only thing in golf you liked better than putting was cheating.*

It took Mathew a second or two to wish he could take it back. The lack of laughter must've been his first clue. He turned red and promptly launched into a recitation of Jason's various kind deeds. Donating to the local food bank during COVID, starting a cancer charity at work in honor of a lost colleague.

The service continued.

Several other friends spoke after him.

I had already declined.

Everyone knew how Jason died. And with whom. And if they didn't, now they could simply ask the person next to them why no one laughed when Mathew made the joke about cheating. They'd be waiting for the spectacle of his wife at the podium, like a jury waiting for a defendant in the box. What would I say? What would I acknowledge? How would I appear?

I'd decided to deny them that pleasure.

I remained a passive listener, still wrapped in the kind of numbness that follows a brutal and unexpected impact just before the pain takes over. The other night I wrote a reminder to myself: *Tell Jason to call exterminator to spray garden for ticks.* It took me a moment to process the fact that Jason was incapable of being told anything. Jason was dead.

I was learning that shock is a seismic event. The aftershocks keep coming every time you allow yourself to forget.

After the funeral, I had to stand there next to Jason's frail mother as the mourners formed a kind of receiving line in reverse—murmurs of *sorry; so sorry; really, really sorry; if there's anything I can do*—as they made their way out the door of the church. My father, permanently attached to an oxygen tank due to acute emphysema, hadn't made the trip.

It was the cusp of late winter and early spring, and every time the door opened as someone left, a gust of frigid chill would sweep in and over me. *Like Jason's spirit*, I would've said if I believed in things like that. If I believed in stories like *The Haunting of Hill House*. My Catholic girlhood had made me a fervid believer in guilt.

Not in an afterlife.

Cedar Lawn Cemetery was just outside town. According to Janice, it was considered the Nick & Toni's of Hampton cemeteries. Meaning people were dying to get into it and so you needed to book well in advance. And you were very likely to run into a celebrity or two as well. Cliff Robertson and Joseph Heller were buried in Cedar Lawn. There were your two.

Now Jason Mooney would be buried there. Mathew had pulled strings.

Jason had grown up in Brooklyn—not the gentrified Brooklyn of today, but the homogenous Brooklyn of before—in a section called Red Hook, which was Irish/Italian and rough around the edges. Jason liked to relate stories about his Brooklyn childhood to impress upon people just how far he'd come. Or maybe as a simple affirmation to himself. Home had been a two-bedroom walk-up with a single bathroom. He'd taken me back there once on the drive out east—looping around the BQE and exiting before we hit Coney Island. We'd sat in the car and stared up at the gray graffiti-scarred building while Jason recounted stories about dodging cars during stickball and being chased down the block by Italians intent on murdering him. The neighborhood was already changing. We'd passed a few hipster bars and warehouses newly renovated into condos, and we could smell weed wafting through the open car window.

Jason thought about going in, knocking on the door, and asking if we could look around for old time's sake. But we were flirting with rush hour and the only thing Jason hated more than driving out east was driving out east in standstill traffic.

We left.

They don't lower caskets by hand anymore. That's the image most of us retain, but it's the wrong one. They use mechanical contraptions that slowly winch the casket down into the black rectangular hole. It reminded me of those staircase lifts for wheelchair users that they used to constantly advertise on late-night TV. People who looked half-dead being slowly lowered down the steps as if into purgatory.

Jason being fully dead, the priest recited the requisite prayer.

Ashes to ashes. Dust to dust. In sure and certain hope of the Resurrection to eternal life.

Father Jordan had pumped me for information on Jason before the funeral service. After all, he didn't know him—Jason and I weren't parishioners. Having attended Catholic school where the nuns routinely smacked his knuckles with a wooden ruler, Jason had lost his appetite for Communion wafers. I toted my Catholic guilt around like an unwanted heirloom I was unable to dispose of.

"What was your husband like?" Father Jordan asked me.

I was wondering how much he knew. Everything, probably. My girlhood recollection of Catholic priests was that they reveled in neighborhood gossip, served in generous portions along with the rest of the Sunday dinners my mother frequently offered at our home. It was only their second-most grievous sin.

"Jason was loved by almost everybody," I answered Father Jordan. Only later did I realize how that might have sounded. *Jason was loved by almost everybody.*

Including her, of course.

They'd buried her the day before, I'd heard. A temple service with the burial in a Jewish cemetery shaded by hundreds of ancient weeping willows.

I felt a sudden hot flash of anger—and wondered if meno-pause would be like this. Searing heat incapacitating me at inconvenient moments and leaving me sweaty and shaken.

"More details would be helpful," Father Jordan said.

"He liked to golf," I said. "He liked to do the Sunday cross-word puzzle. He liked to water our tomato plants even though he wasn't partial to tomatoes. He liked to give toasts—birthdays, anniversaries, weddings, you name it." I kept going. "He liked to bicycle to the beach. He liked Egyptian dates. He liked books about the Civil War. He liked Silver Oak Cabernet. Sometimes he liked to cheat on me."

Father Jordan stared.

"I'm sorry," I said. "That was ungracious of me. Or untimely. Or inappropriate. One of those things."

"You don't have to apologize," he said.

"Fine. I withdraw my apology. Where were we?"

After the funeral I went home with Jason's mother. She'd be stay-ing with me. I wasn't happy about that, but I couldn't exactly banish her to the Maidstone Inn. She was the grieving mother. I was the grieving wife. We were stuck with each other.

We sat in the living room sipping Darjeeling tea before I went up to my bedroom.

"People are fallible," she said, looking up at me.

She didn't bother adding anything to that simple statement. She didn't have to.

"Yes," I said.

When I got to my bedroom I undressed and lay down.

Then I angrily addressed my betrayer.

How could you do that me?

How could you destroy what we had?

How could you betray me like that?

How? How? How?

They say heartache is figurative; they're wrong. The numbness was beginning to wear off like the effects of the morphine drip they'd given me after I was sideswiped by a car on an early-morning run a few years ago. *What's the pain, one to ten?* the ER attendant kept pestering me. *Ten,* I'd reply. *Ten.* This was more like *a hundred and eleven.* Morphine would be of no help here.

My cell rang.

It was Frank DeMarco from the fire investigator's office. He was calling me unofficially, he said. Frank and I had a professional relationship of sorts, since he'd once helped me out on a big arson case.

"Hello, Caron," he began. "I'm very sorry for your loss." Everyone's go-to cliché. "I wanted to give you a heads-up. I'm sure somebody from the police will be contacting you sooner rather than later."

"The *police?*"

"Yeah. The police. We're still investigating, obviously. This is all very preliminary. But we're pretty damn sure it wasn't an accident."

"*What...?*"

"The explosion. It wasn't an accident."

"I don't understand. They told me it was a *gas explosion...*"

"Yeah. Sure. It was a gas explosion. But somebody cut the line. Understand what I'm saying here? Somebody fucked with the gas line."

"I still don't..."

"When they lit the fireplace. That did it. *Boom.* Sorry, thought you'd want to know. Remember, this is strictly unofficial. And again, I'm very sorry."

"Sure. Thanks."

I hung up. Clutched at my chest where my aching heart was furiously pounding against my rib cage as if it were a locked door it desperately needed to open.

Boom, Frank had said.

Boom. Boom. Boom, my heart echoed.

My husband had died. My husband had died next to a naked woman named Emma.

Now Frank Demarco had called to tell me he'd been murdered.

CHAPTER FIVE

It's always the husband. Or the boyfriend. Or the ex-husband. Or the ex-boyfriend.

A cliché that almost always turns out to be true.

I didn't wait for the police to contact me.

The next morning I called Joe Rawlings, who used to be a police detective but had retired on full pension and gone private—my go-to investigator. Joe was damaged in the way most ex-police are—too much alcohol and too many skeletons—but he was dogged, savvy, and thorough.

I asked Joe to ask his buddies at the force for an update. Was there a full-fledged investigation going on?

"I don't have any buddies at the force," he said. Right. When police went private, they automatically became members of the opposing team, the one always getting in the police's way. And Joe had gotten a reputation before retiring—too chummy with Internal Affairs. They must've had something on Joe, I figured, and used it to turn him into a reluctant snitch. I'd never asked him. You can't.

"Try your ex-buddies, then," I said.

"I'm sorry, Caron," he said. "About your husband. It sucks."

By now, Joe must've known what everyone else did. It wouldn't have surprised him much—a husband cheating on his wife. He spent enough hours parked outside dingy motel windows with his telephoto-lensed Nikon for him not to be surprised by that. Many of those hours paid for by me. Still, Joe was a friend. He was sorry for me.

"Thanks, Joe. Will you let me know?"

"Sure. And it's strictly gratis."

"You're a peach."

"I'm a crab apple."

"I'm partial to crab apples."

The crab apple called me back later that same afternoon.

"Her ex-husband," he said.

The woman who'd died naked next to my husband. Emma Shipman. They were focusing on her ex-husband, Joe was saying. Neil Shipman.

It was always the husband.

"A person of interest?"

"*The* person of interest. She had a restraining order against him," Joe said. "Domestic battery. Stalking. Typical prick stuff. And a security camera picked him up on the street by their house that morning."

"Are they going to arrest?"

"Not yet. They brought him in, though."

"And?"

"And nothing. He lawyered up. "

"Who?" The lawyer, I meant. Which one?

"Someone I never heard of. Sam White."

"*Sam White?* Really?" I'd heard of him—hadn't everybody?

"He's not a defense attorney, Joe. Strictly divorce. C'mon, don't tell me you've never heard that nauseating jingle? 'Santini and White … di-vorce attorneys … 800-888-8888 …'"

"That's *him*?"

"He must be the only lawyer he knows. You're stuck in a room with the police asking if you murdered your ex-wife and her lover, you call a lawyer. Any lawyer."

"Right."

I thanked Joe. I asked him to keep checking for me. If he wouldn't mind.

He didn't.

I spent that afternoon with Jason's mom. It was uncomfortable. Not so much because of what we talked about. Because of what we didn't. Aside from her brief statement concerning human fallibility, she kept clear of the circumstances surrounding Jason's death.

She reminisced about Brooklyn instead. She'd come pretty far from that two-bedroom walk-up herself. Jason had seen to that, setting her up in a gated community in Boca Raton, where she played canasta and did daily pool aerobics. Still, Brooklyn retained its pull. A more idealized Brooklyn than it had ever been in actuality, I think. A Brooklyn where neighbors of different ethnicities sat on stoops and exchanged pleasantries. Where all the kids—including Jason— got along swimmingly. A virtual Benetton ad of idyllic diversity. Very different from Jason's recollections of being chased down the block by murderous Italians.

I didn't bother correcting her.

I was wondering how long she was intending to stay. There was no polite way to ask. *What would you like for dinner?* was fine. *When are you leaving my house?* wasn't. Still, I nibbled at the edges. I probed.

"Who's watching Paisley?" I asked her. Paisley was her cat. The one she kept posting pictures of on Facebook and putting on Christmas cards. Paisley and her. *Merry Cat-mas*, the last one said.

"Dora," she replied.

Dora was her neighbor and tippling partner. They'd taken to drinking Manhattans every afternoon, Jason once told me.

"People still drink Manhattans?" I'd asked.

"People in Boca Raton."

"You must miss her," I said to her. I meant Paisley the cat, though she might've thought I was referring to Dora the neighbor. It didn't really matter.

"I do. I'm used to finding her on top of me when I wake up."

I hoped she was referring to Paisley.

"This is the loveliest time of year in Florida, isn't it?" I offered. "Warm but not brutal."

The truth was, I didn't think any time of the year was lovely in Florida. It had always struck me as one large hospice with the heat set too high. I know—a caustic generalization. Maybe because I'd only been to that one gated community where the atmosphere was decidedly geriatric. Still, we always passed plenty of carbon copies on the way from the airport. Golden Gates. Serenity Glen. Mystic Meadows. They could've been the names of cemeteries.

"I *like* summer there," she said, sticking up for her adopted home. "The pool. Playing cards in the lounge."

"Right. Sounds lovely. I was just remarking that it's *particularly* nice now."

That's as far as I pushed trying to elicit a departure date from her.

"I'm worried about you, Caron," she said.

"Why?"

"Being alone, I mean."

"*You're* alone."

"Yes. It's no picnic." Jason's father had passed away from a heart attack twelve years ago while sitting on the toilet. For a while, Brenda thought he was just taking an exceedingly long time in there.

"You just mentioned how nice it is playing cards with your friends. Doing your aerobics in the pool."

"It is nice. That's all it is. Nice. And I'm a lot older than you."

"I'll be fine."

"I'm not sure."

I wondered if that's why she was making her stay open-ended. She was worried about leaving me alone.

"Honestly, no need to worry about me. I'm a trooper."

"You just lost your husband. You're a widow."

"I have my work. I have my friends. I have this house." I wasn't sure why I'd added the house as a bulwark against loneliness. If anything, its excessive roominess exacerbated it.

"*Wait*," she said. "It creeps up on you."

When I was a kid, I used to read *Mad* magazine—a favorite of Daniel's that had migrated to me along with a few other hand-me-downs. You know, Alfred E. Neuman. *Spy vs Spy.* They had a section where they personified expressions—drawing them more like monsters, actually. *Gnawing Fear. Chilling Thought. Gripping Melodrama.*

I imagined a new one. *Creeping Loneliness.*

"If I get lonely, I'll FaceTime you," I said. "And Paisley. Promise."

"Fine."

That evening over dinner—we were still making our way through the mounds of food that had turned the house into a mini–food bank—she told me she'd booked a flight home the next day.

"I'll call you an Uber," I said.

CHAPTER SIX

The papers got hold of it.

Initially there'd been one or two articles simply focusing on the explosion. The two dead. They'd even named them: *Jason Mooney… Emma Shipman.* But nothing salacious. Not yet. Nothing about one of the unfortunate victims being married to someone other than the woman he was found with. About them being found naked. In front of a fireplace.

It was a story about a gas explosion, like other stories about natural and unnatural disasters that keep insurance actuaries up at night. Head-on collisions, small-aircraft crashes, people being swallowed by sinkholes.

Now it was a story about something else.

"POLICE SUSPECT MURDER," blared the headline of a Long Island newspaper.

The police had probably leaked it, I figured. They did that when they wanted to build pressure on a suspect. Make it intolerable for them. Suspects do crazy things under pressure. Run. Confess. Kill themselves.

This article turned the story in a distinctly lascivious direction. Mentioned the fact that Jason Mooney was married to one Caron Mooney but was found in flagrante delicto with one Emma Shipman. Not exactly—not using those words, of course. Not stating that Jason Mooney died in the act of *fucking Emma Shipman.* But strongly intimating it. They mentioned the fireplace, for instance. What else do a man and woman do in front of a fireplace? Not play chess.

And they gave their readers a suspect. A fine one. The current and only person of interest. Neil Shipman—the jealous and violent ex-husband. He'd been stalking her, showing up uninvited at restaurant lunches, backyard parties, and beach soirees. Confronting her. Threatening her. Scaring her.

He once had to be physically thrown out of a major Hamptons bash by police officers moonlighting as security. Wrestled to the ground in front of his ex-wife and escorted through the gates.

She'd gotten an ironclad order of protection against him.

Not ironclad enough.

It was only a matter of time, I knew, before they'd work the other angle in this charming triangle and come for me. The betrayed widow.

The call came to the office.

I'd decided to go back—I had a trial looming, after all. My embezzler's—Jefrey with one *f*, who'd sent me an email masquerading as a sympathy note, but really as a way to ask me if I could still competently defend him given that my husband had been blown to kingdom come. He was worried I might be distracted by that.

I assured him I wasn't. All systems go. What I didn't tell him was that escaping into work was an escape from pain. Even if it was momentary.

Jennifer buzzed me as I was going through pretrial motion filings. A *reporter* was on the line. Did I want to speak with him?

I did not.

Then another reporter called.

I didn't want to speak to her either.

And another. And so on and so on.

Usually the only honking you hear in the Hamptons is from migrating geese.

Not tonight.

When I arrived home that evening, I was forced to honk my way through a crowd of satellite trucks and reporters gathered

outside my electric fence. It looked like a candlelight vigil, with their black mics as stand-ins for lit candles.

Caron, they shouted at me, *Caron*, as if we were old friends.

For once the spaciousness of this place—not just the house but the eleven sprawling acres it sat on—appealed to me. By the time I made it up the gravel drive and parked the car, I could barely hear them.

Once inside, I poured myself a drink in the living room. Johnnie Walker Black with one cube of ice. Not my usual, but then these were unusual times.

I needed a game plan.

Reporters are lazy by nature but dogged by necessity. They weren't going to simply call it a day. They weren't going to quit hounding me.

I called one of those friends of mine who were more friends of *his*. Of Jason's. Maggie, of Terence and Maggie. Prominent Princess of PR—her public relations firm had handled some notorious people in the past. Now I was notorious. Or at least tainted by notoriety. Reluctantly along for the ride.

Maggie had been at the funeral. One of the people who'd told me how sorry they were on their way out the church door.

"I need your help," I told her.

"Yeah. I've been reading the paper. So sorry, Caron. It's unfair. Him dying. And now all *this*."

"I don't think fairness is part of the equation."

"Indeed. But still."

"I was thinking, Maggie."

"Yes?"

"A onetime statement. To buy me some breathing room."

"Sure."

"You know. 'Mrs. Mooney is grieving the loss of her husband. She's awaiting the results of the investigation like everyone else. She politely requests her privacy during this very tragic time.' That kind of thing."

"Are you?"

"What?"

"Grieving the loss of your husband?"

That was Maggie—frank to the point of rudeness. A prerequuisite of her job as a New York City publicist. Picture a female Sidney Falco.

"Yes."

"It's intolerable, isn't it? One thing robbing you of permission to feel the other thing."

My husband's infidelity robbing me of the ability to mourn my husband's death. That's what she meant.

"Yes."

"You can overcome things like that, you know. With practice."

Maggie's frankness extended to herself. Word was Terence had cheated on her, and more than once.

"People are fallible," I said, echoing Jason's mother.

"People are *stupid*."

"That too."

"I'll prepare the statement," she said.

"Thanks."

Now that the story had been leaked to the public—an accidental gas explosion turned into a homicide investigation complete with sex, sensationalism, and an actual suspect—the police must've realized they'd forgotten something.

Me.

The police detective who'd called me that morning and later escorted me into that suffocating room in the morgue called back.

Detective Solano.

He asked if he could stop by and chat with me.

Sure, I said.

He came by the office around noon. I had a legal office on Forty-Eighth and Sixth in the city, but as we'd morphed into more or less permanent Hamptonites, greatly accelerated by the COVID pandemic, which caused a migration akin to the Irish potato famine's—substitute nouveau riche for starving Irish peasants—I'd opened up an office in Water Mill, where I could see that iconic windmill directly out my front window.

Detective Solano was partnerless. I wondered if that had to do with post-COVID budget cuts, which had caused municipalities to severely cut back—even ones with envious tax bases like this one. Or maybe this was just a courtesy call.

Jennifer offered him something to drink.

"Thanks," he declined, "I'm fine."

She shut the door.

"So...?" I said.

"So. I'm sorry you had to read about this in the paper instead of hear it from us. I don't know how they got hold of it."

I did. But there was no point in bringing it up.

"I know this has got to be a double shock for you. Again, you have my condolences."

"It's a *homicide*, then?" I asked.

"We're still waiting on the fire investigator's report. But they've given us their preliminary findings. It seems clear to them that someone cut the gas line—sliced it neatly; it couldn't have been a natural break. In their professional opinion at least."

"So how did that work exactly?"

"Work?"

"The explosion. Why didn't they just pass out from the gas?"

It felt odd talking about my husband and his lover as *they*. A twosome totally separate from me. His wife.

"They would've. Eventually. They lit the fireplace instead. It worked as a natural accelerant. Lit it all up."

"I see."

"Mrs. Mooney. Did you know anyone who would've wanted to kill your husband?"

"No. But you seem to."

He cleared his throat. "I assume you're talking about her ex-husband?"

"Like you said. I read it in the paper."

"He's a current person of interest."

"How much interest?"

"Sorry?"

"Do you think he did it?"

"It's an ongoing investigation. I really can't comment on that."

"Nothing to prevent me, is there? They said he showed up in security camera footage. Around the house that morning—around the time of the explosion."

"Like I said—I can't comment."

"Sure."

"So no enemies of your husband as far as you can tell?"

"As far as I can tell, no."

"No threatening notes? Unsavory incidents? What have you?"

"We got an unsavory note from our neighbor about cutting off some branches of her Japanese cherry tree. Our landscaper, Freddy, must've done it. It was overhanging our property."

"Was it threatening?"

"In a purely litigious way. She threatened to sue us."

"Did she?"

"No."

"Could it have gone beyond that? Could she have taken it to a more violent level?"

"I don't think so. She's eighty-four."

"Okay." He looked upset with me now. Like maybe I'd been playing with him a little.

He'd be right.

"That morning. Did you see your husband?"

"Yes. I usually saw my husband in the mornings."

"What time was this?"

"Eight o'clock or so."

"Did you talk to him?"

"Yes."

"And … ?"

"And?"

"What did you talk about?"

"I asked him if he wanted hazelnut coffee or regular—our machine does both. I asked him if he'd bought a new almond milk. I told him have a nice day when he walked out the door."

"That's it?"

"That's it."

"Did you know where he was going?"

"I assumed he was going to work."

"His office is in Wainscott?"

"He has two offices. One of them is in Wainscott, yes."

"So you had no inkling … you weren't aware that he *wasn't* going to his office?"

"No."

"Mrs. Mooney. Were you aware … Did you suspect at all that your husband might've been seeing someone?"

"*Seeing* … ?"

"Having an affair?"

How to answer that?

"No."

"So there were no … I don't know … late-night meetings? Unexplained disappearances? Things of that nature?"

"Not that I recall."

"Even if you rewind the tape a little?"

Rewinding the tape—like they'd done with that security camera footage.

"I can't say. I've been too busy dealing with him dying."

"Sure. Sorry to have to ask you this. But I have to ... I'm sure you understand. Where were you that morning at approximately 10:30 a.m.?"

I was waiting for that. Even with a suspect who all but had *I did it* stamped on his forehead—they'd have to ask. He wasn't the only one with a motive.

"I was with a client. Here."

"Which client? If you don't mind?"

I gave Detective Solano my embezzler's name. "I think you two may already be on a first-name basis. I believe he spent some time as a guest at your facility."

The detective smiled—that was the kind of humor he appreciated. All was forgiven.

"I'll need to check with him, of course. Your client."

"Of course."

"Oh. One other thing," he said. As if it had just occurred to him as he was already lifting himself off the chair on his way out the door.

"Emma Shipman? The woman your husband was found with. Did you know her?"

"Yes," I said.

Yes, I did.

CHAPTER SEVEN

They call it the seven-year itch, but that's purely anecdotal. Infidelity isn't a science after all.

Yes, it can be seven years. Or, thanks to the wonders of modern medicine, seventy years. Or anywhere in between.

At some point in many marriages—not all, no, but many, both happy marriages and unhappy ones—the day-to-day begins to dull ardor. *Familiarity breeds contempt*, the old expression goes. It also breeds restlessness, a sense of ennui, and sometimes unfettered libidinousness.

I'm a legal counselor, not a marriage counselor. But so many of the things my clients are accused of spring from marriages. Attempting to keep them, attempting to leave them, attempting to financially fortify them. Ask my embezzler, whose wife seemed to enjoy the finer things in life—even if they happened to be purchased with clearly ill-gotten gains. When she'd shown up with him at our first interview, it was clear she hadn't exactly been blindsided by his arrest.

When did the itch in *our* marriage begin?

Hard to say.

But let's rewind the tape, to borrow Detective Solano's expression.

Maybe at Maggie's pool party. The house off Sagg Main. With its own boardwalk to the beach that cuts through soft dunes dotted with seagrass. A modern design complete with a kind of crow's nest at the very tip-top where you can survey miles of unobstructed coastline.

I'd climbed all the way up there on our first house tour. Jason had begged off—his back was acting up. It was left to me to do the requisite tour, which, given the home's dimensions—including three separate levels—reminded me of the tour Jason and I had taken through the Vatican. All those endless rooms leading to more endless rooms. We'd finally ditched our audio-tour headphones in a conveniently located trash receptacle and run.

That wasn't an option at Maggie's.

When Maggie and I finally made it to the crow's nest, I was ready to collapse on one of those white daybeds she had sprinkled around their pool. I could see them from way up here—they looked impossibly inviting and incredibly far off.

I can't remember if we went up to the crow's nest the day of the party.

I remember drinking a bit more than usual. Proseccos mainly. But somewhere along the way I'd added in a blue frozen margarita. It was hot, the way it can sometimes get in August on days when the wind decides to take a holiday. One of the waiters had a tray of them and I plucked one on my way past, more interested in the frozen part of the frozen margarita than in the actual margarita part.

Let's call me mildly inebriated.

We liked to mingle at these things. Or I should say Jason liked to mingle. He was in his natural element. Where he could impart his considerable charm, doling it out like a host handing out canapés. Where he could regale people with stories, jokes, and reasonably witty observations complete with enough self-deprecation to avoid being insufferable. Many of those people were women. Yes. Jason was a flirt. But he was my flirt.

We'd walked into the party together. Had our first drinks together. Then did our normal splitting up, he going in one direction—toward his partner, Mathew, it appeared—and I in another. Toward Janice, who was dangling her legs in the shimmering oval pool while nursing a Pinot Grigio.

We'd occasionally bump into each other during the day. Like dance partners at a quadrille, lurching from one partner to another while occasionally ending up with each other. Only briefly.

Having fun? we'd ask each other.

Yes. Yes.

Then we'd be back on our way.

Jason was having a bit more fun than me. Like I said, he was a people person. I was a private person. I'd hit a wall at these things, when the thought of one more line of small talk became intolerable and I'd find myself sneaking peeks with intense longing at the front door, the pool gate, the path to the parking area, anyplace that led to the way out.

I hit a wall that day.

Which is when I began looking for Jason. It would be a process getting him to leave, I knew, every time having to enact a kind of long goodbye. It needed to be accomplished in stages. First disengaging him from whomever he was currently conversing with, then needing to deal with whomever he'd start conversing with on our protracted way out. Which was everybody. As if he couldn't bear to leave them. Not without another story, another joke.

I didn't spot him at first.

Like usual at one of Maggie's soirees, the crowd was huge. A mass of bodies in swimsuits, cover-ups, and white linen pants. It was like trying to see through the trees at the nearby nature preserve when Jason would whisper *osprey at four o'clock.* You had to *peer* in order to find it.

Then I did.

He was talking to a woman in a black one-piece bathing suit, her hip cocked, a drink being loosely dangled in her left hand. She was laughing at something.

I'd seen Jason speaking to women at parties before.

This time, I felt something lurch inside me. Shift. I suddenly felt dizzy.

The drinks, I thought.

I made my way over there. Reflexively took his arm—no, *not* reflexively. Deliberately. Laying claim to my territory the way the early explorers planted flags.

"Hey, Caron," Jason said, his teeth seeming oddly whiter than normal. That's right... he'd recently had a procedure done at the dentist. "This is Emma...?"

"Shipman," she said, extending her hand.

It was fourteen years into our marriage.

We'd doubled the cliché.

CHAPTER EIGHT

My assistant thought it was a joke.

That it wasn't him.

Then she thought, yes, it was him, but that *he* was making a joke. He had to be, right?

She explained this all to me in shorthand, because he was sitting there waiting on the other end of the phone. Did I want to talk to him or should she tell him I was unavailable? Permanently?

"I'll talk to him," I said.

This surprised Jennifer.

"*Really?*"

"Really."

"Hello," I said when I picked up. "Caron Mooney."

"I know. We're members of the same club."

For a second, I thought he was referring to the East Hampton Golf Club. Then I got it.

"What's on your mind?" I asked him. Asked Neil Shipman.

"Nothing much. Mostly trying to keep out of Dannemora state prison. Mostly that. I hear the food sucks."

"They have Taco Tuesdays according to an ex-client of mine."

"An unhappy ex-client I'm guessing."

"Pretty much."

"I didn't do it," he said.

"I didn't ask you."

"No. But I'm telling you. I didn't do it. I'm not a murderer."

"Just a domestic abuser." I shouldn't have said that. But hey, *it's my nature.* If you've never heard that particular fable, it involves a frog and a scorpion who wants a lift across the pond. *Don't worry*, the scorpion assures the reluctant frog, *I won't sting you. If I sting you we both drown.* Halfway across the pond—you guessed it—the scorpion stings the frog. *Why?* the frog exclaims on their way to the bottom. *It's my nature*, the scorpion replies.

"I never *hit* her," Neil said.

"That's not what it says in the police reports," replied the scorpion.

"Don't believe everything you read. For instance, what you're reading now. Don't believe it, okay? I didn't do it."

"You called me to tell me you didn't do it?"

"No. I called you to hire you."

That's why Jennifer had thought it was a joke. That it must be. The ex-husband and suspected murderer of the woman having an affair with my also murdered husband calling up the grieving widow to defend him.

"It's not a joke," I told her later.

This was after I'd hung up with Neil. After I'd told him I'd think about it.

"I don't understand."

"It's brilliant, isn't it? Why would a wife defend you from murdering her husband if she didn't believe you were entirely innocent? Why even bother making an opening statement? Just walking into the courtroom with him would make one without me ever having to open my mouth. Every day the jury sees me sitting there with him would continue making that statement."

Jennifer looked puzzled. She was going to night school for a law degree and was trying to learn from me. Her first lesson had been watching me in court defending her husband, an academic who'd picked up a two-hundred-dollar-a-day heroin habit and then thought he might as well move the stuff on his own. The DEA had noticed. He'd been facing twenty-five years in federal prison, but I'd managed to get him ten, something Jennifer had been extremely grateful for, at least until her husband dumped her for a yoga instructor he'd begun corresponding with from his prison cell. By then, she was already working for me.

"Excuse me," she said now. "Why would he think you would *accept*? That you'd ever take his case? Given, you know...the circumstances."

"The police think he was angry enough at his ex-wife and her new lover to kill them. He probably was. He's hoping I'm angry enough at my dead husband and his dead lover to defend him. I probably am."

"You're going to *do* it?"

"I'm considering it."

"Really?"

"Yes."

I already told you.

This is a hate story.

That afternoon I had another meeting with my embezzler. His nose was still running. So was his mouth.

"You sure you're properly *focused* on this?" he asked me. "On me?"

"Like a laser beam." We were going to trial in two weeks.

"You're all over the papers."

"Yes. I've noticed."

"Is that bad for me? All that publicity?"

"No. The eight million five hundred thousand dollars you erased from the books is bad for you."

"What are my odds here?" He looked a bit nervous now.

"Sixty/forty."

"Which one is the sixty? To be acquitted?"

"No. That's the forty."

"Jesus. Why didn't you tell me that?"

"You didn't ask."

"You said we had a good shot. That's what you said."

"We do. A forty percent one."

"That doesn't sound very good to me."

"You could've taken the plea."

An eight-year sentence in a minimum-security lockup. Assuming they didn't catch him smuggling in an eight-ball, he could've been out in four.

"Oh, thanks. Eight years in prison sounds *really* terrific. Wonder why I didn't grab it."

"Me too."

"Wait a minute. I don't remember you recommending I take the plea. You didn't."

"I didn't recommend you refuse it either. I was simply the messenger. They made an offer. It was my job to tell you. It was your job to choose. You chose to go to trial. So here we are."

"Sixty/forty, huh?"

"About that."

"Jesus." Jefrey sighed. Crumpled a bit in his chair. "Maybe we should go over my testimony again."

"Maybe so."

Before I left that afternoon, I called Joe Rawlings.

"Hey, Joe."

"Hey there. You doing okay? You got a visit from the goon squad, I hear."

"A squad of one."

"Which one?"

"Solano."

"Good cop."

"You know him?"

"Just by reputation. Clean as a baby's bottom."

"Baby's bottoms are clean?"

"We're talking about the Ffuck." The nickname for the Suffolk PD—pragmatically shortened to Ffolk, affectionately bastardized by those who'd served in it to Ffuck.

"Okay. I'm thinking I may need your services, Joe. Not a hundred percent there yet. But strongly leaning."

"Should I be cleaning my plate?"

"How about just making some room for the vegetables."

"I hate vegetables."

"You'll hate him."

"*Him?*"

"My client. The one I'm leaning toward taking."

"Mind if I ask who?"

"Kind of. But I'll tell you anyway. Neil Shipman."

Silence.

"You're not joking."

"You're not laughing."

"You're taking the *prick?*"

"I don't know if you noticed, but most of my clients are pricks. That's why they're facing jail time."

"Okay. This particular prick is personally offensive."

"To mc. Or you?"

"You. Which makes him personally offensive to me."

"I think you just said something nice to me, Joe."

"Don't let it go to your head."

"I won't."

"Caron?"

"Yes?"

"You know what you're doing here?"

"I know exactly what I'm doing."

"Okay. I'll make room for the peas and carrots."

"Appreciate it, Joe."

CHAPTER NINE

L et's rewind the tape back even further.

Before the party at Maggie's near Sagg Main.

Before I searched the crowd for my husband, Jason, and spotted him talking to a woman in a black one-piece bathing suit.

Let's rewind the tape and talk about marital sex.

I know, boring.

Still, it's what married women do a lot of. Talk about marital sex with other married women. Put down your fork at Babette's in East Hampton on any given afternoon in June, and listen carefully.

House talk, sure. What someone was having done—a new pool, a new wing, a new kitchen—and which newly celebrated contractor/architect was doing it. Parties, definitely. Who had given what party where, and most importantly, who'd attended. But always in there, fitted between the Bellinis, Proseccos, and Chardonnays, sex.

What kind of marital sex they were having. Or what kind of marital sex someone else was having. Not always with their actual spouses, which would make it *extra*marital sex. Sex sells, the old expression goes. It also titillates, entertains, and passes the time at Babette's.

For the record, I wasn't one of those women. The women who talked about marital sex.

I was too private. Too infused with Catholic guilt. Too something.

It had taken me a long while to even get around to sex. To introduce myself to its many pleasures and disappointments.

I was a virgin until sophomore year of college.

It wasn't like I hadn't been asked. Cajoled. Pleaded with. Begged.

It just hadn't relented. Memories of the yawing confessional in Our Lady of Sorrows Church in Urbana, Illinois, were still too fresh. I used to trek there with my brother, Daniel, who'd dutifully clutch my hand for the entire six-block walk. To an eight-year-old trying to come up with a list of confession-worthy sins, it seemed more like six miles. Daniel would carry the *Altar Boy Handbook* in his other hand; he took his duties seriously. So did I. Confession became internalized for me. Talking back to my mother had seemed to threaten me with the torments of eternal damnation. Letting a man into my underwear would've sealed the deal.

Eventually a man miraculously made it there. With the help of several plastic cups of Jägermeister and some potent weed. I wasn't a habitual pot smoker or much of a drinker. I just knew I wasn't going to make it into the ranks of the sexually initiated without them. I needed some enablers that I could later blame for my descent into moral depravity.

I can't say the first time was exactly pleasurable.

There was a lot of wincing involved. After all, blood was shed. In the end I didn't feel satiated as much as relieved—when I wasn't feeling the weight of the self-imposed hair shirt that had dutifully appeared under my Dave Matthews tee.

I've never entirely lost that feeling of guilt. Maybe it's a blessing in disguise—just not the kind I used to receive from Father McCrary. *The best sex is dirty sex*, someone once whispered to me. Jason whispered it. *Fine*, I'd thought. Sex was *always* dirty for me.

Which brings us around to the subject at hand.

Marital sex.

The best sex is dirty sex, Jason whispered.

Then he'd shown me.

Nothing too extreme. Honest. At least not to the average woman in twenty-first-century America, who's grown up on celebrity sex tapes, triple-X-rated rap music, and nude selfies. For an ex-denizen of the Our Lady of Sorrows confessional—sure, it took some getting used to.

"Don't," Jason said to me once. This was as I was slipping on panties after a shower as the first step in getting dressed for a night out.

"Don't what?" I needed to ask.

"Put them on," he said.

"My panties? I thought we're going to dinner."

We were. But Jason thought it'd be *hot* if, well, I went to dinner without wearing any. Panties. The thought of me sitting there in the American Hotel bar in Sag Harbor without anything under my leather skirt was *arousing as hell.*

I'll attest to that. That Jason was aroused.

Aroused enough to drive the car to the tip of the Sag Harbor pier after dinner and act like a teenager out in his father's car. Where even in the very thick of winter, someone could have driven past or parked directly next to us. Could've seen us.

The best sex is dirty sex.

Maybe.

There were other little experiments into lasciviousness that I'll keep to myself. Like I said—I'm not one of those women. The women who talk about sex.

I'll just mention one other thing.

We regularly incorporated porn into our lovemaking.

Yes, I know. Nothing to excitedly blab to a table of friends over lunch at Babette's. Doesn't everyone these days? Flip open the computer and peruse a virtual smorgasbord of sexual activity? Spice things up with the help of this handy and seemingly societally acceptable visual aid?

You get to be a connoisseur after a while. Familiar with the lingo.

BJs. Doggie. B&D. Group. Girl-girl. As if you've studied the Rosetta Stone of sex and mastered an entirely new language.

The best sex is dirty sex.

What was dirtier than this?

Even if the acting was mostly wanting, and the plotlines mostly ridiculous. Not to mention boring. After all, the endings were always the same.

I began noticing something.

Jason—who seemed to dominate the computer touch pad like he dominated the TV remote—seemed to end up in the same place. He might meander through oral, scan some MILF, and flirt with bondage, but he seemed to always make his way to the same destination—like a homing pigeon passing through exotic and uninhabitable landscapes on his way home.

Threesomes.

Sure. One of the more Porn 101 expressions. Its meaning pretty self-evident—even to a novice.

A woman. A man. And another woman.

That's where we kept ending up.

Making love to the sounds of a three-person chorus.

CHAPTER TEN

"Thanks," Neil said.

"You're welcome. For what?"

"Taking me on as a client."

I'd taken a few days to mull it over, then I'd called him back and accepted. We made an appointment for him to come into the office.

He'd shown up fifteen minutes late.

"One thing," I said. "Time is money."

"Yeah. Sorry about that."

"Don't be. You're being charged for those fifteen minutes. That's the money part."

"Fine."

"One other thing. What's with the hoodie and Ray-Bans?"

He looked like he was auditioning for 2 Live Crew.

"Oh. Yeah. The scumbags are following me."

"Which scumbags? The press scumbags or the police?"

"The reporters."

"Figure the police are too."

"Why?"

"They don't want you running off to Guadalajara. They don't have the budget to go get you. Not after COVID."

"I haven't noticed them. Following me, I mean."

"Trust me. They are. By the way, you aren't thinking about it, are you?"

"What?"

"Running off to Guadalajara?"

"I hate Mexico. I always end up with my head over the toilet."

"I wouldn't run off to Costa Rica either."

"I'm not running."

"Good. Because *I* have the budget to go get you. If you decided to run out on the bill, I mean."

"Are you kidding?"

"No."

"I'm not running anywhere. I'm not stiffing you."

"I know. You're paying me in advance."

"Fine. Great. Whatever you say. Are they going to arrest me?"

"I don't know. Should they be?"

"I *told* you. I didn't do it."

"And I told you. I didn't ask."

"I want you to *believe* me."

"Why?"

"*Why...?*"

"Yes. Why?"

"Because you're defending me. That's why."

"I already said I'm defending you."

"Jesus. I want you to have a little conviction here, okay?"

"You want me to prevent a conviction here. That's the way it works."

He looked exasperated with me. He took off the Ray-Bans and stuffed them into his coat pocket. Pulled back the hoodie. He looked like an ex-athlete now, I thought. Not that he'd probably ever dribbled a basketball in Madison Square Garden. There was a thickness to his neck. I could see blue veins protruding from it.

"Did you *know*?" he asked.

"Did I know what?"

"That your husband was fucking my wife?"

I leaned forward—the way I do with juries when I need to make a point. To drive it home.

"Look. Just so there's no confusion going forward. I'm your lawyer. I'm not here to commiserate with you. I'm here to defend you. What I knew or didn't know about what my husband was doing with your ex-wife is immaterial to that defense. Oh, one other thing. *It's none of* your *fucking business.* That too. We clear on this?"

Now he looked embarrassed. And angry. Which looked certifiably scary on him—those veins in his neck seemed more like cords of rope. This was the person who could stalk and harass—show up unannounced and uninvited and need to get escorted off the premises by moonlighting police officers dressed in black. Look at him and you could think this also was a person who could cut a gas line in the home he used to live in that had his ex-wife sitting in it, then sit back and watch as it blew sky-high.

"I was just asking," he said. "I was curious."

"You were inappropriate."

"Okay. Fine. I'll shut up."

"Great. On that subject. The press. Don't talk to them."

"I'm not."

"You'll want to. When their articles get uglier."

"They're pretty ugly now."

"They're just getting started."

"So? Are they going to arrest me?" he asked again.

"More than likely."

"Jesus."

"I'm not entirely sure what they have on you yet. I'll work on that."

"They have *nothing.* Because I *did* nothing."

"They have the restraining order. They have you being forcibly removed from a party you weren't invited to."

"I just wanted to talk to her."

"Fine. Ever hear of cell phones?"

"She never answered her phone."

"Maybe she didn't feel like talking to you. Maybe she had a reason."

"Hey. Aren't you supposed to be on my side?"

"I'm letting you know what *their* side sounds like."

"I went to the party to talk to her. She wouldn't answer the phone. She wouldn't answer my emails. What else was I supposed to do?"

"I don't know. Obey the restraining order, maybe."

"I wasn't violent at that party. *They* were. Those asshole security guys. They like looking tough."

"Some of them are tough. They're cops."

"Sure. They're tough when there's four of them jumping me."

"You were violating an order of protection. On that subject. There's a police report that says you *were* violent with her. With your ex-wife."

"It's total bullshit. Her lawyer made her put that stuff in there. Swear to God. So the judge would feel sorry for her. So she'd raise the monthly support. To make me look like the bad guy."

I didn't tell him that the bad guy is pretty much what he did look like—someone with a short fuse it didn't take much to light.

"There's one more thing they have on you," I said. "Security camera footage."

He looked down, sighed, shook his head.

"Yeah. About that."

"I'm listening."

"Sometimes I would drive past her house. That's all. Just to see what was going on."

"Right. It's called stalking."

"I wasn't *stalking* her."

"What would you call it?"

"I was still paying for that house. I had a right to drive past it."

"Not according to the restraining order. According to that, you didn't have a right to be anywhere near it."

"I didn't go into the house. I didn't go near *her*. I drove past it. That's it."

"The camera has you driving past about fifteen minutes before the house exploded."

"Right. Driving *past*. Continuing on my merry way."

"You could've parked the car. You could've walked back."

"I could've done a lot of things. I didn't."

"Okay. Is that what you told the police? When they brought you in for a chat?"

"Yes."

"What else?"

"Nothing else. I stopped talking. I called my lawyer."

"Sam White."

"Yeah."

"Your divorce lawyer."

"I didn't know any criminal defense ones."

"Yeah. But *Sam White*?"

"You have something against him?"

"Plenty."

"What?"

"That jingle of his. I can't drive two minutes in my car without hearing it."

"I think it's catchy."

"I think its excruciating. Sorry. I've strayed off topic."

I asked him if anyone saw him that morning. After he'd gone on his merry way.

Not till he'd gotten to the office around noon, he said. He was a venture capitalist—another profession I couldn't competently define. I told you. Finance isn't my thing. Just financial people. My dead husband. My embezzler. Neil Shipman. The Hamptons is swimming in them. *Beware of Sharks*, you'll sometimes see posted by the ocean. They should be warning the people on dry land instead.

There was just one more thing. I told him he'd need to sign a waiver.

"For what?"

"To acknowledge the potential conflict of interest."

"What conflict of interest?"

"One of your alleged victims was married to me. That conflict of interest."

"Oh. Sure."

I told him I'd work on finding out what the police had on him. I reminded him not to talk to anyone.

Then I went for a drive.

Down 27 into Bridgehampton—past Bobby Van's and Pierre's and Almond—places we used to go to for brunch on spring Sundays. That we might've gone to this Sunday—scarfed down Bloody Marys as we digested the Sunday *Times* while reading select articles to each other. Once upon a time, that's what we'd done.

I made a left off 27.

I passed a winery, a farm stand, palatial gardens with burlap still shrouding the shrubbery. Almost time to take those coverings off, but not yet— there was still the threat of killer frost.

If you asked me where I was going, why I'd turned left on Mitchell Lane, then right on Scuttle Hole Road, I would've said I don't know. I would've said I had no plan in mind, no destination. I was on my merry way to nowhere.

Then I saw the weeping willows.

It's true—they do look like they're weeping. Their leaves are the first to sprout and the last to fall, their branches scraping the ground like trails of cascading tears.

I drove through the iron fence. I pulled into the nearly deserted lot and got out.

I looked for a plot with a temporary marker.

There wouldn't be a headstone there. Not yet.

Just a mound of newly filled-in dirt and a sign so people could find it among the rows of dead. So they could stand there, head bowed, and express their grief.

Or their anger.

So they could cry, *Why?*

Emma Alice Shipman, the sign said.

Someone had already placed a stone on it, a way to keep the soul from escaping its earthbound resting place.

I knocked it off.

It wasn't allowed yet, I knew.

It wasn't time.

CHAPTER ELEVEN

We were knee-deep in jury selection.

My embezzler was scrawling on his notepad, which he was supposed to use for taking notes on the trial but which he was evidently using to write various lineups for his fantasy baseball team. *Lindor. LeMahieu. Trout. Bellinger.*

Jefrey was bored.

He was wearing a drab gray off-the rack suit. I'd told him to ditch the Hugo Boss. His wife was sitting directly behind us next to his mother, who'd flown in from Arizona. I would've had the kids there, but turning them into truants wouldn't have played well with the jury.

Speaking of the jury. I'd already used half of my preemptory challenges, which is courtroom-speak for *The door's that way.*

Most people think this is where the jury selection begins and ends. During voir dire—which is courtroom-speak for *grilling the shit out of the unhappy bastards.* They're wrong.

This is where it ends, sure.

It begins with Harry Lockman.

My jury selection does. Harry was an old-hand political pollster who switched to jury consulting when he realized there was more money in it and he wouldn't have to deal with candidates' wives. Or these days, husbands.

The career was new, but the principle was the same. He'd run a poll presenting arguments for and against a defendant and tally up the results. He wasn't looking for winners and losers exactly. He was looking for markers. Characteristics that could prove beneficial or detrimental to our case. Then he'd run focus groups with representative populations of the prospective jury pool, which either confirmed or disproved those markers.

In this case? People averse to regulations were our sweet spot. You know, stockbrokers, bankers, any Hamptons builder forced to deal with a bewildering bureaucracy of dos and don'ts. Fences in the Hamptons, for example, could be six feet high, unless they bordered a wetland, in which case they needed to be four feet high so Bambi wouldn't get hurt if he decided to jump it, but only on the side or back of a house, since you weren't allowed to have fences at all in the front of one. Don't even ask about sheds, guest cottages, pools, flagstone paths, septic tanks, and anything else involving laying brick to mortar. There were regulations upon regulations—and when you satisfied those regulations, there were other regulations you needed to deal with.

People who abhorred regulations would be less likely to convict someone who circumvented one or two of them by taking an unofficial loan.

Harry had handed me some supplemental additions to the questionnaires given the jury pool. Judges generally allowed minor defense requests like this since they didn't want their cases thrown out on appeal—it looked bad on their records. Judge Mandy Jessup was no different. She was looking to move up the judicial ladder—state supreme court, so rumor had it, so why let a few added questions to a jury questionnaire get in the way?

The questions we added?

Do you admire people who do what it takes to get something done, or people who go strictly by the book?

Do you think someone well-off got there on his own initiative or more likely inherited his wealth?

In other words, are you okay with embezzlers, and do you have anything against the filthy rich?

We'd gotten the list a week previous to trial.

That gave Harry enough time to check out each and every Facebook page—not to mention Instagram and Twitter. Some of the potential jurors he actually needed to friend in order to gain access to their pages. That's not for public consumption. Harry is one of those people who don't particularly like regulations. Meaning we could've used him on the jury.

I had a list in front of me.

Jurors we wanted.

Jurors we could live with.

Jurors we desperately needed to dump.

Like I said, I'd already used some of my preemptory strikes. Which means I didn't have to give Jessup a reason to get rid of them. Like emperors from ancient Rome, I could do a simple thumbs-down.

For others I needed to come up with *cause*. These didn't have to be important things, just things that sounded halfway reasonable. *Juror number 17 has an uncle who works for the IRS. Juror number 22 once accused her maid of stealing money.* Things like that. Where we could intimate a possible bias against my client.

Realmuto. Alonso. Altuve. Baez.

He was still filling out his Murderers' Row.

"Maybe you want to lay off the baseball Strat-O-Matic for a while?" I whispered to him.

"*Huh?* What's *that*?" he said.

"I just think you might want to concentrate on the jury. You know, the people who'll actually to vote to acquit you or not. I don't think José Altuve is in the jury pool."

He looked surprised—either because I was reprimanding him and he still wasn't used to that, or because I knew who José Altuve was. My father had liked boxing and baseball; it had rubbed off. Jason had been an all-out baseball junkie, and for some inexplicable reason an Astros fan. I wished José Altuve had been in the jury pool—someone who'd given the Black Sox a run for their money probably wouldn't have minded my client taking more than eight million of his company's.

"This is fucking endless," he said.

"Wait till we start the trial. It'll go better if you look like you care."

"You said I could take notes."

"Right. Not fill out a lineup card."

"How do *they* know what I'm writing?" He nodded toward the jury box.

"It would help if you looked at them occasionally. Like you're actually aware they're there."

"Oh, I'm aware they're there. Trust me."

The Suffolk County Criminal Court was located in Riverhead, which is located at the fork where Long Island splits into two. The more rustic rolling-vineyards-working-farms-and-houses-you-can-still-pick-up-for-under-half-a-million-dollars *North Fork*, and the less rustic loss-leader-designer-shops-no-one-shops-in-and-homes-you-can't-pick-up-for-under-several-million-dollars *South Fork*—otherwise known as the Hamptons.

Riverhead is neither North Forth or South Fork. It's the ass-end of actual Long Island, where people who don't make wine or spend thousands drinking it live their middle-class lives.

It's where they put the criminal courthouse.

The courtroom itself looks purely functional—they'd gone for pragmatism over majesty. Wood paneling instead of wood. *In God We Trust*, it states on the wall behind the judge's chair—which has always struck me as an example of wishful thinking.

I knocked a few more jurors off the pool.

My client stopped writing his fantasy baseball lineup and pretended to pay attention. Maybe he was. He leaned over at one point and whispered to me.

"She's looking at me funny." Juror number 29.

"Don't worry about it."

"She's giving me the evil eye."

"She's been fighting a tax lien for ten years and advocates abolishing the IRS on her Facebook page. We want her."

"You sure?"

"I'm sure. You should be worrying more about juror 32."

"*Her*... She *smiled* at me."

"Great. She'll still be smiling when she recommends they remand you to Dannemora."

"I can tell about women. She thinks I'm cute."

"She can think you're cute and still think you're guilty. I'm sure she'll agree to be your pen pal after she helps put you away."

He looked morose. "Great. So you're going to bounce her?"

"I'm going to try."

I did try.

And failed. I brought up the fact that juror number 32 had spoken disparagingly about Bernie Madoff in some decade-old online posts.

Jessup peered at me over her half-glasses.

"Everybody's spoken disparagingly about Bernie Madoff," she said. "Denied."

My client didn't seem upset at this turn of events. He smiled and whispered, "Trust me. She's got a hard-on for me."

"I'd avoid flirting with her. Your wife is sitting right behind us."

"Ha. I'll be discreet."

Jury selection dragged on until one, when Jessup called lunch.

I was barely out the door when I got a call from Jennifer.

"They arrested him," she said.

"*Him?*"

"Neil Shipman."

"Picked him up ... or let him turn himself in?"

"Picked him up. It's on the news."

There was a TV in the cafeteria set to Long Island 12. The sound was turned off but you didn't need any. Neil was being

escorted out of a squad car in handcuffs. Which means they'd
alerted the media so everyone could see Neil being escorted out
of a squad car in handcuffs. They wanted a show.

I called my friend at the prosecutor's office.

"Hello, Eileen." Eileen DeBorgia was an assistant prosecutor who'd begun to assist on some newsworthy cases. Not front-
page ones—not yet, but it was just a matter of time. I wondered if
they'd stick her on this one. They'd want a woman sitting at the
prosecutor's table.

"Hey, Caron. Look... I'm so sorry. I meant to reach out."

"Thanks." We'd come up against each other a few years ago
in an assault case. Things usually went one of two ways with
female prosecutors and female defense attorneys. A descent into
cattiness or a bond of sisterhood. Patronization, mansplaining,
and outright sexual harassment exist on both sides of the courtroom. We'd opted for sisterhood.

"I think you have something of mine," I said.

"What would that be?"

"My client."

"*Huh?*"

"Neil Shipman."

Silence. The same silence Joe Rawlings had presented me
with at the news I was defending my husband's alleged killer. I
empathized.

"I thought..." She hesitated. "Isn't he using some divorce
attorney?"

"*The* divorce attorney. Sam White. You know... with the
jingle you hear ad nauseam. He *was* using Sam White. Now he's
using me." I tried to remember if we'd notified the prosecutor's
office about Neil's change in legal representation. If Jennifer had.
Or if given that no one had actually arrested Neil Shipman yet,
we hadn't bothered.

"Can I ask you a question?" she said. "Strictly between
friends. We are friends, right?"

"Last time I checked you were definitely on my Christmas card list."

"Why?"

"Why what?"

"You *know* what. Why on earth are you representing Neil Shipman? Without going into detail—sorry, I have to put my professional hat back on for just a moment—our case is dead solid. Oh. And one of those dead is Jason. The person you used to be married to."

"Yes. I'm aware it looks odd."

"It looks grotesque. Sorry. Just being honest."

"I have my reasons," I said. "I also have my client. Who could've been *asked* to turn himself in. Or you could've asked Sam White to bring him in and picked up some free legal divorce advice while you werc at it. Or Sam would've told you to contact me and I could've brought him in. You didn't have to do a perp walk."

"Sorry. Not my purview. You know how it is when there's cameras around."

"They're around because your office told them to be around."

"Like I said, Caron. Not my decision."

I denoted something in her voice. A tautness more apropos of one of her closing arguments. A tell that her professional hat hadn't been removed quite yet. Or maybe never would be.

"Are you going to assist on this, Eileen?"

"I serve at the pleasure of the district attorney."

"Is that a yes?"

"That's a maybe. That's an I've heard some talk but maybe it's just talk so who the fuck knows."

"They could do worse."

"Appreciate the high praise."

"I'm just getting into the proper headspace to take you on. I can't be extolling your prosecutorial virtues all over the place, can I?"

"I'll let you know, Caron."

"You'll have to let me know. I'm his defense attorney. Bye."

"Bye."

My client was eyeing me from a lunch table where he was sitting with his wife and mother. He was making a face—either at the soggy tuna sandwich he'd taken two bites of, or at me for taking a work call that, odds were, had nothing to do with him.

"Ready?" I said to him. "We've got half a jury to go."

CHAPTER TWELVE

I hadn't gotten around to getting rid of Jason's things.

Jason hadn't been a clotheshorse—more of a show pony.

He liked to look good. Nice suits. Nice leisurewear, including nice golfing outfits—which is clearly an oxymoron, since I think the only people who might dress worse than golfers are bowlers. It's close. But then, I'm not a golfer.

Jason had tried to recruit me into the ranks. I'd taken a few lessons. Accompanied him to the driving range in Sagaponack. I'd even gone out on the course with him once nearing off-season, so we wouldn't be pestered by foursomes begging us to let them play through.

The game doesn't suit me.

I'm not leisurely inclined. I'd categorize myself as more of an obsessive workaholic—always focusing on what I need to be doing instead of what I'm doing in that actual moment.

Not Jason. I'd bought him a mug with quote emblazoned on it:

Golf is a good walk spoiled.

The problem is, you wouldn't catch me taking a good walk either. A good run, sure—I used to be obsessive about running until I was sideswiped by that Chevy and spent a month hobbling around on crutches. That day on the golf course, I was bored by the second hole. I began checking my iPhone for work emails between swings. We made it through nine before Jason gave up. I think he was more taken with the thought of sharing golf with his wife than with the reality of it, and secretly relieved it would remain estrogen-free.

I opened his closet door the night after the bail hearing.

I was all prepared to start dumping.

It was time.

I'd dragged a few empty boxes up from the basement. *Goodwill,* I thought. *I'll call Goodwill and let them cart it away.* For just a moment, I pictured a homeless-shelter resident dressed in Ralph Lauren and Burberry and found the image painfully funny. Unintentionally farcical.

His suits were lined up by color. Black, blue, gray.

I pulled the first one out and immediately smelled him. As if he'd just walked out of our master bathroom and into the bedroom to begin dressing for the workday. Creed Aventus. His go-to $285-a-bottle scent, mixed in with a $5.40 container of talcum powder. Which admirably summed up Jason. Someone who'd earned the finer things in life but hadn't completely washed off the stench of Red Hook. A man with enough accumulated toys to resent, but enough self-awareness to know that those toys were just that—toys for over-adolescent men—to avoid ever being disliked too much.

Smell is to memory what lighter fluid is to charcoal. It inflames.

I dropped the suit onto the floor—where the arms splayed out like those chalk outlines they used to draw at murder scenes. Showing where the dead body lay before being carted off to the morgue.

I followed the suit to the floor. Not intentionally.

I sank. I collapsed. I fell, as if off a cliff—the second time in a week I became up close and personal with carpeting—in this case the blue-weave Persian rug we'd purchased on a long-ago trip to Istanbul. It was becoming a habit.

I sat there on my knees, my hand pressed to my chest, feeling my heart flutter like a bird with a crushed wing.

I pictured the way I would look to someone else right now. To Jason's mother, for example, if she hadn't decided to head back to the pool in Boca Raton. It would confirm everything she'd feared.

I'm worried about you, Caron, she'd said. The widow alone. Brought to her knees on her own bedroom floor. At that moment, I was worried about myself.

Stop.

I got up off the floor, dragging the suit up with me.

Then I did something reflexive. What I used to do before sending Jason's suits to the cleaners. It's what a wife does, a simple act of housecleaning as opposed to a conscious act of snooping. I went through the pockets.

Something hard and thin was in one of them.

I pulled it out.

A bracelet. Diamonds and white gold.

For a moment, my heart stopped fluttering and instead did something Georgia O'Keeffe might have painted. It *flowered*. It was close to our anniversary when Jason died. Mere weeks away.

I held the bracelet up to the light to see it sparkle.

And caught the inscription.

To E.S. from J.M. With love.

The flower withered and died—snapped shut like a Venus flytrap killing whatever had been suckered into it.

My old friend entered the room—the one I'd just discarded in a weak moment of nostalgia.

Welcome back, hate.

This is still your story.

CHAPTER THIRTEEN

They say everyone's entitled to their own opinion, but not their own facts.

In bail hearings you're allowed your own facts.

One set of facts—the prosecutor's—stated that Neil Shipman was a violent abuser who'd murdered two people in cold blood and was someone with unlimited funds and a strong motive to use them to flee the country. To take that private plane to Guadalajara, where he'd lie on a beach and stick his tongue out at the authorities, including the judge who'd made the mistake of allowing him to be bonded out.

The other set of facts—mine—stated that Neil Shipman was a law-abiding citizen who'd never been arrested (until now), was innocent of all charges and looking forward to proving it in court, and was a well-established member of the community from which he'd never, ever, think of fleeing.

The judge, of course, was the ultimate arbiter.

Judge Moronis—burdened with an unfortunate last name that had sometimes been shortened by certain defense attorneys after trials didn't go their way. Dropping the last two letters for the benefit of reporters and a cheap joke.

Yes. He was known as a prosecutor's judge. The empirical evidence would back that up.

"It's iffy," I said to Neil's question about being granted bail. Not so much a question as a desperate plea. He needed to get out of there.

I'd met him at the Suffolk lockup, where he emerged disheveled and disheartened. There's thinking you might get arrested, and then there's actually getting arrested. The reality of it had clearly hit him hard.

The local lockup wasn't a max penitentiary. But it wasn't a weekend at Gurney's either. It reeked of BO and urine.

"I saw a rat last night," he said. "A *fucking rat.*"

"Animal or human?" I was trying to lighten the mood. Hard to do when you're sitting in jail with MS-13 gang members named Loco.

"You got to get me out of here. I'm *innocent,* for chrissakes."

That again.

"I'll do my best. Promise."

"I can make bail. Two million. Three million. I don't care. So what's the problem?"

"The prosecutors. They're going to be doing their best as well."

"I'll wear an ankle bracelet."

"That's very accommodating of you. Ankle bracelets can be cut off."

"I'll sign a statement. Put up everything I own. Whatever. I'll do it."

"A signed statement? Well, in that case …" I hadn't intended to descend into sarcasm. Not here. Still, I had—and he looked almost disappointed in me.

"For fuck's sake," he said.

"Sorry. I apologize. Look, they've already put you on the front page. They want to keep you there. They just look tougher if they keep you locked up, that's all."

I didn't tell him that Jordan Sizemore was prosecuting. The DA's top prosecutor, who was well on his way to better things and no doubt intending that Neil play the part of steppingstone.

"Good for them. I think I was talking about me. I'm talking about hearing people screaming all night and not being able to sleep anyway because I'm worried somebody's going to shiv me in the back. I'm talking about being stuck here ... *how* long would that be? Till we'd actually go to trial?"

"I wouldn't be buying a new suit yet. They're pretty backed up because of COVID."

"Right. Terrific. So I could sit here a *year*. Or more. That's what you're telling me. A *year* in fucking jail for something I didn't do."

"I'm not saying you won't make bail. I'm saying it's iffy. I'm saying I don't know. This judge likes to side with the prosecution. Not all the time. A lot of the time. You don't have a record. That's good. You have a history. That's not so good. I'm talking about violating those restraining orders. You could put up a significant bail. That's good. You have a significant bank account. That's not so good. They'll claim you can use that money to hire Get Me the Fuck Out of Here Jet Airways and take off for parts unknown. We'll make our argument. We'll see. But I don't want to BS you and say you can start making lunch dates at Bobby Van's. Actually, if we do manage to get you out, I still don't want you making lunch dates at Bobby Van's."

"Why not? Have you seen what they feed you in here?"

"Because you might make those lunch dates with a woman. And one of those reporters you mentioned that's been following you around might take a picture of that. Even if you make a lunch date with yourself, it still wouldn't exactly look good. No one wants you having any fun when you're out on bail for your wife's murder."

"You forgot something."

"What's that."

"Your husband. They're saying I murdered him too. Forget already? They're trying to nail me with a double homicide."

I hadn't forgotten. Two naked bodies. *From J.M. to E.S. With love.*

"Thanks for reminding me. No one who's out on bail for a double homicide should be ordering oysters Rockefeller at Bobby Van's, we clear?"

In the end, it didn't matter. Where Neil should or shouldn't eat.

Eileen made the case for the prosecution. Yes—I'd been right after all. She was assisting Sizemore—and he'd decided to trot her out for the bail hearing. And no—she hadn't given me a heads-up. So much for the bond of sisterhood.

She was wearing a severe-looking pants suit, which given her natural femininity made her look like someone a man might want to follow into a back alley but then not be the one who emerges from it. In other words, she looked both alluring and tough.

Sometimes at bail hearings, you get a taste for the prosecution's case. Not the full five-course dinner, of course. Just an appetizer—a tidbit that tides you over but doesn't ruin your appetite. Just enough to let the judge know he was dealing with a guilty defendant here and so he might not want to let him loose upon the world. But not enough to give the defense a head start on defending him—unless they were looking to force you into a plea deal to save the taxpayers the expense of a long trial. They weren't looking to save the taxpayers any money on this one. They wouldn't give me discovery until they had to. It was a game. A petty one, sure. But that's how it was played.

That tidbit?

Eileen saved it till the end.

After she'd recited the horror of two people being found dead in the rubble of an exploded house. She left out that those two people were found naked. And that they'd surely been getting ready to have sex—or were in the middle of having sex. Or had already finished having sex. She concentrated on them simply being dead. On them being murdered.

And on the murderer.

Who'd stalked and harassed and battered one of them. His ex-wife. Emma Shipman. Who'd taken out a restraining order on him. Why? Because she was frightened for her very life. It turned out she'd had good reason to be. This person—this defendant—was seen at the very scene of the crime. Caught on camera within minutes of the house going up. A house where the fire investigators determined the gas line had been neatly cut in two.

Which is where she dropped in that tidbit. Which was really more of a bomb.

That gas line. His DNA had been found on it.

Neil's.

I tried not to look surprised or flustered. I calmly wrote something down on my pad.

This:

Motherfuckingcocksucker.

After she finished, I laid out my facts to the judge. The ones I'd already discussed with Neil. How Neil Shipman had always been a law-abiding and reputable citizen. Not even a parking ticket to his name. How he was totally innocent of this crime and was determined to prove that in court. I mentioned his strong ties to the community and his ability to put up a sum of money that would strongly deter him from leaving it behind. I ended by reiterating that innocence and stating that an innocent man shouldn't have to spend a year or more in prison until he was given a chance to prove it.

I sat down.

Some judges like to take a little time to give their decision. At least a lunch recess, where they retire to chambers and at least pretend to be going over the arguments for and against.

Some judges don't. The ones who've made up their minds before either side has even presented their case.

Judge Moron.

Who said bail is denied and the defendant will be remanded to the county jail to await trial.

Before they took a stricken-looking Neil away, before I told him that I'd be appealing the bail decision, before I even got to say to him, *What the fuck was your DNA doing on that gas line?* he whispered something to me.

"I liked to fix things around the house. The boiler. The sprinkler system. The gas line. I checked it out once when I thought I smelled something."

"You should've called the gas company," I said.

CHAPTER FOURTEEN

I saw the red flash even before I made the turn to my front gate.

Something was floating on the air. The last remnants of an alarm—like the fading echo of a scream.

It looked like East Hampton's annual July Fourth parade, where seemingly every fire truck on the South Fork lines up end to end with their lights flashing.

It wasn't July Fourth—the fire trucks weren't parading down a crowded main street filled with lawn chairs and limp American flags.

They were congregated by my front gate.

I pulled up and sprang out of my car, thinking this is the way the firemen must've exited their trucks before—the ones lined up by the gate as if waiting for a starting gun.

"What's going on?" I shouted.

A ruddy-cheeked fireman strode up to me. "Is this your house, ma'am?"

"Yes. What's happening? Is there a *fire*?"

"Someone called in an alarm."

I felt a chill in the pit of my stomach. I clicked the small remote attached to my key chain. Before the gate was fully open, the firemen scrambled back onto their trucks like those old Keystone Cops reels where everyone moves in impossibly fast motion.

I followed the fire trucks up to the house.

Where there's smoke, there's fire, I thought, but does that mean where there *isn't* any smoke, there isn't any fire?

The house looked unperturbed. I couldn't see any leaping flames, flying cinders, burst windows. Nothing.

The firemen were about to charge into my house.

"Wait a minute," I said. "Who said there was a fire?"

The ruddy-cheeked fireman shrugged.

"Who phoned it in?" he asked someone on another fire truck.

That fireman shrugged too.

A *passerby*, apparently. One of the fireman finally confirmed someone passing my house had reported seeing a fire.

"Hold your hoses," I said. I was going for levity, but no one laughed. I don't blame them; fighting fires is serious business. "I don't see any fire. I don't smell any smoke. Do you?"

The fireman had to admit no, he didn't. He said he should probably make sure, though. Him and the rest of his company—who were milling by my front door like a frustrated baseball team whose game has been rained out.

"If there's no fire, I don't need any firemen," I said. "Tell you what. I'll take a look. If I see even one spark, you'll be the first person I tell."

"It's your house" he said.

He looked unhappy that I wasn't going to open the door and let him in to play. That he'd possibly been called out to what amounted to a fire drill. He had better things to do with his time.

When I entered the house, it was confirmed. No fire. I scoured every single room in the house to make sure, and there are fifteen rooms in our house if you count the two powder rooms and the three half-finished ones down in the basement. I checked those out too.

I went back upstairs and peeked my head out the front door to give them the news.

"Nothing here, guys. False alarm."

Grumble, grumble, grumble…

"You sure you don't want us to do a quick scan of the house?" the fireman asked. "Just to be sure?"

"No, thanks," I said. "I want you to find the person who reported the fire and turn your hoses on him."

He shook his head. They piled back onto their trucks. They drove away.

I poured myself a Johnnie to calm down.

It took a while; false alarms are still alarming.

I went online to see what the papers would make of me in the morning. That was the benefit of the internet—you didn't have to wait till morning.

Reporters had ambushed me as soon as I'd walked out of the courthouse—mostly local ones.

Chris Policano had been a page 12 guy in the city who'd moved east and become page 1. *Newsday's Senior Crime Correspondent*, it said on his byline. He was *Newsday's* only crime correspondent. Like every other newspaper in America they'd slashed their staff to bare bones in a nod to economic reality.

I liked Chris.

He'd told me a sad-sack story once while we were sitting at a diner counter waiting for a jury verdict. In the nineties, Chris wrote a piece on the ex-NYC mayor who'd just suffered a severe heart attack. Unfortunately it was on the same day Jerry Garcia died. *No wood for you*, his editor told him—tabloid-speak for cover story. *Your guy didn't die.* Then purely by happenstance Chris became the only reporter who actually got through to the ex-mayor's hospital bed. Which made it an *exclusive*—which made it *wood*, according to the editor.

"Then Mickey Mantle died," Chris said dourly.

He'd had better luck on Long Island. A virtual scrapbook of front pages, most of them with pictures of sagging crime tape strung between street poles.

He was the first reporter to ask me a question.

The question.

"Why are you representing the person who murdered your husband?"

"Because he didn't murder my husband. Neil Shipman didn't murder anyone. He's innocent of these charges and we look forward to proving it in court."

There—I'd just given him his headline.

"How does your innocent client feel about not getting bail?"

"How would you feel?"

"Pissed."

"That accurately sums up my client's feelings."

I went to *Newsday*'s website first; Chris had himself another cover story.

"WIFE DEFENDING HER HUSBAND AND LOVER'S ALLEGED KILLER DECLARES HIS INNOCENCE." Dark, twisty, and complicated—front-page-worthy for sure.

The phone rang.

"Guess you weren't kidding," Joe Rawlings said.

"Guess not."

"You have a shot?"

"Possibly. I don't know what they have."

"They have his DNA on that gas line."

"Right. He likes to fix things."

"I think maybe he likes to blow up things."

"You working for me or them?"

"I don't know. Am I working for you?"

"I was hoping. Yeah."

"So it's a go?"

"Afraid so. Time to eat your vegetables."

"I told you. I hate vegetables."

"Let's start with a timeline. It'd be lovely if we can put him fifteen minutes away from the house fifteen minutes after he passed it."

"Where does he say he was?"

"Driving."

"Driving where?"

"Away from the house."

"On his way where?"

"Work."

"Great. Did he get there?"

"At noon."

"Where's work?"

"Southampton."

"Was he driving five miles an hour?"

"Maybe. I did mention him never even getting a traffic ticket in my argument today."

"He had his phone on I hope?"

"I hope."

"Okay. We'll start there. Caron?"

"Yes, Joe?"

"Mind if I ask if you know what you're doing again?"

"Yes."

"Too bad. Do you know what you're doing?"

"Yes."

"You think he didn't do it?"

"I have no idea."

"So why are you defending him?"

"I'm a defense lawyer. That's what I do. Defend people."

"Okay. I'll shut up."

"Thanks, Joe."

After I hung up, I went back to my computer and logged on to the home's security system. We have a camera mounted on the front gate. I started scrolling through the footage searching for passersby.

A few cars whizzed past. A garbage collection truck. A cable TV van. A landscaping truck lugging four trees to some nearby estate.

A car crawled by, stopped, parked up on the other side of the road. The door opened; a stout-looking man got out and slowly walked up to my front gate. He stood there for a while.

He pulled what looked like piece of paper out of his coat pocket, slowly unfolded it, then looked straight up at the lens, holding it out where the camera could clearly see it.

FIRE.

CHAPTER FIFTEEN

We ran into Emma again on a Sunday afternoon in September. The Wölffer winery holds outdoor concerts by their wine stand. People settle down by tables or spread out on blankets across the grass. Somebody with a guitar usually sings Jackson, Joni, and James. That's Browne, Mitchell, and Taylor for anyone who's never listened to Classic Folk Rock 102 FM. Little kids chase each other between the blankets as their parents get bombed on Chardonnay. Some bring whatever sections of the Sunday *Times* they hadn't gotten to that morning. By the end of the festivities they're being used as face coverings to shield inebriated and sometimes slumbering concertgoers from the still-potent sun.

I enjoyed these concerts.

It felt a little like an extended-family gathering—the kind they like to show in those saccharine holiday commercials that bombard the airwaves from Thanksgiving to Christmas. Multigenerational get-togethers where everyone seems to be having a terrific time. The kind of family mine wasn't. Not After Daniel. After the twelve-year-old boy who used to hold my hand all the way to church climbed onto a step stool in his bedroom closet one fine morning and hung himself. He used a tie, gold with black stripes—a Christmas present from Aunt Josephine. Grief and embarrassment descended on my house, slowly cocooning us from Josephine and seemingly everyone else in the family. Maybe my father just couldn't bear the sight of his sister's three sons scampering around our backyard anymore. I remember they suddenly stopped coming over. And I remember intuiting the void in my father's soul—an emptiness that seemed as vast as the Sahara desert in the *World Book Encyclopedia*'s global map. An emptiness I tried to fill by *being* Daniel—crawling onto my father's lap to watch Iron Mike Tyson administer another first-round knockout. Cajoling him to teach me Tyson's left uppercut, later estimated by a Stanford physics study to be the equivalent of being hit by a medium-sized Vespa. I'd watch baseball games with Dad too—tag along with him to lumberyards and hardware stores—once the sole preserve of Daniel. I was a poor substitute, I knew—a knockoff, like those cheap designer bags they hawk on New York City's Canal Street. Okay-looking from a distance but on closer inspection made from inferior and flimsier stuff. I forced myself to toughen up. There was a commercial back then for the Amazing Moppomatic, guaranteed to soak up voluminous amounts of spilled milk, knocked-over coffee, you name it. They'd demonstrate its wondrous capabilities by wringing it out over a plastic garbage can. The Amazing Moppomatic would fill the garbage can all the way up to the brim. How could so much liquid come out of that small mop? The same way so much came out of small me. After that, I was wrung dry.

I was the one who'd found my brother.

I'd gone to wake him for school.

Danny, stop loafing, I'd screamed though his bedroom door. *Loafing* was my dad's expression, and I'd eagerly appropriated it along with his annoying habit—annoying to Daniel, hysterical to me—of singing "Danny Boy" to him during September's back-to-school week ... "the summer's gone and ye must go ..."

I don't remember if I sang it to Danny through the door that morning.

The bedroom looked empty when I walked in.

I thought I'd catch him still lounging in bed, still dressed in his pj's, and I'd run down to the kitchen to tell my mom, who'd give him what for. Then I saw the half-open closet door, with

8 5

the *Star Wars* poster taped to the inside. And Danny. It looked like he was reaching for something—like he'd pulled the step stool in there to maybe grab his baseball glove or stash of *Mad* magazines.

When I swung the closet door open, I noticed the step stool had been knocked on its side.

And this: Danny was completely still, the way he'd manage to freeze himself when we played endless games of Red Light, Green Light in the driveway.

Danny, I shouted, trying to get him to move.

That's when I saw the tie wrapped around his neck.

Danny wasn't reaching for his baseball glove.

God was reaching for Danny.

So the priest explained during the funeral service. *God wanted another angel*, he stated, though it seemed to me that he had more than enough of those already.

My family had cracked into pieces when I was eight years old.

For two hours or so on an early fall Sunday at the Wölffer wine stand, I could pretend otherwise.

Their wine isn't bad either.

I highly recommend their Summer in a Bottle White. It promises the possibility of being able to bottle June, July, and August—not just the wine itself, which is sweet and lingering, but the bottle, decorated with ferns, flowers, birds, and crabs— not the kind that sometimes befall hedonistic partygoers at Montauk's Surf Club—the kind you find scuttling across the wet pockmarked sand.

I was loading up on Summer in a Bottle White that Sunday. I was trying to hold on to the summer itself—to wring the last dregs of sun and that languorous haze that hits you around midafternoon on most summer Sundays—a combination of sea air and alcohol, where the ocean seems to merge with the horizon, or if you happen to be sitting at a table at Wölffer's wine stand, where the lawn seems to merge with the clouds in a swirling layer of mist.

I was feeling nostalgic for another lost summer.

I was feeling at one with the world.

With Jason.

Like any marriage, we'd had our ups and downs. Our fights about nothing, where we'd descend into petty one-upmanship and exchange brittle barbs that pricked. We always recovered—one or the other of us offering an olive branch that was usually accepted on the spot. We were good at making up. We were good at makeup sex. We were good in general, I thought.

He spotted her first.

Sitting by herself on a log meant as a makeshift bench, dangling a half-drained wineglass, which in the middle of a crowd that was otherwise attached made her seem even more alone. Like those quizzes you get in first grade: A pig. A chicken. A horse. A fire. Which one doesn't belong here?

She was the fire we both mentally circled, I think.

"The woman from Maggie's party," Jason said. "Maybe we should ask her to come over?"

Maybe we shouldn't, I thought. But I didn't say it.

She did look alone. I was half-inebriated. I was ready to be kind to strangers. An *almost* stranger that we'd spent ten minutes or so conversing with—at least I had. Jason, I remembered, had already been talking to her when I'd sauntered over and laid claim to him. I didn't remember what we'd been talking about. Probably nothing.

"Sure," I said, but in a tone that must've sounded half-hearted.

"We don't have to," he said. "She just looks … I don't know …"

"Solitary."

"I was going to say *sad*. She looks sad and solitary. She's recently divorced."

Right—that was what we'd talked about. Her divorce. I don't remember the context—how we'd gotten there. But I remembered she'd talked about being divorced only recently, and how these parties were like auditions for her new role—that of an available woman in the Hamptons. I'd gripped Jason's arm a bit tighter.

"Okay," I said. "Let's bring sad and solitary over to drunk and married."

"You sure?"

"Sure."

Jason got up and walked over to the log. I saw her look up—quizzically at first. Then a look of recognition, a smile, a glance over at me.

I smiled back.

He helped her up off the log. I remember thinking how courteous that gesture looked, almost chivalric, the way knights supposedly lowered their coats over puddles so ladies wouldn't soil their shoes. That kind of courtesy had gone out of fashion—if it ever existed in the first place. Jason had never covered a puddle with his Burberry coat for me. He would've balked at the cleaning bill, and I would've laughed out loud.

When she came over, she reached out her hand.

"Nice to see you again. Thanks for asking me to join."

She might've thought it was nice seeing me, but I couldn't see her. Her head was directly backlit by the sun, which gave her a kind of celestial glow—the way they'd painted angels in the Vatican, I remembered. It wasn't until she sat down at our table that her features came into view.

Jason was always surprised at the way women were so easily able to compliment each other on their looks.

"I've never said, 'You look handsome today, Mathew,'" he once said to me. "It wouldn't fly."

"Don't worry. Most of the time, we don't mean it."

"Good to know."

Sometimes we did.

Emma Shipman had the kind of face that appeared different depending on which angle you were gazing at it from. When she looked directly at me she looked one way. When she turned to speak to Jason, another. Both were beautiful. That's why I'd gripped his arm that day and refused to let go.

Directly facing me she looked like a humbler version of Elizabeth Hurley. Was that her name? The English actress who'd romanced Hugh Grant until he was picked up soliciting a transvestite on Hollywood Boulevard. From time to time she still popped up on Instagram under titles like *Fabulous at Fifty*. She was. Emma had rich brunette hair, which seemed even richer in comparison to my own—Jason's pet name for me was Blondilocks. Her eyes were the kind of green you see in retouched photos of Ireland.

Her profile—which I was unconsciously hoping would prove deficient and shatter the illusion of Hurley-like beauty—confirmed it, albeit in a somewhat sharper version, mostly in the chin and nose, but the kind of sharpness that added strength to that beauty, not detracted from it.

Yes, women are easily able to compliment each other. Or sometimes uneasily able to.

That's how I felt at the table. Uneasy.

I can't tell you exactly why. I'll amend that. I couldn't tell you then.

"Do you come here often?" I asked her. I was trying to be funny—using a pickup line mostly spoken in bars—or maybe just in movies about people picking up people in bars.

I don't think she got it. The trying-to-be-funny part.

"First time. A friend mentioned it to me. The same friend who said I should get out and do things. I decided to take her advice."

"You got out to Maggie's party." I'm not sure why I said that—as if I were challenging her assertion about being a wallflower. Was it possible to kick yourself under the table?

"Yeah. She actually brought me to that ... *dragged* me there, really. Honestly, I'm glad she did. It was nice to be among people other than lawyers."

"I have terrible news for you. I'm a lawyer."

"Whoops." She looked genuinely embarrassed. "Okay. I was referring to ones I was paying four hundred dollars an hour. And the ones accusing me of moral turpitude."

"Let me guess," Jason said. "You're speaking about your divorce."

"How'd you know?"

"Somebody said death and divorce are the two worst things that can happen to someone," I said. "I think death was second."

"It's close."

"Got a little nasty, huh?" I asked.

"Just nasty."

"Sorry."

"It's fine. It's over. At least I hope it is."

Jason changed the subject.

The music. The woman in retro bell-bottoms was singing a song I vaguely remembered but have forgotten the name of. About the seasons going round and round, the world a kind of carousel we're unable to jump off.

Maybe it was because it was the end of summer and the season was about to change. Or because I'd had two glasses of Summer in a Bottle. Or because I was sitting there with my husband and a strange woman. The song moved me.

I might've even started swaying to it, which is something I last remembered doing when I was thirteen at a slumber party in Alicia Samuel's house.

"I used to have a poster of her," Emma said.

"Who?" I asked.

"Joni Mitchell."

"Not New Kids on the Block?"

"My mom loved her. She used to vacuum the house to 'Big Yellow Taxi.' She would've named me after her but we needed an *E* for my grandmother."

"My mom loved Caroline Kennedy. She did name me after her—sort of. She dropped a few letters out of piety."

"I think Caron's a pretty name," Emma said.

"Thanks. But it doesn't shorten. Jennifer to Jen. Margaret to Mags. Caron to what … *Car*?"

"What kind of law do you practice, *Car*? I don't know"—she smiled—"works for me."

"The kind that makes people tell lawyer jokes."

"Hard for me to find lawyers funny. They cost too much."

"C'mon. We're hysterical. Why won't sharks attack lawyers?"

"Why?"

"Professional courtesy."

"Okay. That's funny."

"Why did God make snakes before lawyers?"

"I give up."

"*Practice.* See, I told you. We're a barrel of laughs."

"Seriously. What kind of law?"

"Criminal."

"Which side?"

"The one that pays."

"Great. If I ever kill my ex-husband, I'll know who to call."

I'd remember that later. When I got the call about my husband dying naked in a house explosion next to a naked woman who also died. The same woman who on a September afternoon at the Wölffer wine stand said she'd know whom to call if she ever murdered her ex-husband. The ex-husband accused of murdering *her*, who did call me.

Jason asked what kind of work Emma did.

"I used to be in fashion."

I could see that. Emma being in fashion. One of those women jumping out of a cab on Seventh Avenue dressed head to toe in Gucci.

"Now. Not sure," Emma continued. "Aren't divorced women in the Hamptons forced to sell real estate?"

"Yes. It's a local ordinance." Jason said. All white teeth.

"Fine," she said. "Hope I don't have to start with mine."

"Part of the settlement?" I asked, then regretted it. It was too nosy for someone I hardly knew.

"Still up for discussion. He paid for the house—I made it a home. More like a haven, really."

"Where is it?" Jason asked.

Sycamore Lane in East Hampton, she said. Not in the way most people in the Hamptons tell you their addresses—as if offering up their bank statements. The physical address didn't seem important to her—it was all about the emotional. She'd constructed a shelter from the storm that had become her recent life. She wanted to hold on to it.

The conversation went round and round like the seasons. Flowed like the Summer in a Bottle—Jason ordered another bottle plus a platter of charcuterie that he rightfully insisted on paying for. I can't remember the rest of what we talked about. Just pieces of it. I remember feeling jealous when Jason and she leaned in a little farther than necessary toward each other. I remember chiding myself for feeling jealous. Mostly I remember the way the sun seared the edges of everything, like the fiery corona that appears around a total eclipse. The lush trees, the bell-bottomed singer onstage, the empty bottle of wine, Emma. Circled by rings of fire.

And I remember being serenaded by a song about the vagaries of love as we stumbled off to our respective cars with a casual invitation to do this again. *Such fun. Really nice time.*

We should do it again real soon.

CHAPTER SIXTEEN

I had my first dream about Jason. The first one since he'd died.

We were out back at the pool.

He said he was going to get something from the shed.

It was the place we stored everything we were too lazy to throw out. Broken lounge chairs. Ripped table covers. Old grills with the residue of a thousand jalapeño cheeseburgers encrusted on them. A place I avoided because it was filled with spiders. Venomous ones, I was convinced.

Ever since I read as a kid that black widows devour their mates after sex, I was revolted by them over and above my natural and understandable aversion to poisonous eight-legged insects with multiple eyes. Eating their partners was macabre and grotesque, not to mention sickeningly deceitful.

In the dream, Jason didn't come back to the pool.

I felt a growing dread. The sun turned to ice.

I felt the necessity to go look for him. Even though it meant opening the door to that shed.

I was greeted with black. The kind of black that black spiders can disappear right into. I called out his name.

He answered me. Asked me to come inside.

I walked in and saw him half-hidden in the dark. Smiling.

His face was covered with them. With black widow spiders.

I screamed.

And woke up.

I was drenched in sweat. My heart was thudding.

I flicked on the light and sat up in bed. Fright slowly morphed into emptiness. He was alive in my dream, but not in my house. It still shocked me—that I was alone. Brenda was right—it was no picnic.

It being the middle of the night didn't help matters.

It's happened to me before, of course. Waking up at three in the morning and not being able to get back to sleep. That feeling that you're the only one alive on the planet. Back then, there'd been someone else sleeping beside me.

Now there was a sad sterility emanating from the other side of the bed. Not even the depression of a body, just a clean sheet tautly tucked under the mattress, unoccupied and undisturbed.

I grabbed my laptop and went online. I thought I might as well do some housecleaning.

I was an inveterate email hoarder. I currently had 10,338 of them piled up in my personal account. I'm not sure why I didn't erase them after reading—maybe there was the nagging thought I'd need them one day. That a client might've inadvertently sent something to my personal email address instead of my legal one. Maybe it'd prove to be important. Maybe I was trying to set the Guinness World Record for most emails stuffed into a single address. Sometimes the sheer number shocked me and I'd think I should really get around to removing them. But how? In bulk, with one click—or would I need to go one by one? The magnitude of that effort cowed me from ever starting.

But now it was the witching hour and I knew I'd never make it back to sleep. That dream had unnerved me. Seeing my dead husband. Seeing him with a blanket of spiders covering his smiling face. I was afraid that if I did make it back to sleep, I'd find myself in that shed again, like a Netflix horror movie picking up where you last left off. I used to have nightmares about walking into a boy's bedroom closet. I'd often wake to the sound of my own screaming.

So emails.

The first were the ones I'd received since Jason's death. People didn't need to send you sympathy cards in the mail anymore. They could just send them online—most of them designed like the kinds of cards they'd replaced. *Sorry for Your Loss* on a what looked like an actual card cover—you needed to click on it to see who it was from and read the personalized message.

Some of the messages were simple homilies—the kind they used to needlepoint onto wall samplers.

When someone you love becomes a memory, the memory becomes a treasure.

Life isn't eternal, but love is immortal.

Those we love don't go away, they walk beside us every day.

Reducing loss to a Hallmark card is the way I would've summed it up to Jason—had Jason been there, as opposed to being the person these homilies were about.

Click. Click. Click. Click. Click. Click. Click. Click. Click. Click.

Only 10,328 emails to go.

I got into a rhythm—scanning and dumping, scanning and dumping. I must've stayed at it for more than an hour, but every time I looked at the figure in the upper right-hand corner it hadn't seemed to decrease very much.

It reminded me of the time our basement flooded on a Sunday in the middle of the night—meaning we weren't going to be able to get someone from Roto-Rooter out of bed. We'd had four days of constant rain, and it seemed like our sump pump had given up out of sheer exhaustion. It was left to us— Jason and me—to head down there in fishing boots (Jason had read a book about trout fishing and imagined spending weekends lazily casting on a Montana river) and lugging pails up and down the staircase. It was a pathetically inefficient method of flood control, and the black swirling water never seemed to dip below our knees.

The flood of emails felt the same. I could keep dumping them nonstop for days and it wouldn't make a difference. That number in the upper right-hand corner would just keep sticking its tongue out at me.

I was ready to give up and take half an Ambien—a last resort for me.

Then I noticed a word.

Scent.

I stopped and read the whole email.

It was about *my* scent.

From the love of my life who was no longer in my life.

Who was now dead. Blown to smithereens.

An email from my betrayer, who would usually tell me things face-to-face or on the phone or lying next to me in bed— but occasionally in *emails* after we'd fought and things were still touchy. Still raw.

Yes. We'd had a fight, I remembered now.

Darling Caron.

I still smell you from last night. Your scent. I'm not talking about the Guerlain I bought you. I'm talking about YOUR scent. What I can still smell on my hands and on my face. Yeah, I know this will probably make you blush or possibly even gag but it's a reminder, I think. Even when you push me away, you still end up clinging to me.

I felt myself making up all over again. In my thudding heart I did.

I felt something else.

This will *make you blush* the email said. It also made me, well, hot.

It'd been weeks since I'd felt anything remotely sexual. Death will do that to you. Banish those feelings to a subterranean chamber where they're expected to stay for a respectable amount of time. They have no place in a story about grief and loss.

Or in a story about hate.

This story.

But they'd come out of that dark chamber and into the light of day. Or more accurately—the middle of the night.

I'll confess something.

I touched myself. Here in my empty marital bed at four in the morning, surrounded by half-filled boxes of Jason's clothing and a computer opened to online mail. I touched myself.

Your scent. What I can still smell on my hands and on my face…

After my breathing had come back down to earth and I went into the bathroom and splashed cold water on my face, then came back into the room and slapped the computer shut, I felt another old friend creep into bed with me.

The one I'd had since childhood.

Hello, guilt. Introduce yourself to hate.

Hail Mary, full of grace, the Lord is with thee. Pray for us sinners now.

Hail Mary, full of grace, the Lord is with thee. Pray for us sinners now.

Hail Mary, full of grace, the Lord is with thee. Pray for us sinners now.

I'm sorry.

It's a habit.

CHAPTER SEVENTEEN

I n chess matches, each side gets the chance to go first.

In trials, it's always the prosecution.

That mostly benefits the defense, since you get to see their case in its entirety and then figure out where you can poke holes in it.

In the case of my embezzler, the prosecutor trotted out the first three names on their witness list and they all said more or less what you'd expect them to.

A co-owner of my client's company testified how he'd first become aware of a shortfall in funds. A shortfall in the millions of dollars. He'd notified the company accountant to investigate.

The company accountant testified that he'd immediately suspected fraud. The books had been doctored. Unusual checks were made out to LLCs with no known provenance. With the co-owner's permission, he'd referred the matter to a forensic accountant better equipped to deal with these matters.

The forensic accountant testified it had taken him three weeks to untangle the carefully spun web. Those LLCs were companies with PO boxes in the Turks and Caicos that seemingly did no legitimate business. Newsflash: they'd been incorporated by none other than—drumroll, please ... my client. It was embezzlement pure and simple.

The co-owner had notified the authorities.

I did what little touching up I could do on cross. The facts of this case weren't in dispute—money had been taken and it'd been taken by my client. *Taken*, not *stolen*. The semantics were important here. You can take something with the intention of returning it. When you steal something, no one's giving it back.

I mostly did a little character polishing.

Had my client been a good, productive worker? I asked the co-owner.

"Up to the point he robbed us?"

I admonished him to give a yes-or-no answer—and for the judge to strike his answer from the record. I went one for two—which in baseball will get you into the Hall of Fame, but in the courtroom will simply keep you afloat.

Was my client a good, productive worker? I repeated the question.

"I suppose."

"So that's a *yes*? For fifteen years my client was a good, productive worker? An asset to your company?"

"He was okay."

"Just okay? He received sterling year-end reviews, didn't he?"

"I don't remember."

"Let's see if I can refresh your memory." I asked the judge to allow those year-end reviews into evidence.

The prosecutor perfunctorily objected—his work records had nothing to do with the crime he was charged with. It was immaterial.

I explained that the prosecution was trying to paint my client as a thief. We intended to show that my client was no such thing. He merely borrowed funds with the intention of returning them. His work records played to character and showed no pattern of disreputable behavior while in fact showing just the opposite—that my client was a productive and valuable member of the company.

Objection overruled.

I put my client's last year-end review into the co-owner's hands.

"Is this the year-end review you yourself gave my client?"

"It looks to be."

"It looks to be because it is. Yes?"

"If you say so."

"With all due respect, I'm trying to get you to say so. Is this his last year-end review or isn't it?"

"It is."

"Can you read it for the jury, please?"

He looked to the judge and asked if he had to.

"Assuming you're capable of reading," Jessup replied.

The year-end review included words like *diligent, industrious,* and *conscientious.* The witness spoke in a lower-than-normal voice, as if hoping the jury wouldn't hear. Perfectly fine, since I was able to ask him to repeat select words for their benefit.

The word *conscientious,* for example.

"Do you know the definition of the word *conscientious?*" I asked him.

"Of course," he answered.

"Well, in the interest of exactitude, I'll provide it for the court. *Conscientious* is *wishing to do what is right, especially to do one's work or duty well.* You wrote in your year-end review that my client was wishing to do what is right. Right?"

"I wrote he was *conscientious.*"

"Which, as I've just defined for the court, means he was wishing to do what is right." I gave the jury a lingering look here—I wouldn't swear on the courtroom Bible, but juror number 32 seemed a little less dour today.

I decided to finish cross on a high note. When I sat back down at the defense table, my client was smiling.

"Knock it off," I whispered.

"Knock what off?"

"That smile. There's no gloating in jury trials. Certainly not by the defendant."

"You did great. *Conscientious.* That's me."

My cross was followed by the prosecution's re-direct, where he got the co-owner to repeat that my client had stolen eight million five hundred thousand dollars by *conscientiously* creating fictitious companies, writing checks to them, and then doctoring the books.

My client lost his smile.

Still, for a day in which my client's sins were enumerated by three respectable witnesses, it wasn't a total loss. I'd planted a seed, and with a little watering and careful nurturing, it was just possible we might be able to grow some nascent doubt.

On the way out of the courtroom as we were waiting for Jefrey to emerge from the bathroom, his wife asked me if it was okay if the house and other assets were transferred to her name. You know, in case he lost and they went after the money.

"I'm afraid the state wouldn't appreciate that. They might notice and decide to bring it to the jury's attention."

"It's not *illegal*, is it?"

"If the funds that purchased the house were illegal, then yes. It's illegal."

"Oh." She looked unhappy about that.

The courtroom steps were empty of reporters. This was your run-of-the-mill embezzlement case. It didn't involve sex or death and a lawyer defending the person accused of murdering her husband. It wasn't *wood*.

Jefrey asked me if I wanted to grab a drink with them.

I desperately wanted to say no.

I desperately wanted a drink.

I'd been doing more than usual of that lately. Drinking. Johnnie Walker Black with one cube of ice. I'd play a game to see if I could down the glass before the ice melted. Sometimes yes. Sometimes no.

Jefrey told me to follow their car on the way back from Riverhead.

Down 32 then left onto 27 East.

It wasn't until I parked and exited my car after following him onto a gravel drive somewhere off exit 66 that I noticed where we were.

The Dove-Tail Inn.

CHAPTER EIGHTEEN

I don't remember who chose it.

Jason? Or was it her?

We'd exchanged cell phone numbers as we left the Wölffer wine stand that September Sunday, pledging to keep in touch and do it again.

She had kept in touch.

She'd texted me a political meme, as I recall—memes about the orange-haired resident of the White House had become a national rage back then, a word that aptly summed up the nation's mood. Rage at the president, rage at people who raged against him.

I don't remember what the meme was. I can safely say it made fun of the forty-fifth president of the United States, which, after all, was the whole point of memes.

I texted her back—*LOL* probably. Something short and to the point.

I wasn't much of a texter. The smartphone has made constant social interaction the new norm—though I consider it more of a constant social intrusion. You're expected to answer texts promptly, and if you don't, you can expect to receive more texts asking you if you're actually still alive. Phone calls have beginnings and ends, but texts are as endless as the universe. They just keep expanding.

I did answer Emma Shipman. With that *LOL* or *HA*.

And then perhaps a week later, I received another text from her.

This one I remember. A picture of my namesake, six-year-old Caroline Kennedy, standing at attention next to John Jr. at their father's funeral. Emma had come across it somewhere and immediately thought of me.

Thanks, I texted back. *I wonder what it was like to become a symbol of national mourning?*

I think she was too wrapped up in her own mourning then. If she even understood what death was at that age.

I'm not sure you know what death is at any age.

So true. My father passed away when I was 22 and it took me months to actually believe it, Emma texted.. *To not pick up the phone and tell him what I was up to that day.*

My mom died of breast cancer when I was 31, I answered. *I bought her a birthday present the next year. It's what I did on my mom's birthday—buy her a present. I'd forgotten she wasn't actually there to receive it.*

This was already a lengthy conversation for me. Way past a normal text chat, and a lot more personal than I generally got with people—never mind someone I'd spent a single Sunday afternoon with.

Who knows. Maybe your mom and my dad are dancing right now, she texted.

The line struck me as odd. It wasn't just the allusion to an afterlife—a belief that seemed out of vogue these days—but the image of our two dead parents waltzing across a celestial cloud together.

I'm guessing you don't believe in heaven... she wrote.

I'd broken the rhythm of our growing text-a-thon. She'd noticed.

Sure I do. Heaven is a hot-stone massage at Gurney's Inn.

A smile emoji. Then: *I suppose the good news would be there's no hell either then. Can I stop recycling?*

No. We have to save the planet for the children both of us don't have.

She'd mentioned that to us at Wölffer's. *Thank God I never had kids with him*, she'd said, referring to her ex-husband. Was that why we got along? When you don't have kids to talk about, you have to find other interests, which possibly makes you more interesting. Or maybe just makes you transfer those maternal feelings elsewhere.

Her house maybe. *My baby*, she called it, that safe haven she was still fighting tooth and nail to retain.

I'm not sure where my maternal instincts were. Maybe under the same Oval Office couch where W had searched for those WMDs.

Do you have kids? is usually the second question out of everyone's mouth when they meet you, right after *What's your name?* It's always struck me as egregiously personal, as if they're asking if you have any money in your bank account.

Not a one, I answer, then wait to read their expressions, which vary from thinly disguised pity to something more questioning. The presumption being that something might be wrong with me.

There's plenty wrong with me, I think. *Just not this.*

Okay. You convinced me. I'll keep recycling. But I'm going to start asking for plastic bags at the Stop & Shop. The paper ones always break just as I get through the door.

We kept on like this for a bit.

Then I got a work call and had to run.

The next time I was the one texting her, and we slowly became texting friends—which is one level up from Facebook friends who aren't actual friends at all.

At some point one of us—she or I—asked about the three of us getting together for that drink again. Someone recommended a place off exit 66 that had a lovely bar facing a kind of glen.

The Dove-Tail Inn.

When I walked in with Jefrey and his wife, the receptionist glanced at me with something akin to recognition. It looked like she was about to greet me with a full-smile welcome back. She didn't—glancing down at her ledger instead, then back up with a look cleansed of all familiarity. I wondered if that was hotel reception tradecraft—a carefully honed reticence to acknowledge too much.

"The bar's pretty nice here," Jefrey said, and I momentarily wavered on how to answer that. *Yes, it is,* or *Sounds lovely.*

Or maybe: *I just remembered I have to leave.*

I was struggling for an excuse that wouldn't seem like an unabashed lie and coming up empty. I simply nodded and followed them in.

A second look of recognition came from the bartender. Teddy.

A toddy, Teddy… we'd caroled him with during holiday season, which sounds less funny than it did after our first round of his specially concocted cider that came with an overly generous portion of eighty-proof rum topped off with a peppermint cinnamon stick.

The bar had been festooned with sprigs of pine, sagging Santa hats, and striped Christmas stockings. Out in the glen they'd constructed a manger with a bodacious-looking Mary who might have been sculpted by Jeff Koons.

Guess there was no room at the inn… Jason had joked.

The two of us had dutifully laughed.

Is there… one of us had asked. I don't remember who.

Is there…?

"Hello," Teddy said once we'd settled down at the bar. "Nice to see you again."

Bartenders must be exempt from Inn School, where they teach the ins and outs of proper guest etiquette. Maybe he'd simply flunked out, while the receptionist was busy graduating summa cum laude.

"You too," I said.

"You've been here before?" Jefrey asked.

"Right. I'd forgotten."

Teddy asked us what we wanted.

I ordered a Johnnie with one cube of ice. Jefrey demanded a wine list and then took five minutes perusing it with an exaggeratedly attenuated eye before choosing a Pinot Noir from the Willamette Valley. His wife went for a piña colada.

"How we doing?" Jefrey asked after downing half his glass.

"We aren't doing. We haven't gotten to the plate yet." I thought I might as well go for a baseball metaphor given his evident interest in fantasy play.

"Right. Okay. So how are they doing?"

"A solid double into the right-field corner."

"Hey, I said I was sorry for doing my lineup. I was bored."

"Actually, you didn't say you were sorry."

"I *stopped*, didn't I?"

"Yes. You stopped. I'm over it. I was just trying to answer your question in layman's terms."

"*Huh?* Okay. So they just did okay."

"They did okay. So did we—we were able to lay a little foundation."

"Right. Conscientious. That was good."

"Thanks."

Teddy was staring at me. He was ostensibly wiping down a glass with singular devotion, but what he was actually doing was peeking sideways at me. He must've read the paper. He was trying to remember things.

"Is that it for them?" Jefrey's wife. Who had a coconut mustache from her frothy colada.

"*It…?*"

"Their case. Is that it?"

"Afraid not. They have a few more witnesses."

"When do we get to go?"

"When they're done."

"When's *that* going to be?"

"A few more days."

"Are you sure about putting *him* on?" She nodded toward her husband, who seemed to be eyeing a woman at the opposite end of the bar. She knew him. Over the years she'd probably heard him try to worm his way out of this and that as he twisted himself into pretzels. Like many wives, she'd become adept at knowing when he was lying. She was imagining him up on the stand doing it. *I swear on a stack of Bibles*, he'd probably said to her more than once when he'd come back with lipstick on his collar and booze on his breath. Now he'd be swearing on a single Bible. She was skeptical of our prospects for success.

"He'll be fine," I said.

"If you say so."

"We've been *practicing*," Jefrey told her.

"You'd better."

She was scared of him going to jail. Of all their money going *poof*. She didn't have a job—it seemed like being married to Jefrey was enough of one. And then there were the kids.

"Don't worry. He's going to nail it," I said and reached over and patted her hand. Suddenly it was someone else's hand.

I snatched my hand back. So quickly that Jefrey's wife stared down at hers as if something might be wrong with it. As if it were sweaty or dirty or in some way physically offensive.

"Sorry," I said. "Some people don't like to be touched. I didn't know if you're one of them."

"Oh … that's okay. I don't mind. If you say he's going to fine up there, I believe you."

Guess there was no room at the inn … Jason laughed.

Is there … ? It was me. I was the one who'd said it.

"Maybe we should have another session," Jefrey said.

"*Session … ?*" I wasn't focusing. What was he talking about?

"You know … where you play the prosecutor."

"Sure. Tomorrow night."

"You think I should cry?"

"*What ...?*"

"On the stand. Do you think I should cry?"

"You mean force yourself to cry?"

"Correct."

"I'd advise against it."

"Why?"

"Because it'll *look* like you're forcing yourself to cry. Like you're not being genuine. Juries don't appreciate that."

"You've never seen me cry."

"I can imagine."

He looked down at his lap. Sighed. When he looked back up there were tears in his eyes.

"Very impressive," I said.

"Told you."

I was going to tell him to save it for if and when the jury found him guilty. I didn't.

"I would lay off the tears," I said.

"You sure?"

"I'm sure."

"Another round?"

"No. I have some work to do."

"On my case, I hope?"

"Don't worry. I'm an excellent multitasker." When he looked offended, I lied: "Sure, on your case."

I had to go the bathroom before leaving.

I offered to pay—Jefrey thought about it before dismissing the notion. I said goodbye to them. As I got off my stool and began making my way to the corner of the room, I could see Teddy still peeking at me.

The bathroom had that all-white Hamptons look. Some genius had figured out that stripping décor down to bare white screamed luxury. Maybe because it invited you to fill all that white—to make your mark on it. Leave an imprint worthy of your stature in life.

Why do women go to the bathroom together? she'd asked me in this bathroom. *Men don't.*

Because men are strong and independent, and women are clinging vines incapable of carrying out the most rudimentary bodily functions without assistance.

You're joking.

Yes.

So why do women go to the bathroom together?

Because we can.

CHAPTER NINETEEN

"He didn't keep driving," Joe Rawlings said calmly.
Joe had stopped by the office. We had a day off due to a juror's illness and Joe thought he'd deliver the news in person.

"Care to elaborate?"

"That morning. The prick told you he drove by the house and kept going. He didn't."

"Since he's officially my client now, is it okay if we refrain from calling him the *prick*? Not that it offends my sensibilities. Just my professionalism. After all, I'm taking the prick's money."

"If you don't want me to call the prick a prick, I won't, Caron."

"Thanks, Joe. You were saying…?" Joe had managed to get hold of Neil's cell phone location data in the way that Joe managed to get hold of everything. By hook or by crook. Mostly by crook.

"If he'd kept driving toward Southampton he would've switched to another cell tower. He didn't. Not until five minutes till noon—which is five minutes before he showed up to work."

"I see."

"Do you? He stayed in the general vicinity of her house for over forty-five minutes. Enough time to slice a gas line, do a crossword puzzle, and grab a skinny vanilla latte at Starbucks."

"How big is the general in-general vicinity?"

"I don't know. Twenty-five square miles. Maybe more."

"So he could've been twenty-five square miles away from her house for most of that time."

"He could've been father of the year if he had kids. Last time I checked, he doesn't have any."

"I think you need a refresher course in defense investigation work, Joe. It's where you find me things that help exonerate my client. The *other* side looks for things that implicate him."

"He blew up your husband, Caron. Jason. Remember *him*? Sure, maybe Jason was fucking around on you. Maybe he was a louse and maybe you were going to kick him out the door. I don't know. None of my business. But he was your husband and this prick blew him up."

"Sorry, I forgot you've turned up proof of that. Oh, wait a minute. You haven't. Here's an actual possibility—the closest he came to that house was when he drove past it. Oh, one more thing. You were going to stop calling him a prick, remember?"

"Caron." He leaned forward. It's what Joe did when he decided to act fatherly with me. He didn't get to do it with his own daughter, whom he was long estranged from, the occupational hazard of being a cop and seldom being around while she was growing up. Being busy solving murders didn't cut it with nine-year-olds waiting for piggyback rides. "I get you're pissed. No one enjoys getting cheated on. To be betrayed. It sucks. It hurts. It tears your guts out. I get it. But Jesus Christ . . . to *defend* this guy? To go into court and try to get him off? He had a restraining order—know why? Because he beat the shit out of his wife. That's why. *Two* fucking people, Caron. One of them was your husband."

"I appreciate your concern, Joe. But right now I'm actually defending him. I have my reasons why I'm defending him, honest, but if it's okay with you, I'd prefer to keep those to myself. I owe you a paycheck but I don't owe you an explanation. I'm saying this with all due affection."

"Okay. I said my piece."

"You have."

"Speaking of owing me a paycheck."

"It's in the mail."

"Seriously. Pensions aren't what they used to be."

"Seriously. It's in the mail."

"One more question."

"Shoot."

"You haven't cried."

"*Huh?*"

"Tears. I haven't seen you shed any. I was at the funeral...I know, I didn't do the reception line. Never can think of anything to say. I sat way in the back so I could get up and leave. I saw you handholding your mother-in-law but I didn't see any tears."

"Are you asking me this for a reason?"

"Yeah."

"Which is...?"

"Maybe you need to talk to someone."

"Jesus, Joe. Really?"

"Really."

"First a lecture about my client list and now about my mental health."

"It wasn't a list. It was one name on the list."

"Sue me. I was exaggerating in order to make a point. How do you know I haven't cried my eyes out every single night at home?"

"Have you?"

"No. I take Sundays off." I could have told him that I'd stopped crying a long time ago, right after my brother and number one protector walked into his closet and didn't come out. After this human equivalent of the Amazing Moppomatic had filled several industrial-sized garbage pails. I could've told Joe how I'd put myself through a kind of emotional boot camp in an effort to replace him. Daniel didn't cry; neither would I. I'd learned to hold everything in, even as I ignored the cost, pushing the payment due to a much later date. Like those sucker deals on TV that promise no money down for the first five years. Sooner or later you have to pay up. Alex, the boyfriend I'd summarily dismissed in Chicago, had accused me of *emotional constipation* on his way out the door. Guilty. It had been a matter of survival once. The air in my childhood house had become thick enough to squeeze the breath out of me.

"It doesn't hurt to talk to someone, Caron. Really."

"Actually, it does. I went to someone when my mother passed. It hurt a lot. It hurt so much I went once and stopped." The therapist had seemed intent on steering me back to the place I had no intention of going. "I'm fine, Joe. My husband died and I'm dealing with it. I lost my mother but I still have a father. When I need a replacement, you're the first name on my list. Okay?"

"Okay," he grumbled. He had one more question before leaving. "I'm assuming there's money to run some DNA samples?"

"Which DNA samples are you talking about?"

"The ones we probably won't find on the boiler and sprinkler systems. You know, the things our home improvement guy supposedly fixed with his own two hands. You mentioned me finding things that might help exonerate him, didn't you? If we can show that he was a regular Bob Vila, it'd help."

"I'll have to petition the court."

"Petition away."

I told Joe I had an embezzler I needed to get off.

As Joe sauntered out of the room, I thought the day was coming soon when I would need a replacement for my father.

I could do worse than Joe.

CHAPTER TWENTY

"One for My Baby."

You know … the Frank Sinatra song. Someone had sent it to me in a one-word email.

That word?

Talk … ?

That's all. That's it.

It arrived in my professional email account after another day at trial. A day the prosecution had put a few more people on the stand, one of whom—a forensic accountant hired by the state—meticulously went over my client's material possessions. They were considerable. They set up a TV screen facing the jury box in order to display my client's house in full technicolor glory—courtesy of a video taken by Corcoran Real Estate before my client purchased the home. Complete with a white electric front gate that slowly opened like a sweeping invitation for the jury to step inside. The massive front hall. The two-fireplace living room with skylit ceiling. The gleaming kitchen with basalt island. A separate den with recessed flooring and wraparound windows that faced the blue gunite pool and green Har-Tru tennis court.

I objected. Not because I expected the judge to sustain. Because it allowed me to accuse the prosecutor of *rich shaming*, which may or may not be an actual word.

The prosecutor was Harold Loman, whom most would politely term *workmanlike*. Someone who'd never absconded for greener pastures—yes, I'm referring to the color of money—a middling prosecutor who was generally given lesser cases that wouldn't soil the DA's conviction rate too badly if he happened to fuck up. Harold responded to my objection by pointing out that he was simply showing what my client had *done* with that eight million five hundred thousand dollars. In other words, presenting my client's *motive* for stealing all that money.

Jessup agreed with him.

My client seemed to have mixed emotions during the video presentation. On the one hand, clearly pissed that the jurors were seeing he'd put the money into a big Hamptons home, as opposed to, say, a house for needy orphans. On the other hand, unable to prevent his pride in owning that big Hamptons home from seeping into his otherwise sour expression. I noticed an actual smile when they showed off the tennis court.

I leaned over and politely whispered to him to lose the smile. Okay, I wasn't polite. *Lose that fucking smile.*

We hadn't even gotten to the upstairs yet. Six bedrooms. Four bathrooms with built-in saunas and Jacuzzi tubs. A library with floor-to-ceiling bookshelves, which something told me they'd never put any actual books into. Maybe just those hollowed-out leather decorative ones meant to represent the essential classics no one actually reads.

They went over his cars.

A Lamborghini. An Escalade. A Range Rover convertible. I didn't even know Range Rover made a convertible.

I asked one question on cross. Just one.

"Would you say my client was living above his means?"

"I wouldn't know how to answer that."

"With a yes or no."

"I wouldn't know whether he was living beyond his means or not."

"Well, that's a lot of stuff you just showed us, isn't it?"

"I'd say so."

"More than you'd expect his bank account and salary to be able to support? Correct?"

"I suppose."

"Thank you. I have no further questions."

If you think I was buttressing the prosecutor's case you'd be half-right. And you'd be half-wrong. Yes. My client had blown the money on a lavish lifestyle. Yes. The reason my client needed to *borrow* that money was so he wouldn't have that lifestyle yanked away from him. So his wife and two kids wouldn't be thrown out on the street. It was an act of a man in the throes of desperation. A man trapped in financial quicksand who'd reached for the nearest branch to survive, committing an act contrary to his basic principles and moral compass. A *conscientious* man, who'd always intended to make restitution.

To borrow a golf expression from my late husband, I was teeing things up.

When we walked out of court, Jefrey didn't invite me for a drink this time.

"What was that?" he asked me.

"What was what?"

"*Living above my means.*"

"You weren't?"

"What's that got to do with anything? With getting me off?"

"Plenty, actually."

"Huh?"

"If you weren't living above your means and you took eight million five hundred thousand dollars, that would make you a simple run-of-the-mill thief."

He looked puzzled.

"You took that money because you needed to. Because you put yourself in an untenable position where not having it would've meant complete and utter ruin for your family. Sure, it was highly unethical and technically illegal, but you felt you had no choice. You were always going to pay it back a little at a time. Understand?"

He nodded. Yes, this was *exactly* what he'd intended to do. His wife looked dubious.

"See you tomorrow," I told them.

Coming home was accomplished in three parts.

Walking in.

Pulling off my bra—nothing too fancy—a simple white Cosabella that I threw on my hall table and left there, it beginning to resemble the unmentionables bin at Walmart. There was no one else in the house to notice.

Pouring myself a Johnnie Walker Black on the rock, singular. Racing to see who would melt first—the rock or me.

Opening my computer sometimes followed this third part.

"One for My Baby."

I wasn't sure, but I thought I might actually have that plaintive standard on my Spotify. The Smiths, Springsteen, Talking Heads, and Dolly Parton taking up the bulk of space, but with some Sinatra sprinkled in. After all, who was immune to Ol' Blue Eyes? A singer who wasn't a crooner like most everyone else from that era—more of a storyteller.

He was telling a story in this one. I'd pressed play.

A man walks into a bar—like the beginning of a thousand bad jokes. But this was no joke. He asks the bartender for a drink. Two really. One for his lost flame, and another for the road.

A different game commenced between me and that half-melted cube of ice.

Trying to determine which one of us was colder.

I'd made the mistake of playing the song all the way to its plaintive ending, where Frank laments the burden of carrying a torch that needs to be extinguished before it, well … explodes.

After all, it's a torch song. About a thwarted passion. A wounded soul. An imminent explosion. And a bartender named Joe wearily listening to another patron's sob story.

Not Joe, though.

Teddy.

CHAPTER TWENTY-ONE

" Hard night?" Jefrey was appraising me at the defense table.

He wasn't wrong. My mascara deserved hazard pay today. The circles under my eyes were more like sinkholes. I hadn't slept much. That's what happens when you play "One for My Baby" twenty times, and in between start and stop writing the same email.

Talk? he'd written to me.

The only possible answer was *yes* or *no*— what I'd told a million people in the witness box. I suddenly appreciated their difficulty in answering.

A money grab.

What else?

He'd go to the papers and get nothing or come to me and get an early Christmas bonus. To stop him from going to the papers. That's the way he'd put it—that he was doing me some kind of favor.

"You okay?"

I hadn't answered my client. He looked concerned in a purely self-interested way.

"More importantly, are you?"

This was our big day. My client was taking the stand. *It just takes one juror for a mistrial*, I'd reminded him this morning.

"And go through all this again?" he'd sneered.

"Ten to one they'd offer a plea deal. They don't have the money to try an embezzlement case twice. Or the inclination."

"Wonderful," he said sarcastically. "They offered me a plea deal before, remember?"

"This would be a better plea deal."

"How much better?"

"Probation and restitution, if I had to guess."

Jefrey brightened at that.

"I'm ready to rumble," he said.

"Fine. Remember this isn't the WWE"

"It's an expression."

"Right. Keep your answers simple and to the point."

"Got it."

"Rumble. Don't ramble."

"I said I *got* it."

The seats were barely filled. Embezzlement trials don't draw reporters—or much of a crowd. A few familiar denizens of the courts were there—mostly seniors who came for the daily entertainment. It was better than Netflix. One of them—a woman who looked to be in her mideighties—smiled at me. I remembered her from other trials—she'd once congratulated me after a win. *I bet my friend five dollars you'd get him off,* she'd told me. I'd thought about asking for a cut of her winnings as a joke. I hadn't. Today I smiled back at her.

"I swear to tell the whole truth and nothing but the truth, so help me God," my client intoned with one hand on the Bible. If you didn't know any better, you might have even believed him.

Once I'd yelled *objection* when a jailhouse snitch took the stand against the client I'd defended in that big arson case. The judge wasn't amused.

What on earth are you objecting to? he'd asked me. *This witness is merely taking the oath.*

This witness wouldn't know the truth if he fell over it, I replied. Which earned me a counterobjection from the prosecution, an *overruled* from the judge, and a stern admonition to never do it again. My words were stricken from the record.

I started my examination with the basic particulars—*what's your name, where do you live, do you have a family, what's your profession?*

The same basic questions they ask in lie detector tests to put the subject at ease. There's a more devious reason, of course—setting a baseline they can use to measure any deviation into deceit.

I needed Jefrey to be at ease today—to answer these perfunctory questions in a tone that wouldn't waver when we got to the more problematic ones. If he sounded the same when asked his name and when asked if he'd intentionally stolen eight million five hundred thousand dollars, then a jury might believe he was telling the truth.

I asked him to take me through his career. His promotions. His devotion to the company. His pretty much unblemished record of advancement and achievement.

Then we got to the blemish.

I'd decided to begin with a complete acknowledgment of the crime—if a somewhat semantically altered one. *See*, I was saying to the jury, *we have nothing to hide.*

"Did you take eight million five hundred thousand dollars from your company?" I asked him.

"Yes."

I allowed that to sink in—to let the jury wonder why we'd begin our defense with what sounded like a clear-cut admission of guilt.

"Did you ever intend to *steal* that eight million five hundred thousand dollars?"

"Absolutely not."

"Then why did you doctor the books? Cover your trail, so to speak? Was it so they wouldn't *notice* you'd taken that money?"

"Yes."

Another grievous admission. Another self-inflicted body blow. I could almost hear a gasp from the jury box. *What's going on here?* they must've been thinking. A guilty client represented by a clearly incompetent defense attorney—that's what.

"I don't understand. You say you never intended to *steal* that money, but you went to some lengths to *conceal* it?"

"I didn't want them to notice I'd taken the money because I was going to pay it all back. Every single cent of it. I needed some time to do that. I'm not a *thief*."

"Then can you tell us why you took that money in the first place?"

"I'd gotten in over my head. I wanted to give my family—my kids—a good life. A better one than I had growing up. My kids mean the world to me. Everything. I wanted them to be proud of me. I was foolish. I was wrong. I spent more than I had. Then suddenly it was all going to come crashing down. I didn't know what to do."

"So what did you do?"

Jefrey hung his head. Shook it slowly back and forth like someone who can't quite believe what circumstances have led him to. I wondered if he'd been practicing that.

"I borrowed money from the company."

"*Borrowed...?*"

"Yes. I figured I would borrow the money, then give myself time to pay it back by adjusting the books. I would put the money back bit by bit until the loan was paid off."

"But it wasn't a loan, was it?"

Sometimes the best way to do the defense's work is by doing the prosecution's. Blunting the force of their cross by getting there first, albeit without the overt hostility. *Steal their thunder by setting off a few firecrackers*, was the way my law professor at Northwestern used to phrase it.

"I was in a hole. I was desperate. There was no other way to make up the money. We would've been out on the street. My family. My kids. This seemed like the only way out."

"The money. How exactly were you going to pay it back?"

"By increments. You know, keep adding a little here and there and adjusting the books accordingly."

"All right. So did you begin paying it back?"

"I couldn't. They discovered it before I could ever start."

"Did you *tell* them that you never intended to keep the money? That you were just borrowing it?"

"I never got the chance. I was arrested at my home. Taken to jail like a ... a common thief."

"What was that like?"

"Going to jail?"

"Yes."

Jefrey hung his head again. When he raised it, I felt like hitting it with the nearest blunt instrument—the judge's gavel maybe, nearly within arm's reach.

He had tears in his eyes.

"To be handcuffed in front of my children is something I'll never live down. It's the worst punishment you could ever give me. I'd done it for *them*. My *kids*. And now here I was being carted off to jail as they watched."

I was trying to do two things at once. Keep my examination going while attempting to determine if those tears looked half-way authentic. If the jury was remotely buying it.

I glanced at the jury box—at one juror in particular. Juror number 32.

She was biting her lip as if trying to hold back tears.

Defense lesson number one: you never know about juries. Even Harry Lockman would agree with that.

"I understand this is traumatic for you. Do you need a min-ute to collect yourself?"

"No. That's all right. It's just when I think about my kids I get kind of emotional."

"I understand. Every parent would." Just ask juror number 32, who must've been a parent herself.

I asked the judge to enter an exhibit. Defense Exhibit C-3.

I'd been holding it back for my close.

Not now.

I'd asked Jefrey to send me a picture of his family. The one he would've chosen the day they hauled him to jail if he'd known he'd be there for a while as opposed to being quickly bailed out. The one he would've placed over his bunk bed so he could stare at it every night before closing his eyes.

I'd blown it up to large-screen TV size.

The four of them were curled up on the couch. The younger child barefoot in pajamas—she looked to be around four or five at the time the picture was taken. She was nestled in Jefrey's arms fast asleep as he stared at her with naked adoration. His son, older by a few years, was leaning his head against his father's shoulder as if trying to burrow right into him. Jefrey's wife was lodged against his other shoulder, rounding out the family tableau. It was Jefrey your eye went to, though. The center that held it all together. The source of this family's strength. Without it, the family would fragment and collapse.

I'd intended to hand it off to the jury before starting my closing argument. To make sure it was slowly passed from hand to hand, from front row to back row, forcing the jury to focus on it long and hard before a word had even left my mouth.

You not only hold my client's future in your hands today; you're holding theirs, I was going to start off.

Jefrey's crocodile tears had circumvented that plan.

I saw an opportunity.

"Objection," Loman nasally intoned. "A picture of the defendant's family has absolutely nothing to do with the charges against him, Your Honor."

"Counsel … ?" Jessup asked me.

"The prosecution exhibited my client's house in an attempt to prove motive, Your Honor. I'm asking the opportunity to do the same."

Jessup rearranged her glasses. "Objection overruled. I'll allow."

I held the picture catty-corner to the jury box so both my client and the jurors could drink it in.

"Is this your family?" I asked Jefrey.

"Yes," he said, still teary.

"What are their names?"

"Rebecca, Joshua, and Stella."

"Who did you take that money for?"

"For *them*," he blubbered. He hung his head again, shook it, sniffled.

"Were you going to pay back each and every cent of that money?"

"Yes."

"Remember you're under oath. You swore on a Bible to tell the truth."

"I swear on their *lives* I'm telling the truth. On the lives of my children, I was going to pay back every single cent."

Loman looked like he was going to stand up and object, but somewhere on the way out of his chair he must've realized he couldn't think of one. *I object to this defendant swearing on his children's lives* was unlikely to be sustained. Instead he looked like someone trying to surreptitiously pass gas, a small lift and resettle, while grimly wincing with the effort.

By now juror number 32 looked like someone in need of an entire tissue factory.

"Thank you," I said. "That's all I have for this witness."

I'd tried to time everything—to finish my examination with the judge's gavel hitting the sound block with the resounding smack of finality. A loud period put on the end of a suitably emotional crescendo.

It worked.

"Court is adjourned for the day," Jessup said.

CHAPTER TWENTY-TWO

April showers bring May flowers.

One aphorism that seemed decidedly spot-on. April had been good for Bible literalists—if it didn't quite rain for forty day and forty nights, it seemed like it. Now the Hamptons were in full bloom.

The grounds of the Topping Rose were topped off with roses the color of mauve. Blue hydrangeas lined both sides of the East Hampton Town Green. Red and yellow tulips circled the windmill across from my office.

Hyacinths, azaleas, and black-eyed Susans bordered the drive up to Neil and Emma Shipman's missing front door.

The court had agreed to our petition.

I was meeting Joe there. Not just Joe. Someone from our DNA lab as well. Meeting the three of us would be a crime scene investigator from the Suffolk PD to verify the chain of custody. We couldn't just pull DNA on our own—someone from their side had to stand guard and Big Brother it.

During the pandemic, a video had made the rounds—someone zooming in on a Brunello sports jacket and Lacroix tie who stood up believing his business meeting was over and revealed nothing below. Not even a pair of dingy boxers.

Nothing. The contrast had been shocking.

The flower-festooned front drive was like that man's sports jacket and tie.

The house it led to was the nakedness below.

What was left of it.

Yellow crime tape strung from tree to tree circled its remains.

The foundation was basically intact, and various pieces of the actual house were still standing—some with windows that had shards of glass embedded in the sills, like misshapen teeth stuck in Halloween pumpkin grins.

The roof was gone.

When I exited my car, some crows shot out of what would've been the entry hall. Their cawing echoed across the lawn. I stepped on something—what looked like a wall clock half-embedded in the ground. The hour hand was pointing at nothing.

I was trying to keep myself together. To rein in the panic.

The cemetery had simply been a final resting place.

This was the killing ground.

It looks like a bomb hit it, we say of things like messy rooms and houses after an all-night party. But this is what it really looks like when a bomb hits something. Like utter devastation. I'd once opened a fat law book in school, turned the pages to somewhere in the middle, and found an entire chunk of the book ripped out—tiny teeth of paper where august pages had once adhered to the spine. It had shocked and revolted me. Their yawing absence.

That's what I felt walking up to the crime tape facing what used to be Emma and Neil's front door, where Joe and the man from the DNA lab were silently waiting.

Absence. An absence so acute and all-encompassing I felt hollowed out—as if the slightest spring breeze might knock me on my ass.

Joe could sense it. Wise, weather-beaten, crab-apple Joe.

He reached out to take my arm and steady me. He'd warned me not to come. Why did I want to do that to myself? he'd asked. *Why?*

"Let me help you," he said now. I didn't say *all right*. I didn't say *go fuck yourself* either.

"The basement was pretty untouched," Joe said. "The sprinkler pipes and boiler. The gas line too, of course."

I glanced at our DNA expert for confirmation. He looked familiar. Small and rumpled, matching the black leather briefcase he held in his left hand.

"Len Dawson," he introduced himself. "If his DNA is on anything we should find it," he assured me.

"Great."

"This must've made one hell of a bang," he said, surveying the damage.

"This is the Hamptons," I said. "The ordinances insist you build the houses far enough apart so that if one of them blows up it won't disturb your neighbor's dinner party."

I was trying to be my usual acerbic self, but standing before the house where two people died, it didn't land. I was trying hard not to focus on who those two people were. Joe was still supporting my arm like a father walking a panicked daughter to the altar, as we waited for the investigator from Suffolk PD to show up in order to all enter the house together.

Just then I spotted a car crawling up the driveway spitting gravel from all four tires.

It lurched to a stop next to ours and parked.

You made it, she'd said to us, after we'd pulled up to her house and Jason handed her a gift-wrapped bottle of Chivas Regal. She'd appeared in the floodlights wearing a Japanese robe decorated with serpents.

A tall man extricated himself from the front seat and introduced himself.

"Mark Schriff. Criminal investigator." He handed me his card, as if we were meeting at a convention. I'd once gone to Vegas for a criminal defense conference where we attended lectures on the latest DNA technology and jury selection algorithms, but spent most of our time doing shots in stripper bars. One of the strippers had given me a lap dance, as everyone else— mostly men—hooted their approval. Her name was Sapphire. It wasn't her given name.

"Shall we?" Joe said.

Mark nodded and the four of us ducked under the crime tape and walked toward what used to be the front door but now looked like an empty frame in a Lego set.

Nice knockers, Jason had quipped when Emma had led us inside. He was referring to the two antique knockers fastened to a thick mahogany double door.

Thanks, she'd replied, *I've had work done on them*. It was the first time we'd seen her since the Dove-Tail Inn, but the repartee was still flowing. It had sounded more sophisticated when we were sloshed.

The basement staircase was intact.

Joe produced a flashlight. The sun illuminated the stairs all the way to the bottom step, but once we were down there a flashlight would be needed.

As we walked down the stairs—Joe still attached to my arm— two butterflies erupted from the basement and flitted around my head.

Butterflies are my thing, she'd told us. There were butterfly mosaics in the kitchen she'd designed to look like somewhere in Provence. A print of Van Gogh's *Butterflies and Poppies* sat in an upstairs hallway—or maybe it wasn't a print. Maybe it was the real thing. She had butterfly-decorated satin pillows spread across her bed.

Why butterflies? I'd asked.

Blame Emily Dickinson. "Because he travels freely, and wears a proper coat, the circumspect are certain, that he is dissolute."

I must've missed that one, I said.

It's a Smith thing. Dickinson yes. Dick no.

If you didn't know there wasn't an actual house upstairs you might've felt completely at home in this basement. It was impeccably finished: tile floors, ochre-colored walls, and expensive furniture spread across several rooms. We passed the home gym first—a Peloton, treadmill, and weights still sitting in there, as if simply waiting for the woman of the house to come down and resume her workouts. Sometimes they'd used it together.

It was my little joke, she said. *If someone called me down here and asked if my husband and I were working out, I'd say no. We're not.*

The gym led to a kind of TV room. The kind where the men might descend in the middle of a party and turn on some golf tournament. Where they'd swap stories of dubious appropriateness and say whatever they couldn't say among their wives.

There was a wet bar tucked into the left corner of the room. It seemed a bit anachronistic, like a leftover from *Mad Men* days. The husband arriving on the 5:30 out of Penn Station and the wife, Emma, standing there with a freshly stirred martini to hand him.

The image was all wrong. That wasn't her.

We walked through the room and entered a small door where the finished part of the finished basement ended. Here were the inner workings—pipes and boilers and circuit breakers and a bunch of other things I wouldn't know the first thing about.

But Neil did. That's what he said anyway. He liked to fix things. He liked to tinker. We'd see.

Joe shone his flashlight on the boiler.

Len said he'd start there. Mark took out his phone to video it.

Len placed his briefcase on the floor and unbuckled it, like a doctor about to do an examination. More like a surgeon in an operating theater—talking his way through the delicate surgery step by step.

"We'll be going for touch DNA," he said, pulling on a pair of latex gloves. "I'll be using a self-saturating foam-tipped swab." He held the swabs tip down where Mark—and Joe—could see them.

"I'm squeezing the handle to release the liquid to the tips," he said. "We'll start with the control panel. If someone was trying to fix a boiler, he'd start there."

Joe shone his flashlight on the panel.

Len placed the tip of the swab to the boiler panel. Gently—as if he were about to clean an infant's ear.

"Swabbing now." That took him a good minute or two.

"Gently peeling foam tip from swab," he said, as he did exactly that. "Placing in sterile container."

He placed the swab tip in a clear plastic tube that he quickly sealed, then dropped the tube into a larger envelope that he sealed as well.

Mark nodded.

That was the first swab. He did four more on the boiler around the various connections.

The sprinkler system was in a different corner of the room—a mass of pipes and rubber fittings. Len repeated the step-by-step narration as he swabbed it in three different areas.

"Swabbing for touch DNA done," he said. "Seven sealed envelopes on their way to the lab."

That was it.

Joe reached for my arm again. We'd be walking back up the stairway to nowhere.

"I'm okay now," I said.

"You sure?"

"Pretty sure."

"All right, then."

We walked up the stairs, Len and Mark going first, busy talking shop. Then Joe and I saying nothing.

When we made it back up to ground zero, Mark stopped and pointed at something. The stone chimney. It was still standing upright even though the wall it'd been embedded in was no longer there. It reminded me of something—a picture of Hiroshima after the bomb, a lone chimney surrounded by miles of eerie flatness—a macabre testament to survival amid a nuclear Armageddon.

It reminded Mark of something else.

"That's where they found them, isn't it?" Mark said. "Lying by the fireplace?"

Joe stared at him—the kind of stare that must've had suspects begging for a lawyer back in his cop days. "Do you *mind*?" he said.

"Do I mind what?"

Maybe Mark didn't read the papers. They'd called him to bear witness at a DNA pull—he'd said yes. Where he'd met the usual—an investigator, the DNA collector, and the defense lawyer. He didn't know the defense lawyer had been married to one of the victims—they don't usually represent the person charged with murdering their husbands.

"Never mind," Joe said. He must've realized Mark wasn't familiar with the players. There'd be no point in enlightening him.

Has anyone actually roasted chestnuts on an open fire? Emma had asked, Nat King Cole warbling away on her Sonos. The three of us were roasting by it instead. Three glasses of amber Scotch reflected flickering tongues of fire. There were other flickering tongues involved here. The Japanese robe had been dropped too close to the fire, I noticed at one point.

It'll get burned, I said.

"I'll let you know as soon as we get results," Len said before turning toward his car. "Figure a week or so. We're kind of backed up."

"Have we met?" I asked him. He still looked familiar.

"That arson case. I testified for the prosecution. Remember?"

"Sure," I said. Then shivered, as if—*what's that old expression?*—right, as if someone had just tiptoed across my grave. "I remember."

CHAPTER TWENTY-THREE

Jewish lightning, they used to call it, before referring to it like that would get you hauled off to political correctness court and canceled like a bad subscription. Fair enough. The client accused of torching his business to the ground was Greek Orthodox and wore a thick gold crucifix around his neck. He did have a fondness for lox and bagels.

He owned a container factory on Long Island.

He was dangerously in debt.

Too many trips to Atlantic City, and too much competition from cheap-labor countries like Mexico and local undercutting competitors.

The factory went up on a Sunday night, which is a good night for those kinds of things because cops need a night off too, and Sunday nights serve as a kind of unofficial one. (FYI—if you're going to get assaulted, raped, burglarized, pickpocketed, or otherwise victimized, don't let it happen on a Sunday night.)

My client's only alibi was his wife, who swore he was home all night with her watching *Law & Order: SVU*.

There were a few problems with that.

One was that *Law & Order: SVU* wasn't on that night.

Right, she said, they'd previously recorded it. Sorry, she'd forgotten.

Another was the CCTV camera that seemed to show a car that looked suspiciously like her husband's—a silver Lexus SUV—entering the factory gate at about 1 a.m. Then leaving about ten minutes later.

Then there were the traces of turpentine found in the area where the cardboard containers had been piled to the ceiling—meaning if you wanted to burn down the factory, it would be the most likely place to start.

Oh. And there were those receipts from Home Depot for three gallons of turpentine purchased on my client's credit card just two days before. And just in case there was any doubt my *client* was the one wielding that credit card, there he was at the checkout counter in the extraordinarily clear Home Depot security camera footage.

Last, and certainly not least, a book of matches was found in the trash bin just outside the factory entrance. It had my client's DNA all over it—this according to Len Dawson, the prosecutor's crack DNA expert who'd testify at trial.

Of course it was my client's factory—*of course* you'd find a matchbook with his DNA on it sitting on the bottom of the factory trash bin, I'd been ready to argue.

Not so fast.

It had rained up until 8 that night. Meaning everything in the bin was thoroughly soaked. With one exception—that matchbook, which was apparently as dry as the Kalahari. Meaning someone had deposited it there after 8 p.m. when it had finally stopped pouring. Someone who for some reason had the very same DNA as my client—up to a one hundred millionth probability, according to Len Dawson on the stand.

Actually, that wasn't the last thing.

Sorry.

There was the insurance policy—due to pay out fifteen million dollars if the factory was destroyed by flood or fire or other acts of God—though decidedly not if was destroyed by my client.

No one said criminal defense is easy.

I'd learned that quickly during my one year as a public defender, when I kept getting files with *DBL* scribbled across them. *What's that stand for?* I'd asked a senior lawyer. *Dead-bang loser,* he'd said, but not without smiling. The same public defender told me there were only three words I needed to know in order to do the job: *take a plea.* He'd smiled at that too. When I told him I'd decided to take one of my DBLs to trial, he finally stopped smiling. I learned my own magic word in the public defender's office: *delay.* If you delayed long enough, witnesses ran, died, got arrested, or simply forgot. It helped turn a bunch of dead-bang losers into what-the-fuck winners.

The container factory owner would've no doubt had a big *DBL* stamped across his file.

Joe worked the case for me. He spent six weeks trying to find a homeless man who, word on the street had it—in this case *literally* on the street—was often seen using the factory grounds to bed down in. He'd slip in and out through a rent in the outdoor fence. Maybe this man had been there that night. Maybe he'd seen something.

That hole in the fence was useful as well—it might be big enough to punch a hole in their case if we could squeeze another suspect though it.

Speaking of which.

Those undercutting competitors who'd been turning my client's bottom line red. There was a story attached to that. This was the container industry. Certain men of Sicilian lineage had been asking local factories to become members of their commercial protective organization—strictly out of civic concern, and for these factory owners' own good. My client's included. Apparently my client had yet to become a paying member of this civic-minded organization and the annual dues were in arrears.

This would be the linchpin of our case.

When you need another villain, men with colorful nicknames and a penchant for lounging in Bronx social clubs fit the bill.

My guess? Those social club members might've been threatening his business, but NAFTA had already killed it. He knew that paying those dues would've dropped his bottom line even further into a ditch, but if he didn't pay them there was always a chance he would be found in one.

My client had made that trip to Home Depot.

That was simply my guess.

Not my case.

The jury heard about the shakedowns in the industry. About the specific proposals these civic-minded individuals had made to my client. About my client's demurral. And about some examples of the persuasive tactics these men had been known to use when simple salesmanship failed.

The jury found him innocent.

That's not what I remember about the case, though.

No.

What I remember is the night Joe came in out of the rain, when I was still at the office working on my closing argument with my eyes starting to droop. How Joe's rapping on my door had startled and woken me.

Joe was soaked to the skin because he'd been out prowling around the factory, still looking for that homeless man. That's what he'd come to tell me at two o'clock in the morning.

He'd found him.

CHAPTER TWENTY-FOUR

I can take you through the rest of the embezzlement trial.

The prosecution's cross, where my client wobbled, deflected, and stumbled a bit, but mostly stuck to his story. Where Loman wielded sarcasm as a weapon as he asked my client the cost of seventy-three separate items he'd purchased for his Amagansett manse. These included a tennis-ball launcher, an electric pool cover, and a party tent large enough to house the Romanian army—in each case asking Jefrey if he'd considered using that money to begin paying back that unofficial *loan* he'd helped himself to.

Jefrey had to admit that hadn't exactly occurred to him. Seventy-three times.

I can take you through my follow where we presented those purchases as more evidence of the crater-sized hole he'd desperately needed to dig himself out of, where Jefrey reaffirmed his intention to pay all that money back and affected tears again, given how well it had worked the first time. He even swore on his children's lives again—which, I'll admit, made me worry just a bit for his children.

I can tell you how the jury went out and didn't come back that day. Or the next day either. How they sent a note to the judge saying that after much intense deliberation they were unable to come to a unanimous decision. How Jessup ordered them to keep at it.

I can tell you about the three lunches I was forced to have with Jefrey, his wife, and his mother, who'd reappeared for the jury verdict and kept calling me Kathryn.

I can take you through the moment Jessup called us back in and proclaimed a mistrial. How Jefrey forgot he was supposed to act chagrined at that—his innocence still in question—but given what I'd previously prophesied, how he'd broken into a smug smile and, though I can't be one hundred percent certain of this, gave Loman the middle finger.

I can tell you we did some digging and discovered there'd been a lone holdout in the jury room who'd refused to budge.

Can you guess who?

In the end, the very juror I'd feared the most was the juror who kept my client out of prison.

Juror number 32.

I can tell you how three months later, the prosecution offered us the very deal I'd predicted they would. Probation and restitution. The case lacked juice, it hadn't garnered a whit of media attention, and they were gearing up for something that would.

An ex-husband who'd cut a gas line and murdered two people in cold blood.

Jefrey took the deal.

I can also tell you how I met a bartender named Teddy at Shadmoor State Park, where you can walk half a mile down a scraggly dirt path toward the very edge of the hoodoos. The hoodoos are razor-sharp cliffs that tower over Ditch Plains Beach in Montauk, where surfers in wet suits bob on the waves like black seals. If you didn't know any better you'd swear you were in Monterrey instead of the east end of Long Island. The cliffs are that high.

I can tell you that I met Teddy at the very top of a hoodoo where a sign says:

Danger. Keep Off.

I can tell you I handed him a Christmas bonus in spring.

That I then mentioned some of the people I'd gotten to know intimately through my career in criminal defense. Men facing serious charges like murder one and assault whom I'd managed to get off. Men who seemed to gravitate to careers in sanitation and cement and the container industry. Men who owed me.

I might've even mentioned how many people fall from the hoodoos every year.

That's why they'd put up the signs.

I can tell you Teddy turned a shade of white not much different from the fissures of chalk that permeate the hoodoos like veins of fat on a steak.

I could tell you all this in intricate and laborious detail, but it's time to tell you what happened at the Dove-Tail Inn.

Even a hate story has interludes of affection.

Sorry for the delay.

Some stories just take time.

CHAPTER TWENTY-FIVE

"Jingle bell, jingle bell, jingle bell rock."

"All I Want for Christmas Is You."

"I Saw Mommy Kissing Santa Claus."

The soundtrack that night was decidedly yuletide. One Christmas song after another that either put you in the holiday mood or turned you into Scrooge. For me, it was more the latter—it was as if they were determined to force-feed holiday cheer into you.

Still, the music seemed cheerier as I got drunker.

It wasn't like me to proceed past buzzed, but there was something in the air. I'm not talking about holiday spirit. If you asked me if we'd had an idea what would transpire that night, a plan, a road map with a purposeful destination, I would tell you no.

I would be right, up to a point.

That would ignore the several road signs we'd passed on the way from here to there.

Had Jason mentioned more than once that Emma was beautiful?

Yes. Probably when I mentioned her resemblance to that English actress.

Had he commented on an Instagram photo of her taken in St. Barts? Knee-deep in the turquoise surf, wearing a miniscule French-cut bikini?

I think so.

Had he even—excuse me while I blush—inserted her name during one of our porn-fueled romps on our living room couch?

I can't say for certain, but yes, it's possible. He did that some-times—added a pretend third to the festivities. Whispered a name of someone we knew just as I was starting to scale the heights—softly at first, as if tentatively trotting it out for approval, then, if it seemed to pass muster, louder. I was usually too far gone to protest, even if it was the name of someone I would've easily dismissed playing *Wouldn't Kick Them Out of Bed* back in my college days with Kim.

Speaking of Kim. Speaking of things I don't speak about.

I told you. I'm not one of those women. The women who talk about sex the way men talk about football.

One night Kim and I played Wouldn't Kick Them Out Of Bed with each other and we both chose *wouldn't*. It's what college girls did back then—still do, I'm certain. On the course curricu-lum, it would've fallen under *Lab Experiment*.

I can't tell you it was amazing.

I can tell you that I whispered thirty Hail Marys afterward.

I hadn't ventured to the other side since. Unless you counted Sapphire, who'd nuzzled my ear as she furiously ground herself against my lap in a Las Vegas stripper bar. Did that bring back memories? Had I felt something that night? Anything? Maybe.

Emma walked into the Dove-Tail Inn bar in a black slinky dress that ended far enough above her knees to leave *plenty of playing field*—a Jason expression. She'd finished it off with black lace stockings and black leather boots. A vision in black—the way you might dress the temptress sitting on your left shoulder—the one whispering dirty thoughts into your ear, as the Virgin Mary from the outdoor manger sat primly on your right.

There was one more thing that night that might have por-tended where this was going. Where it was probably fated to go.

The location.

A bar in an inn with rooms. Off an exit that was decidedly out of the way. Had that occurred to us on some barely conscious level—the illicit possibilities—or had it always been there front and center?

I don't know.

I know that I was hyperaware there were *three* of us sitting at that bar. A crooked number in a social setting used to even integers. There wasn't a boyfriend or husband who was taking a bathroom break and about to join the party.

We were the party.

When Jason touched my leg or shoulder, when he briefly kissed the nape of my slightly sweaty neck, I was very cognizant that no one was doing those same things to her. To Emma. Have you ever been on vacation at one of those romantic getaways— Venice or Santorini or St. Barts—and noticed a woman alone, nose intently buried in a guide book or trashy novel as if to prove to the world she's perfectly fine by herself? Have you ever felt guilty you're coupled up, while that pretend reader isn't? Have you ever felt like reaching out and rescuing her—yes, exactly like Jason did at the Wölffer winery?

I was aware of Jason's hands and breath and alcohol-induced ardor.

I was aware they were being lavished on me and only me.

You need to share is the first lesson you learn in kindergarten. Otherwise you grow up selfish and socially inept.

I don't mean to paint any of this in altruistic terms. That would be disingenuous of me. Still, those things, those feelings, did cross my mind.

Other things as well.

For example, a few fleeting scenes from Jason's growing pornucopia. No, not the gynecologically detailed stuff. I'm talking about the badly written precursors. The setups, the meets, what happens before the clothes ever come off.

Three people in a living room. A summer backyard. A bar.

I often found them more erotic than what came after. The flirtation, the checking out, the understanding by both the actors (I use the term loosely here) and the audience where this was headed. To use an overused cliché, the sexual tension.

The tension at the Dove-Tail bar was palpable, or to use another cliché, you could cut it with one of the pâté knives laid lengthwise across the bar.

But then, you'd need to want to cut it.

Once or twice she reached over and grazed my hand, as if trying to get in on the action, the physical intimacy I was hogging for myself. I may have touched her hand back.

The small talk—what she'd done with her beloved house lately, how much Jason's hedge fund was up, a current court case I was handling—seemed to divert into more fervid areas. I don't remember steering the conversation that way exactly—I don't remember anyone doing that. It just did.

The sexual repartee started. The bad sexual repartee.

The unbroken medley of yuletide songs was briefly interrupted by Bryan Adams. You know, "Summer of '69."

Great song, I think I muttered.

Great position, Jason rejoined. Yes, in the light of memory, distinctly juvenile and decidedly unfunny. But in the dim light of the Dove-Tail bar while zoning on three of Teddy's special toddies, it seemed worthy of Dorothy Parker.

I don't know, Emma commented. *I'm a bad multitasker.*

Laughter all around.

Yeah, I said. *You don't know if you're coming or blowing.*

More laughter.

More cider.

A toddy, Teddy…

Another thing. That constant ordering of drinks.

Was there an unspoken acknowledgment that it would render us incapable of leaving the premises? No one was raising their hand to be the designated driver. Instead we were raising our hands to drunkenly toast one another. A designated driver usually wasn't needed with Jason and me—one glass of wine was our general limit—two at the most.

Not that night.

We seemed in a hurry to drink up—as if we were trying to re-create the first night of some long-ago spring break. The kind where you spent the entire next day in the toilet as your friends kept calling from the beach.

Maybe that's exactly what we were doing.

Taking a spring break from convention.

At one point it occurred to us that the bar was going to close and none of us were sober.

At one point Jason pointed to the manger and said, *Guess there was no room at the inn.*

And I said, *Is there?*

A room at the inn, I meant. Because it was last call and we were on our last legs. None of which were wooden.

I think it was Jason who went to ask reception. Lurching off the barstool, which only served to confirm that driving home was probably a bad idea.

We'd asked Teddy first.

Do they have room here? *Two* rooms?

Teddy didn't know.

Jason went to find out.

I've got good news and bad news, he said when he wobbled back.

What's the good news? I asked.

There's room at the inn.

What's the bad news?

There's one room at the inn.

It was Emma who said, *That's fine.*

And me who said, *Sure. Okay. Why not?*

Did we know as Jason paid the bar tab, as he took both my arm and hers, as he stopped at the desk to get the room key, as we dragged ourselves up the stairs to room number 14, what would happen in that room? Were we like those porn actors happy to finally dispose of the chitchat and ready to get down to business? Or were we imagining an innocent kind of pillow party—a quick nightcap maybe and then Emma and I gallantly given the bed to snooze on, while Jason curled up on the couch?

I'm not sure. Maybe both.

I was thinking we'd probably collapse into a post-drinking slumber instead of a postcoital haze. I was thinking we'd slowly undress one another and see how well we could multitask. I was thinking both.

At first we simply lounged. Jason and I sitting on the edge of the bed, Emma perched on the couch. Jason broke open the minibar because why stop drinking simply because we'd left the bar?

At some point Jason turned on the bedside sound system and Bette Midler's "Do You Want to Dance?" floated across the room.

Yes, I do, said Emma.

Yes, she was saying, she did want to dance.

And because Jason springing up to dance with her here in a room at the Dove-Tail Inn would've been too provocative, too much going from point A to point C without stopping at B, because women were allowed to dance with women without reading anything into it, I was the one who sprung up and started doing something slow and sinewy with Emma. Because the *song* was slow and sinewy and achy and a little breathless. The song was one big plea. *Do you … ?* the song kept asking. *Do you … ?*

Yes.

And then Jason got up and tried to either cut in or join in, which still seemed within the bounds of perfectly acceptable behavior. Still seemed like maybe we were just three friends enjoying a night out together. A bit sloshed, sure, a few boundaries being blurred, personal spaces probed. But nothing inappropriate in a court of law, maybe even in the court of public opinion.

Not yet.

Only somewhere in this pas de trois, his arms stopped circling just me and began including her. The arm I'd slung around Jason's neck somehow ended up around hers.

Do you…? Bette kept asking. *Do you…?*

I believe he kissed me first. He was allowed to. I was his wife.

Then he stopped kissing me and looked at me instead. For permission, I think.

It's the moment I keep replaying.

When it could've stopped, when we could've begun an awkward untangling. A few giggles, some remonstrances, a retreat to neutral corners.

I nodded.

Yes.

He kissed her. Emma. It was shocking and it was thrilling and it was detestable and it was delectable. It was all those things at the very same time. It made me turn cold and it got me hot. It unnerved me and it emboldened me.

When she broke the kiss with my husband, she turned toward me.

Your turn.

I leaned in. I kissed her.

I gave it the old college try. Both of us. *Dickinson yes, dick no,* she'd described dorm life at Smith. Why settle when you can have both?

I'd forgotten how soft women's lips were. Like the softest lip gloss on earth.

And how satiny smooth a woman's skin is. So different from Jason's—with its prickles of hair, rough scabs, and sunbaked patches from too many afternoons on too many golf courses.

I won't chronologically detail what happened next.

Not out of prudery. Out of memory blunted by alcohol and obfuscation. Even the next morning—it only came back as a series of snapshots.

Here's one of them.

Emma and I, naked on our sides and facing each other. For just a moment, I thought I was looking into a mirror. At my own rise of hip, distended nipple, vaginal cleft. That's the only place I'd ever witnessed a flesh-and-blood woman's nudity, wasn't it—in my own bedroom mirror. Not on a hotel bed.

Another snapshot.

Watching Jason enter someone other than me.

Watching it as a participant and as a voyeur. *So that's what it looks like*, I thought. *Like that.*

The best sex is dirty sex, Jason had once whispered to me.

It wasn't dirty. It was filthy.

It wasn't filthy. It was rapturous.

It wasn't rapturous. It was egregious.

Alcohol saved us, I think, from confronting its many contradictions at the moment it ended. Kept us from staring at each other in horror or pleasure or embarrassment or remorse. Instead we dropped like lotus-eaters onto the bed and couch. We slept.

It was the next morning when the hangovers hit—from last night's toddies and last night's torridness. Where two reverted to being company, and three to being a crowd. Where we half eyed each other as we stumbled half-dressed to the bathroom. As if we needed to hide the nakedness we'd already seen and reveled in. A Sunday childhood sermon came back to me—the one about Adam and Eve eating from the tree of knowledge and becoming embarrassed by their own natural state. From then on, they'd need to clothe and hide it.

What a night, Jason may have said. Not in a boastful or lascivious way. In the way he may have referred to an alcohol-induced blackout back in his twenties. Something it was okay to chalk up to youthful indiscretion and just forget about.

I may have silently seconded that with a shake of my head.

Only at the very height of awkwardness, when we were fully dressed, patting down our pockets and purses for wallets, scanning the room for leave behinds, as we mostly ignored each other's eyes—Emma said goodbye.

And said hello.

Said, *Wasn't that fun, and let's do this again sometimes. Please.*

Not by saying any of that.

Then how?

She kissed Jason on the lips. She kissed me on the lips.

And smiled.

That's how.

PART TWO

CHAPTER TWENTY-SIX

The cut in the gas line was approximately 1/32 of an inch thick. It's determined the natural gas would have seeped out at an approximate rate of one cubic foot per minute.

Natural gas weighs .0712 kg/m compared to the 1.204 kg/m weight of air. This is primarily due to the abundance of methane. This weight differential causes natural gas to rise.

Given the dimensions of the house, It's determined the natural gas would've taken approximately fifteen to twenty minutes to permeate the basement and ground floor of house.

It's determined the ground floor windows were closed. This is based on post-blast forensic examination of window sills and on an outdoor temperature of 42 degrees which likely would've negated the opening of any windows.

Maximum pressure of natural gas is defined as 101.325 kPa. This could've easily been achieved in that 15 to 20 minute time frame.

The minimum heat necessary for natural gas ignition is 435 degrees Centigrade. The temperature of the fire would've reached approximately 1,000 degrees Centigrade.

Due to shock wave analysis and forensic examination of fireplace, it's determined lighting the fire likely caused the deflagration and the resultant explosion that measured at 2000 m/s. This is an approximation and has a variance of 300 m/s either higher or lower.

Richard Schwabacher
Certified Fire and Explosion Investigator

I was reading our investigator's report in the bathtub—the trial was just weeks away.

When I reached for the loofah sponge, I accidentally splashed water onto the pages.

Water vanquishes fire, I thought. The bathwater had singled out that exact word in the last paragraph of the report...*fire*...smudging it beyond all recognition.

CHAPTER TWENTY-SEVEN

There were five witnesses who swore Neil talked about killing his ex-wife.

The discovery dump had come several months ago. I clicked on my computer to check out the day's mail and there it was. All 1.6 gigabytes of it.

The DA's office used to send it over in boxes, but this saved them money.

I preferred actual paper, where I could scatter the pages across my desk or bedspread like pieces of a jigsaw puzzle, sifting through the pile for various odd-shaped bits as I slowly put their case together.

You were hoping it wouldn't fit. That the pieces would be misaligned or missing. You were hoping for holes.

I made Jennifer print it out, a task she performed only under protest. Printing wasn't millennial.

The discovery should have come sooner—180 days after arrest, according to New York State law. But there were ways around that and the DA had used all of them, though some of the resultant delay was admittedly self-inflicted.

I'd filed an omnibus motion—which sounds more impressive than it is. It's where I basically disputed there being probable cause for Neil's arrest—in this case almost entirely ceremonial since it had no shot of being granted. I filed it to force Sizemore to respond—even though he undoubtedly sloughed it off onto Eileen. I was hoping there might be something in their response

I could make use of. Something they'd throw in out of sloppiness or bravado or simple stupidity.

There wasn't.

The omnibus motion had stopped the clock on discovery. It was as if I'd called a glacial time-out.

Among those 1,243 printed pages dumped onto my bed were the names of five witnesses who had a similar story to tell. A story about Neil, or more accurately about things Neil had told them—in a bar at 1 a.m., at a backyard barbecue on a summer Sunday, driving in a car on a weekday morning, on the fifteenth hole of a golf course on a Thursday afternoon.

I swear to God I'm going to kill that bitch. Variations of that sentiment.

That bitch is as good as dead.

I'm going to fucking bury that bitch.

And this one:

We'll see how much that bitch wants that house when I blow it the fuck up.

The bitch in question was Emma—just in case you're wondering.

I asked Neil about that.

Jail had softened his body but hardened his disposition. He looked overweight and pasty from all that jail starch, except when his face flushed with anger, which was most of the time I was with him. Anger at Judge Moronis for locking him up in here, anger at me for not getting the key.

When he wasn't angry—at his situation or at me—he would turn self-pitying or even reflective. Those were the times he'd talk about Emma.

He'd met her one night at the Stephen Talkhouse, a bar in Amagansett that usually showcased local cover bands. It was Seventies Night, a particularly unfortunate era in music, but one that allowed patrons to dress like Tony Manero in *Saturday Night Fever.* That's how he was dressed that night, he told me, in tight bell-bottoms and an open satin shirt. He'd spotted a woman in flared pants and a black bolero top and, in his words, swept her off her feet. Literally. At one point Emma and Neil had the floor to themselves, he claimed, the crowd circling them and clapping to their flamboyant version of the hustle, which they managed to pull off on multiple Patrón margaritas. Later they went out to the small hot dog stand that sits just outside the club to satisfy their late-night munchies and soak up the excess alcohol. They both took their hot dogs with sauerkraut and ketchup. What were the odds? They had other things in common—both of them were professional purchasers, if on vastly different scales. She bought fashion lines for a Seventh Avenue clothing company—he bought companies. They compared their dating histories; both agreed they didn't want to become one of those long-in-the-tooth Hampton singles, where pathos replaces eros. He was confident, if a touch boastful; she was sexy, if a bit coquettish. They didn't hook up that night, but they did two nights later, when he began a full-court press that had them living together within three months. Marriage followed.

That's what he talked about on days he wasn't angry. Today wasn't one of those days.

"You said you would *appeal* the bail decision?" he accused me.

"I did appeal the bail decision."

"And … ?"

"Waiting on the judge. But don't hold your breath."

"Thanks. You always have good news for me."

"You want me to lie to you?"

"No. I want you to do your job."

"I am doing my job. Speaking of which."

"What?"

"I finally got discovery from the DA."

"*Discovery … ?*"

"Their entire case basically. Everything they have on you and are more than likely to use."

"They don't *have* anything on me because I didn't *do* anything. How many times do I have to tell you?"

"They obviously hold a different opinion on that. They have five witnesses ready to stand up in court and say you threatened to kill your ex-wife."

"What the fuck...?"

"Yeah. Pretty much my reaction."

"That's bullshit."

"You didn't threaten to kill your ex-wife?"

"No."

"You never said *I swear to God I'm going to kill that bitch*?"

"No."

"*No...?*"

"Not like that."

"Like what, then?"

"You know... not like an actual threat. Like actually being serious."

"What were you being?"

"I was blowing off steam."

"Not blowing up houses?"

"I *told* you..."

"*We'll see how much that bitch wants that house when I blow it the fuck up.*"

"Huh...?"

"Another thing you supposedly told someone. Alex Saunders. Who you apparently played golf with at the East Hampton Golf Club in between discussing blowing up your house."

"He *said* that?"

"Yeah. Is he lying?"

"That motherfucker..."

"Is he lying?"

"Yes."

"You never said that?"

"I don't know. No. I can't believe that fucking prick went to the cops."

"It's more likely the cops went to him."

"That fucking cunt ..."

"Did you say it or didn't you?"

"Who the fuck remembers? I wasn't serious."

"So you did say it, but you didn't mean it. You were just joking."

"Yes. Right."

"You can see how it's not going to look that way to a jury, right?"

"You say all kinds of shit when you're pissed. Everybody says stuff. It doesn't mean anything."

"In light of your house blowing up it's going to appear that it did mean something."

"I don't care. This is bullshit."

"There are three more witnesses who say you threatened to kill your ex-wife. Jeff Weston. Tom Klein. Paul Denucious. Friends of yours?"

"*Some* friends."

"Right. But nonetheless."

"I wasn't serious. I didn't mean it."

"That'll be our story. The prosecution's will be you did."

"Those fuckers ..."

"Those fuckers will be on the stand. You won't."

A guard opened the door and asked if I wanted coffee. They'd given us the room reserved for legal meetings. Three chairs and a desk. Someone had carved *Moronis sucks dick* into the desk. Like it was high school.

"No, thanks, Tony." Tony was a fixture in the Suffolk lockup. It's possible I was too now.

"What about me?" Neil asked Tony.

"What *about* you?" Tony closed the door.

"Motherfucker." Nobody was going to escape Neil's wrath today. Including me.

"Aren't you supposed to be doing something about this shit?" he seethed. His face was the color of Rudolph's nose, if Rudolph was severely drunk.

"I am doing something about it."

"What?"

"You want the entire list?"

"Yes."

"Okay. I'm going to file a motion in limine."

"What the fuck is that?"

"A motion to suppress their testimony. Not allow it into trial. That it's hearsay. That its probative value is outweighed by its prejudicial impact. You didn't tell Alex that you blew up the house *after* the house blew up. You didn't make a confession. You were joking around on the golf course like guys do. Allowing those statements into trial would unfairly prejudice the jury."

"Will that work?"

"Maybe. Maybe not. They'll claim it's an exception to hearsay because it's reputational."

"Can I have that in English?"

"It plays to your reputation. They're going to paint you as a violent ex-husband who had a restraining order lodged against him because his wife feared for her life. Telling your golf buddies that you were going to murder her would back that up. If your reputation is of someone who wanted to kill his wife, showed a previous inclination to do that, and even let his friends in on his plans, then maybe you did cut that gas line. Maybe you did murder her. And the person she happened to be sleeping with. Him too. Is that English enough for you?"

"That's it? That's your grand plan? File your motion in lemon and wait for the judge to shoot it down like he does all your fucking motions?"

"Motion in limine. Not lemon. No, that's not everything I'm going to do. You asked for the entire list. I'm going to send my investigator out to investigate. The one charging us one thousand dollars a day."

"Investigate what?"

"*Who.* Alex Saunders. Jeff Weston. Tom Klein. Paul Denucious. And Dan Hess—almost forgot him. He's the one you apparently told, 'I swear to God I'm going to kill that bitch,' at the bar in Cittanuova at one in the morning."

"Investigate them for *what?*"

"We'll see. Have any of them been convicted for perjury before? That would be nice, but okay, not likely. Have they written bad checks? Beaten up their mothers? Robbed any banks? Filched any of those pens they attach to chains by the deposit slips? No? Do they do drugs? Abuse alcohol? Like to down a few on that fifteenth hole while you were blowing off steam? Are they bipolar, depressed, in therapy, on prescription meds? Do any of them have a score to settle with you? Have they been known to make things up now and then? We'll find out."

"They're scumbags."

"Unless they're lying scumbags, that won't discredit their testimony."

"Jesus," Neil said, rubbing his eyes with both hands. Not like he was calling out to Jesus, placing his soul and his fate in Jesus's hands the way a lot of defendants do—as a kind of last resort. *Okay, I've tried everything else, let's try religion.* In Neil's case, it was purely secular.

"That forty-five-minute gap between you driving by your house and showing up at work?"

"Yeah?"

"It doesn't take forty-five minutes to get to Southampton. Did you take the scenic route?" The cell phone data was in the DA's discovery as well. It confirmed what Joe had already told me.

"I took my time. I was pissed off."

"You took a lot of time."

"*So?*"

"They're going to say you passed the house and then parked somewhere. That you walked back—eluded the security camera and entered your house from the back. That you went downstairs and cut the gas line. That you had more than enough time to do that and still make it to your office by noon. Understand our problem here?"

"I told you. I just drove around. I wasn't in a hurry."

"Fine. Drove around where?"

"Just around."

"Could you be a little more specific?"

"No."

The problem with being in the Hamptons as opposed to, say, New York City, was that New York City had CCTV cameras on every block and the Hamptons by and large didn't have blocks. In other words, I couldn't go to the videotape and show Neil merrily meandering up and down the East End's back roads.

"Did you stop somewhere?"

"I may have. Sure."

"Where?"

"I don't know. I may have pulled over. I told you, I was pissed off."

"About your ex-wife?"

"About a lot of things."

"What things?"

"I don't know. The divorce agreement. She was fucking me out of the house."

"The house coming out of the settlement? Deducted from her half?"

"I bought that house. I paid for every fucking thing she put in that house—and she didn't stop putting things into it. It was a fucking money pit."

"That's why they were deducting it from the asset division."

"I don't give a shit. I wanted it sold."

"Right."

"You say *right* like I'm full of shit."

"Not at all. I'm saying it like I believe every word. They will too. They're going to present the crime as a double fuck-you. You blew up your ex-wife and you blew up the house she screwed you out of. Make that a *triple* fuck-you. You also blew up the man who'd replaced you."

"Your husband. That's the man who replaced me."

"Yes."

"You never call him that. *Husband*. You never even say his name. *Jason.* Jason, Jason, Jason." Repeating my husband's name like an obscene taunt. "I find that really strange."

"I told you the first day we met. I'm your lawyer. I'm not here to empathize with you. I'm here to represent you. We need to have boundaries."

"I don't know. You talk about it like it happened to someone else. Like you're not even involved."

"I think we're done for today," I said.

"Oh, we're done. You go back to your cushy office and I go back to my shithole cell."

"I'd trade places with you, but Tony might object."

I tried not to notice Neil glaring at me as I walked out.

CHAPTER TWENTY-EIGHT

Harry Lockman was on one of those diets where all you could eat was steak and more steak. With a side order of steak.

He'd shrunk by thirty pounds, but it had seemingly made him more carnivorous. He'd gotten his teeth into the jury pool and was busy ripping it apart.

"Half the jury list are divorced women," he said snidely.

"Half the country are divorced women," I said. "In the Hamptons, it's probably three-quarters."

"Too bad for us."

"They can't all hate their ex-husbands."

"Want to bet?"

"Okay. Tell me some good news."

"I've lost thirty-two and a half pounds."

Harry used to poll for Senate and congressional races. Even a few presidentials. When I'd asked him why he'd come over to criminal defense, he'd said he was looking to work with more reputable people. I don't think he was joking.

"So what are we looking for?" I asked him.

"The other side of the coin. Divorced men who feel unfairly screwed by their ex-wives. Those are the obvious ones. Republicans more than Democrats. Don't ask me why. It just is. Anti-feminists. People who think Me Too is just he said, she said and what she said is most likely bullshit."

"Fine. Are any of those in the jury pool?"

"Sure. This used to be Trump country."

"Okay, then."

"I'm going to run some focus groups. Want to peek in?"

"No. But send me the video." I'd sat in on a few of Harry's focus groups before, where I'd parked myself behind a one-way mirror and made faces at the participants.

"You sure? I'm ordering steak sandwiches from the Palm."

"I thought you can't have bread."

"I remove the bread."

"I'll probably be sorry for asking, but why don't you just order steak, then?"

Harry seemed to contemplate that as if I might've really stumbled onto something.

"I don't know." He shook his head, which had always struck me as leonine, but now seemed too big for his severely diminished body. "I always order sandwiches at these things."

"It was just a thought. How'd we make out on the poll?"

"Terrific if you're the prosecution."

"How terrific?"

"We've got a lot of work to do."

"No kidding."

"Let's avoid blue collar unless it's blue collar with restraining orders against them. You know the deal. How much do they resent their wives versus how much do they resent the rich? It's close."

"Noted."

"Kudos on the mistrial, by the way." He was talking about my embezzler. We hadn't spoken about it since the trial.

"Thanks. You were instrumental."

"Bull crap. I heard you tried everything short of murder to eighty-six the juror who saved our ass."

"So you weren't instrumental."

"I can take it. I got paid, didn't I?"

"If you didn't, take it up with Jennifer."

"How you doing, Caron?"

"In what context?"

"I don't know. In the context of losing your husband?"

"Is that really what you're asking me, Harry?"

"Okay. In the context of losing your husband and defending the person who more than likely murdered him?"

"I was wondering when you were going to ask me that. You waited long enough."

"Not really my place, is it? You're my client."

"It doesn't stop Joe."

"Joe's used to banging down doors. I come from more refined stock. You know the papers are going to have a field day with this. Once it gets going."

"They had a head start back in April."

"That was just batting practice."

"I read the online comments for laughs. I counted thirty-four *cunts* and forty-five *bitches*. They were talking about me, by the way."

"With any luck some of them are in the jury pool. We could use them."

"About the papers. Sure—they'll love writing about the wife of one of the victims defending his alleged murderer. On balance, that works for us. *Why would she be defending him if he really did it?* She being me."

"Because she being you was a little upset her husband was sleeping with the other victim, who by the way she wouldn't feel very fond of either. Because she thought they both had it coming and the final coup de grâce would be getting off the person who administered a little frontier justice. I'm sorry, have I overstepped my bounds here? If I have, I humbly apologize."

"Don't bother. You may be right."

"About you being angry enough to do something like that?"

"About them thinking that I'm angry enough to do something like that."

"I'm not going to ask if you are."

"Good. I'm not going to tell you."

❧ ❧ ❧

1—*Erase the imprints of betrayal.*

Meditation can help reach the root of former deception and jump-start the healing process.

2—*Forgive.*

Forgiveness breaks us free like a ship dislodging from a dock, because when we pardon the past, life is our open sea.

3—*Regain faith.*

The first person you have to trust is yourself, because if you can't trust yourself, who can you trust?

4—*Detach from people you can't trust.*

Don't put up with people who act in bad faith.

5—*Envision a future free of betrayal.*

Imagine each day that no one will ever hurt you again.

Nothing like a little light reading to get you to sleep.

Beyond Betrayal by Dr. Helene Katzman had cost me $14.95 on Kindle. It came with gold-plated reviews from *Psychology Today* and *Mental Health Magazine*.

It was a five-step program to move past the past. I could already tell I was going to have a problem with step one. *Erasure* was a lot to ask of anyone, wasn't it? Step two, *forgiveness*, wasn't going to be walk in the park for me either. *Regaining faith* was clearly beyond my capabilities. *Detaching from people I couldn't trust* would force me to take a different career path because criminal defense was a cesspool of people incapable of being trusted.

Which meant I'd never make it to step five.

One of the people I did trust called me at 10:15, just as my eyes were starting to droop.

"Did you know Mathew and your husband were having problems?" Joe asked me.

I shut the Kindle.

CHAPTER TWENTY-NINE

H e was nervous.

Latino landscapers in the Hamptons don't usually find themselves sitting on the other side of polished French Provincial desks. Their conversations with the local hoi polloi are usually relegated to fending off complaints about the state of their lawns. An invasive species of Georgia grass that smells awful and looks even worse had recently been making homeowners on the East End apoplectic.

In Miguel's case it wouldn't be lawns he was worried about. It'd be *greens*.

He worked at the East Hampton Golf Club.

Pass the golf course any morning at five o'clock on your way to a beach run, and you'd probably spot him out there drifting through the mist like some sort of ghost, preparing the greens for the onslaught of descending foursomes. Like shoemakers' elves, Miguel and his fellow landscapers were expected to do their job and disappear by morning.

Back before that wayward Chevy brought my running days to an end, I'd probably passed him and felt a bit guilty about it. Not enough to ruin my day. Enough to stop and think that if you had money you could choose to wake up at that ungodly hour but that others were forced to in order to earn a whole lot less.

Sorry.

That's what passes for a social conscience out here.

I was talking about Miguel's nerves. We kept the office at a less-than-balmy sixty-eight degrees, but Miguel was sweating.

The sweatshirt he'd layered on wasn't helping things, even with several enormous holes in it.

"Go ahead," Joe Rawlings told him, perched on the arm of the opposite chair. "Tell her what you told me."

The chairs were French Provincial too, meaning I was usually particular about how people sat on them. I was making an exception in Joe's case. He'd brought Miguel in at 7:45 a.m. because Miguel wanted to avoid regular office hours, Joe said. I assumed that was to avoid any people who might show up during regular office hours. The same kinds of people who regularly showed up at the East Hampton Golf Club.

Miguel mumbled something.

"Qué?" Joe said. The side benefit from years of picking up MS-13 gang members in various Long Island barrios was picking up some rudimentary Spanish.

Miguel seemed to repeat what he'd said before.

"He doesn't think he should be talking to us," Joe said to me.

"Did you tell him it's confidential?"

"I did. Not sure he's ready to take our word on that."

"He spoke to you before, didn't he?"

"I wasn't sitting behind a fancy desk in a fancy office."

"Would he prefer the broom closet?"

"Ask him. I don't think you know how to say broom closet, do you?"

I smiled at Miguel. "Por favor," I said. I did know how to say please.

Miguel's eyes darted around the room. He rubbed his hands together—stained and calloused hands, I noticed.

He spoke.

"It was nine months ago," Joe translated, "when this happened."

That would've been last March. About a month before Jason was killed.

"*Yes … ?*" I said.

Miguel continued.

"He says the course wasn't officially open yet. But sometimes members came in to use it anyway—it was unofficially allowed. That morning—maybe 6:45 he thinks it was, he spotted them out on the tenth hole."

"Who?"

Miguel must've understood a few English words. The word *who*, at least.

"Meester Jason and Meester Mathew," Miguel stammered.

"Jason and Mathew?" I repeated.

"Correct," Joe said.

"Okay." I said. "Sure. Sometimes Jason would get in a round before work."

Joe told Miguel to keep going.

Miguel started to relax—the words tumbling out in a steady if winding stream.

"It's the *reason* he saw them on tenth hole that's important here. He heard something, so he went to see what it was."

"Heard something?" I said. "Heard what? Two guys hitting a golf ball?"

"Two guys hitting each other," Joe said.

"Come again?"

"He heard what sounded like a fight. It was."

"You're telling me Jason and his best friend and business partner were physically *fighting* with each other?"

"No. He's telling me that. He was there. He knew them. Like you said, your husband and Mathew sometimes liked to get a round in before official hours. In this case, even before the official opening. They'd sometimes overlap ... Miguel and them. They even spoke to each other on occasion. One time Jason asked him to rake a sand trap. Apparently your husband spent a lot of time in them. In sand traps."

"Miguel saw them *hitting* each other?"

"Yes. Apparently they stopped hitting each other when Miguel showed up."

"This doesn't make any sense. Mathew gave the fucking eulogy."

"It gets worse. They weren't just using their fists. At least your husband's best friend and business partner wasn't. He was about to clobber Jason with a nine iron when Miguel showed up."

"*A nine iron?*"

"Okay, I'm taking a little creative license. I couldn't tell a nine iron from a putter. He was about to hit your husband with a golf club. Miguel shows up and Mathew sees him and stops. Drops the club."

"Could he tell what they were fighting about?"

Joe asked Miguel. Miguel shook his head.

"What happened then?" I asked. "Did they say anything to Miguel?"

"Apparently so."

"What?"

"Mathew told him they were just arguing about a lie."

"A lie? I don't understand."

"Where one of them had placed the ball. Sometimes golfers move the ball to a more advantageous place. It's called cheating. I don't play golf and even I know that."

"Mathew told him they were arguing about where one of them put the ball? That's what he said? He was going to hit my husband over the head with a metal golf club because he thought Jason cheated? Did Miguel believe him?"

Joe asked Miguel.

"No," Joe translated.

"Anything more?"

"Yeah. Mathew gave Miguel a tip."

"A tip?"

"Five hundred dollars."

"To keep quiet?"

"He didn't say what it was for. He didn't have to."

"Then?"

"Then Miguel golf-carted away and that was it."

"Ask him something else for me?"

"Shoot."

"*Why* didn't he believe Mathew?"

Joe asked. Miguel furtively glanced around the room as if checking to see if anyone else was there before whispering to us like a kid telling a secret.

I recognized one of the words.

Matar.

I'd heard it in a subtitled art film Jason had taken me to when we'd first begun dating, in a theater on Houston Street where you can hear the subways rattling by every five minutes. The movie was about a doomed bullfighter whose job was to *matar* the bull.

"He says the reason he didn't believe Mathew was because Mathew looked like he was going to kill him," Joe translated.

"Yes," I said. "I understand."

I didn't.

After Miguel left, Joe stayed behind.

"You have any idea what they could have been fighting about?" Joe asked me.

"No."

"It wasn't about where your husband placed the ball."

"He never said a word to me about Mathew. About problems with Mathew."

"Fair enough."

"What do you think?"

"They were business partners. I'd bet it was about business."

"The business was doing fine. As far as I know."

"Maybe *they* weren't doing fine. Mathew and Jason. Something made Mathew pissed off enough to want to kill him."

"Wanted to, or looked like he wanted to?"

"Does it matter? I'm sure you could use another suspect for the jury."

"It wouldn't hurt."

"Not just for the jury. Considering we're talking about your husband's murder, you might want to know who did it."

"*Mathew…?*"

"What… are you telling me it isn't possible? Remember the kid they put away for murdering his parents some years back? He woke up one morning and found his mom and pop stabbed to death. They worked that case out of my precinct. A detective who shall remain nameless told the kid his dad had lived long enough to finger him—lied to him, but fine, you're allowed. The kid says maybe he blacked out, lost his mind, confesses. What this detective didn't tell him was that the father's business partner—who it just so happened had been over the house playing poker that night and owed the father a ton of money—had donned a wig, bought an airline ticket, and vamoosed to California the next day. One more thing. This detective didn't tell the kid that he had a side business with that California-bound business partner."

"Sounds like a dirty-cop story." I wondered if that had been the moment Joe became too chummy with IA, and persona non grata around the precinct water cooler.

"Sure. It's also a dirty-business-partner story. Sometimes partners don't get along."

"Now what?"

"Now I keep earning that money you said you sent in the mail but so far hasn't arrived."

"What about the five friends?"

"Some friends."

"That's what Neil said."

"I'll bet he did. I'm working it."

"I would stay aboveboard on this. You know, don't pretend to be whoever it is you pretend to be. I may need you as a witness."

"What about you?"

"What about me?"

"About them calling you as a witness. All they had to do was put you on the witness list and they could've kicked you off the case."

I'd thought about that, of course. I'd planted seeds. "I think they were afraid if they asked me if anyone else wanted my husband dead I might've said sure and given them a list. After all, look who I agreed to defend."

"Too bad. Now you wouldn't even have to make something up."

"You mean Mathew?"

"I mean."

"Did something occur to you like it did me, Joe? About the reason Mathew told Miguel they were fighting?"

"Over a lie?"

"Right. Over a lie. Maybe Mathew wasn't using the golf term."

Joe smiled—he had several types of smiles depending on the situation. I'd categorize this one as sardonic.

Yes. It had occurred to him.

CHAPTER THIRTY

We became accomplished liars. Jason and I.

I already had my PhD in lying. A degree in criminal law. A colleague of mine had once suggested changing *lawyers* to *liars*. The judge would introduce the respective sides in a court case as the *liar* for the state and *liar* for the defense. This way jurors would be under no illusions. The verdict would hinge on who could lie best.

What did Jason and I lie about?

Her.

When Janice asked me what I'd done last night on the morning we stumbled bleary-eyed out of a room at the Dove-Tail Inn, I said nothing. It had been a pretty chill night, I told her. Jason and I had stayed in.

I hadn't prepared this cover story in advance. I hadn't prepared myself for someone asking me about it. It had come spontaneously—the lie. I wasn't going to speak about what we'd done in that room, so I wasn't going to speak about the person we'd done it with.

Later that night, I brought it up with Jason.

We hadn't said one word about it on the drive home. Or during the time we'd showered, dressed, made two cups of coffee, and wished each other a good day. The reticence to meet each other's eyes in the hotel room that morning had continued, as if we'd both signed NDAs we were now obliged to respect.

When Jason walked in that night after work, I ripped the NDA in half.

"I think we should talk about not talking about it."

All right. Confusing. Jason did that thing with his eyes—like when he was perusing indecipherable instructions for assembling a barbecue grill or outdoor table, a purchase he'd assumed would come all put together only to find he'd been brutally let down.

"You mean you and me?" he asked.

"I mean us and anyone else."

"Oh. Right."

"I mean I wouldn't tell Mathew or Larry or your best friend's caddy either."

"Sure. I mean, I wasn't intending to."

Jason had once told me that the greatest pleasure about sex was telling someone about it. For men, he meant. Or at least, men of a certain age—he'd been ostensibly referring to his late teens and early twenties.

"Okay. Just don't."

"Are you … ?"

"Am I what?"

"Okay?"

"Not sure. I'm still processing." I was. It was a little like waking up from a strange dream and then spending all day trying to figure out what it meant. Like a dream, it wasn't entirely coherent or completely whole. The chronology was all over the place—pieces I found hard to lay end to end. Just like the three of us had physically ended up—end to end to end. How did we get from there to there?

"It was … I mean … it was kind of hot," Jason said, a little timidly, as if he wasn't sure I'd be on board with that.

I wasn't ready to say if I was or wasn't. Yes, it had been hot. Searing hot. So was the Catholic guilt racing like antibodies to fortify this shocking breach in my moral defenses. I felt unmoored. I'd been knocked off-kilter.

"Let's just not say anything. To anyone. About her. Or anything."

"Sure. Scout's honor."

"You might want to use a different term. The Boy Scouts are being sued for abusing little boys and covering it up for decades. One of them happens to be a client of mine."

"Will a pinky swear do?"

I held my pinky out the way I used to do as a nine-year-old back in Urbana, Illinois.

Jason hooked it with his.

Done.

We wouldn't talk about it—about her—to anyone. We would hardly talk about it to ourselves.

Then Emma texted me.

Hey stranger.

I'll admit I felt a jolt—of adrenaline or desire or possibly fear. Not the fear of dreading something. More the fear of wanting something.

Hey, I answered.

Miss you guys, she wrote.

The kind of sentiment that means one thing among friends but another thing among friends with benefits. Which one was she speaking as?

I didn't know to respond, so I texted back one of those smile emojis.

You miss me? she texted back.

There it was. One of those blatant queries you either say yes or no to. And if you say yes, you're saying *yessssssss*, and if you say no you're saying go away and don't text me again. Ever. You're shutting the door to room 14 at the Dove-Tail Inn and you're locking it behind you.

Yes, I texted.

A return smile emoji. A red heart added on for good measure.

We texted off and on after that, sometimes descending into the kind of double entendre we'd engaged in that night at the bar. The kind if you heard from anyone else on earth you'd stick a finger in your mouth and pretend to hurl. But this wasn't anyone else and my finger stayed where it was and kept texting.

We were talking about the worst deprivations during the pandemic and I wrote *I missed eating out.*

What did she text back?

You're very good at it.

I didn't text back *Ewwww.* Or *Ugh.* Or *Please stop…*

I texted back: *Really…?*

Yes, really.

One morning I told her Jason was out playing golf in his usual foursome.

Not his usual threesome?

You get the idea. Not exactly sexting. But not exactly not.

At some point, the whole *miss me—miss you* thing needed to be adjudicated, of course. It needed a conclusion.

Jennifer's ex, the one who'd been facing twenty-five years in federal prison for drug smuggling, had been a respected Ivy League academic whose career path took a hard turn left after he became addicted to heroin. He'd been confident his first time would be the only time. It wasn't—he'd gotten hooked. He'd needed to try it again. And then again.

I empathized.

The further I got from that night at the Dove-Tail Inn, the more I wanted to repeat it.

If you asked me why, I might've given you the same answer Jennifer's ex had when I'd asked him why he couldn't have simply abstained. *Abstainers are weak people who yield to the temptation of denying themselves pleasure*, he quoted Ambrose Pierce at me—the kind of response you get from a rising English scholar turned failed international drug smuggler.

It wasn't as simple as that, of course. Not for me. I questioned whether something was wrong with this picture—the one sitting on the rosewood hall table showing a tuxedoed Jason kissing his new virginally clad bride. Did there need to be a lack of something to create the want of something? Were we taking a break from normal or was something irreparably broken? Maybe I was finally acting out against the ties that bind—that Catholic girlhood that shaped me—listening to the voice that had been placed in my head at a too-early age that repeated as if on a loop: *You are a sinner. You are bad.* Maybe I was saying, *Okay, I give up, you're right. If sex is always dirty, let's make it dirtier.*

I'm not sure about any of this.

What I *was* sure about was that I felt something akin to a heart murmur every time her texts popped up on my phone. Or is that being way too genteel? Would it be more accurate to call me Pavlov's dog, with every *brringg* starting me salivating?

"I've been talking to Emma," I told Jason one night, going for offhand casualness. The way I might've said I'd been talking to Janice or Maggie or his mother in Boca.

He perked up—not the reaction I would've elicited if it had been about anyone other than Emma.

"*Oh…?*"

"She was wondering if we wanted to come over to her house. On Saturday night."

Completely innocent on the surface—going over to a friend's house for dinner or a drink. But this wasn't completely innocent because this wasn't exactly a friend.

"Sure," Jason said. "Sounds like fun."

When Maggie called me and asked if we could get together that weekend, I told her no. We already had plans.

What plans? she asked.

A client of Jason's, I said. A couple I'd never met.

The lie was on.

When Emma greeted us that night in her Japanese robe, she was discarding all pretense between us. She was saying we can skip the part where we wonder if anything's going to happen again. We could proceed right to the main event.

I think is where I disrobe, she said by the fire. Funny.

The second time was less clouded by alcohol and hindered by awkwardness. This time we knew what we were doing. We were signing on the dotted line.

The fireplace setting was soft-core cliché—the dancing flames and leaping sparks. It worked.

Jason watched us at one point. That's the thing about being one of three—you're constantly shape-shifting, trading between participant and voyeur. Knowing you're being watched adds its own kind of scintillation. Emma and I weren't just performing the sex act we'd tittered about at the Dove-Tail Inn—we were performing.

In the middle I spotted red satin serpents undulating by the firelight. I warned her to move her robe—the kind of thing a woman would take note of and a man ignore. Jason rescued it and draped it over us like a blanket, then joined us beneath it.

We didn't doze off this time.

If anything, I felt hyperalert. I was trying to determine the rules of disentanglement, to figure out whose arms I was supposed to retreat into. I'd ended up face-to-face in hers, Jason snuggling against my back like a squirming child demanding to be acknowledged.

I couldn't help noticing the inherent symbolism of this. I was turning my back on my husband. I was embracing someone else.

Eventually Jason did doze off.

Not Emma and I.

Let's have a heart-to-heart, she whispered to me.

She was being literal. Our hearts were pressed up against each other. Our breasts. Everything.

CHAPTER THIRTY-ONE

Mort Gluckman was our longtime personal lawyer. He'd been besieging me about reading the will. I'd been resisting. *When I get a moment*, I told him. I wasn't dependent on what Jason had left me; I made a fine living on my own. Maybe I was simply avoiding another widow's task—like cleaning out Jason's closet or answering the onslaught of condolence emails.

Eventually I gave in because Mort told me it was getting a little embarrassing—all that time between Jason's death and the reading of his will. Plus Brenda had been hounding him. She wanted to know her portion of the inheritance.

I told Mort I'd come by on a Tuesday morning. Brenda would phone in from Boca Raton.

Mort had a well-heeled office in the shadow of the Empire State Building. I drove to the city on Monday and spent the night in our apartment. I hadn't been back there since Jason's death.

It was an emotional repeat of walking back into our empty Hamptons house. The palpable presence of a void. Like black holes in Hubble's pictures of the universe, only noticeable by an absence of light. I could feel its enormous pull trying to suck me in, capable of crushing me.

I opened a bottle of wine, ordered in some sushi, and stared at the twinkling lights of Jersey City across the river. I was trying to remember the last time Jason and I had been here. Perhaps a month or so before he'd died.

I ate half the sushi, threw the rest in the garbage, and retired to the bedroom.

I pulled down the duvet, then stood there and stared.

I was compulsive bed maker. Jason used to chide me for making hotel beds just before checking out. *You might want to leave something for the maids to do.*

My father was an army vet who thought making your bed every morning was the key to an orderly and upright life, a way to teach you to not cut corners. It had stuck.

Speaking of corners. He'd taught me the art of making *hospital* ones. How to tuck in the bedsheet between the mattress and box spring so it was taut enough to bounce a dime off of.

Whoever made the bed the last time it was used had neglected to do that. To make hospital corners. It hadn't been me.

I felt dizzy.

I had to sit down on the bed to keep from falling. The heat was rising in me again—the kind that threatened to immolate me.

When I lay back on the pillow, it got worse.

I smelled it on the bedsheets.

Her.

"I hereby nominate, constitute, and appoint my beloved wife, Caron Mooney, to act as the executor of this, my last will and testament. In the event that Caron Mooney shall predecease or chooses to not act for any reason, I nominate and appoint Mathew Gorman to act in her place."

Mort was treating the reading of the will literally—seemingly determined to read every single word of it. Maybe because Brenda was sitting on the other end of the phone.

"How are you, Caron?" she'd coolly asked me over speakerphone. "I haven't heard from you for a while."

The truth is, she hadn't heard from me at all. Jason had been the connective tissue that bound us together. Now that it had been ripped away, there hadn't seemed to be a particular reason to keep in touch.

"Sorry. I've been busy with a couple of trials."

"So I hear. I was hoping you might have told me."

That was the other reason I hadn't kept in touch with Brenda. The touchy subject of who I was defending in one of those trials.

"Sorry. I don't usually clear my client list with you." It came out ruder than I'd intended. It was an occupational reflex: when challenged—attack.

"*Jason's murderer?* That one you maybe should've cleared."

"Alleged murderer. We've pleaded not guilty."

"*Pleaded?*"

"Our case is he didn't do it."

"Your *case*? What about your *belief*? What about your responsibility to your dead husband?"

I was tempted to ask her about my dead husband's responsibility to me—to not be found naked in front of a fireplace next to a naked woman the morning they sifted through the rubble. I reverted to lawyer-speak instead. As if I was talking to Chris Policano instead of the mother of my murdered husband.

"My client's innocent. We intend to prove that in court."

"Well, isn't that golly-gee fantastic for you. I hope it's okay if I don't wish you luck."

Mort cleared his throat.

"I think maybe we should get to the reading," he said.

It was fairly anticlimactic. Jason had left most everything to me. With a few notable exceptions.

"I give and bequeath the sum of five hundred thousand dollars to my beloved mother, Brenda Mooney. In addition, all property expenses for Unit 7A in Magnolia Gardens, Boca Raton, Florida, will be covered by this estate in perpetuity. If Brenda Mooney predeceases me, this sum will revert to Caron Mooney."

I could hear Brenda sniffling over the phone. I wasn't sure if it was because Jason had referred to her as his *beloved* mother or because she'd been hoping for more. Maybe she was still smarting over my recent choice in clients.

Jason left his new Callaway golf clubs to Larry.

He left a generous sum to the cancer charity he'd begun for his co-worker.

The savings he left me were enough to keep me in the style I'd grown accustomed to, even if I weren't a criminal defense attorney charging five hundred dollars an hour.

There was the matter of his hedge fund. Of divvying up Jason's share. There was a liturgy of financial terminology I found hard to follow. After the reading Mort told me all that was still in flux. A contract Jason and Mathew had drawn up at the formation of the fund designated in specificity how a deceased partner's half would be allocated. Mathew had sent over a veritable *War and Peace* of financial statements Mort was still going through. Needless to say, when he sorted it out, he'd let me know. I might want to contact Mathew if I had any questions.

"Can you make copies?" I asked him.

"Of the statements?"

"Yes."

"Sure. Need a little light reading?"

"Maybe. I've already read *War and Peace*."

"Really? I didn't think anyone did." I was packing up to leave. Brenda had hung up after directing her goodbye to Mort and only Mort.

"How are you doing, Caron?" he asked; he'd walked me to the door of his office, which given its dimensions qualified as light exercise. It seemed to be the question of the year—how I was doing. Everyone wanted to know.

"I've got a big trial coming up. Ask me after the verdict."

"Did you think about saying no?" he said.

"To my client?"

"Yes. There are plenty of other ones."

"I thought about it."

"Is this a kind of posthumous FU?"

"Mort…"

"I'm not saying maybe you don't have cause. It just ... when I read about it I was kind of thrown."

"What's that like?"

"Huh?"

"Being thrown. Wait a minute. Don't tell me. I imagine it feels the same as when I got the call from the police detective that morning."

"Okay, Caron. I'll shut up."

"Please get me those papers, Mort. Thanks."

CHAPTER THIRTY-TWO

I couldn't sleep.

I was back in East Hampton.

I waited till the first pale light slowly crept across the bedroom floor. How would *Mad* magazine have drawn *Creeping Light*? Four spindly legs with a lighthouse-shaped head. I threw on some sweats and a heavy parka and drove to the beach.

The parking lot was desolate. In summer, I would've had to wait in line till some pimply high school kid checked the beach pass plastered to my rear passenger window.

Not now. All the high school kids were in high school.

I had my pick of spots. *Eeney, meeny, miney...* I chose the one closest to the beach path.

If the beach lot was desolate, the beach looked apocalyptic. I was used to seeing it crammed with blankets, beach chairs, umbrellas, and oversized coolers. The salt air thick with the shrieks of six-year-olds playing tag with the surf, the *thunks* of hands swatting volleyballs, the soft mash-up of R and B, rap, and indie emanating from various radios at a respectable non–Jones Beach level.

This morning all I could hear was the distant caw of a seagull and the hissing sound of the Atlantic being sucked past pebbles and broken shells. A faint frost clung to the sand.

I walked to the edge of the surf and stopped.

Whitecaps skimmed the surface of the black ocean like latte cream. The waves seemed fiercer in late winter, as if they were driven by roiling anger instead of howling wind.

I used the foot of my sneaker to draw the first letter.

I watched as the surf covered it and withdrew, cleansing the sand of any trace of it.

Then the second letter.

And the third.

Chapter 6 of *Beyond Betrayal*: "Helpful Exercises to Heal." "One: Write each letter of your betrayer's name and let the ocean wash it away. It will take your anger and sadness along with it."

The surf only covered three-quarters of the fourth letter, leaving the upper curve like a hyphen. I waited till the next wave came and erased it.

They say women have an extra sense. Or maybe only certain women do, ones adept at looking over their shoulders.

I felt someone's presence before turning and spotting a lone figure standing way back where the path to the beach ended.

A man. Standing and staring at me.

I began to walk away. Casually at first, the way I used to start a jog back in my running days—limbering up the muscles, getting the kinks out, starting the heart pumping.

It was already pumping.

The man had begun walking toward me.

I picked it up a notch—somewhere between a fast walk and a slow jog.

He mimicked me, looking like a man out for his morning beach jog except for the fact that with an entire beach to choose from he'd decided to jog toward me.

I ratcheted it up two more notches—let's call it actual running now.

When I peeked back—he was still coming.

Right on my heels.

My run-in with that wayward Chevy had left me with stress fractures in both legs my orthopedist had admitted would never fully heal. They wouldn't bother me during normal walking, he'd assured me, but would scream bloody murder if I ever decided to start doing ten-miles runs again.

I hadn't made it half a mile, but they were already whining.

The man kept following.

Running on sand is three times harder than running on asphalt. It's simple physics. You're sinking downward as you're moving forward. My breathing reflected it—I sounded like a broken-down air conditioner just before it stops working—wheezing, rattling, and groaning.

I felt a sudden sharp stitch in my side. What was that mantra my mother murmured to her seven-year-old daughter trying the master the art of knitting...? *Sew one. Stitch two.* Right. There was another saying my mom was fond of: *A stitch in time saves nine.* Nine *what*...? She'd never said.

I peeked back again, trying to determine if the man was getting closer or dropping back. Or if he was still keeping pace—which would be nearly as bad as inching closer, because soon those stress fractures of mine would start bawling and I would stop working like that broken-down air conditioner and begin falling back while the man would keep coming.

Somehow I kept my legs churning.

So did he.

I almost fell into it before actually seeing it. Just over a rise, frigid seawater had cleaved the beach in half, forming a temporary canal. There wasn't a bridge to help me cross it.

I stopped dead at the edge of the water.

The man was shouting something at me.

The water seemed shallow enough, but I knew the cold would be heart-stopping.

I took a deep breath. I plunged forward. The water immediately rose to my knees; in two seconds my legs turned numb. Only for a bit. On the other side of the numbness came searing pain.

I kept going.

When I finally made it to the other side, I stood there gasping before glancing back at my pursuer.

He'd stopped on the opposite bank, bent over his knees—far enough away to appear like an insignificant piece of driftwood in a sea of sand. And just as harmless.

I turned around and walked away—my legs screaming at me to not take one more step, to please, *please* get somewhere warm.

That's when I noticed it. The beach house just over the dune of seagrass.

I walked up and over the dune and found the wooden path. I followed it up to the side door. I rapped on the glass.

"You're *running* again?" Maggie said when she opened the door.

"Trying," I said.

"In a parka?"

"It's cold outside."

"I noticed. How about we get you inside where it isn't."

Then she saw my legs.

"Jesus, Caron. What happened to you? You go for a swim too?"

"I ran a little too close to the surf."

"Well, get in. I'll find you some dry sweatpants."

I changed into a pair of black Lululemons in the downstairs bathroom. Maggie brewed coffee and we settled around the center island in the kitchen.

"How are you, Caron?"

"A little out of breath. Otherwise A-OK."

"I thought your doctor told you not to run anymore."

"It's been a while. I thought I'd see if he actually knew what he was talking about."

"And…?"

"Apparently he does."

"Good to know. If I ever break a leg, he's my guy. How's everything else?"

"Other than experiencing cancel culture up close and personal, terrific."

Those previous friendships Jason and I had nurtured over years had splintered along various fault lines just as I'd predicted. Some by natural attrition, and some because they'd picked up the morning paper and been as horrified as Brenda to discover I was defending my husband's alleged murderer. I'd gotten some acid-tinged emails, a few curt messages left on voicemail, and one or two unfriendly stares on the streets of Water Mill. When I didn't respond to them—the emails, the voicemails, the stares— then nothing. My social universe had contracted accordingly.

It was fine. Like I said, I'm not a people person.

Maggie, however, remained. Given her own marital history, she probably thought I had good reason to be furious at Jason and seemed nonplussed that I'd chosen to represent the person accused of his murder. I was simply engaging in a little *frontier justice*—isn't that what Harry Lockman said?

"Well, people are … fucking *judgmental*," Maggie said.

"If it matters, I believe he didn't do it."

"Well then …" She took a sip of coffee and slowly placed the cup down on the granite counter. "*Screw 'em.*"

Later on, Maggie asked me where my car was. She'd noticed it wasn't sitting in her carport.

"I parked it in the beach lot and decided to run from there."

"How industrious of you. Want a lift back?"

"No, thanks. I'll walk."

I'd been in her house for more than an hour. Waiting.

After I kissed Maggie goodbye and stepped outside, I confirmed the beach was empty.

He'd left.

When I made it back to the lot, I could immediately see the spiderweb covering my entire driver's-side window. As if one of those black widows lurking in my pool shed had decided to hitch a ride.

The man had tried to smash it in. He'd almost succeeded, but not quite. I seemed to remember the Audi dealer telling me how their window glass was specially made to take a frightening level of impact and remain whole. For once, a car dealer had actually been telling the truth.

Still, it would need to be replaced.

Before I opened the door, settled in the front seat, caught my breath, and tried to tamp down a gnawing panic, before that, I spotted a piece of paper stuck in my windshield. Like those ads teenage hawkers are always sticking in there—for new beach clubs, trendy restaurants, impromptu music events.

This wasn't an ad.

The man had written one word.

Why?

CHAPTER THIRTY-THREE

Justin Allen Thompson graduated high school as most likely to paratroop out of an airplane.

He did.

Spending six months on Parris Island, then two years patrolling the arid valleys of Afghanistan as a US Marine. Sometimes they'd parachute him into Taliban territory at night because marching in there by day would've turned him and the rest of his platoon into the equivalent of ducks in a shooting gallery.

You haven't lived until you've seen the world through night vision goggles, Justin emailed a friend from high school. He was being smart-assed and truthful. He'd become a kind of adrenaline junkie out there in the Panjshir Valley, dodging Taliban fire at night, maneuvering through third-world villages by day, wondering whether the friendly guide showing him the way to an elder's hut was leading him into a fatal ambush instead.

When he got back home, he became a different sort of junkie.

Crystal meth replaced adrenaline.

Justin felt conflicted. About his time defending democracy in a country where the elders practiced sexual slavery with twelve-year-old boys. About some choices he'd made over there involving the use of his M27. There were certain pictures in his head that refused to get out.

PTSD was the diagnosis he received when he smashed in his girlfriend's TV one night after being unable to access *American Sniper* for the fifth time, and she made him hump over to the VA the next morning to see what was what.

For a while he attended weekly bitch meetings with a bunch of other PTSD vets in the basement of a church. They'd sit around and relate how they'd lost their jobs, their wives, their sanity. The problem, they believed, was that in Afghanistan or Iraq they'd needed to be on full alert 24/7, but back in the real world they couldn't seem to find the off switch. Being on high alert in a supermarket, a business office, or in bed with your wife was a true recipe for disaster. It's what had brought them to this basement, and in the case of Justin Thompson, to other basements where he cooked and shot meth with a bunch of other junkies.

He stopped going to meetings because he was usually too high or too embarrassed or too busy looking for meth.

His girlfriend kicked him out. He'd started stealing money from her pocketbook, even when she started finding ingenious places to stash it. He'd been a first-class sniffer in Afghanistan—adept at finding hidden guns or bomb ingredients where others saw a harmless wheat bin or nursery. That survival skill helped him in his search for his girlfriend's money. It didn't help him with his girlfriend.

That's how he ended up on the streets.

At first he found couches in the homes of old friends—that high school buddy he'd written from Afghanistan was one of them. But things would go south pretty quickly because he began to do to his friends what he'd done to his girlfriend. That is, steal from them.

He'd own up to it, promise to never to do it again, and beg them to please not kick him out onto the street because he had nowhere to go. That worked for a while. But there were only so many second chances turned into third and fourth ones—and eventually that's where Justin ended up.

On the street with nowhere to go.

Since he couldn't steal from his friends anymore, he started stealing from strangers, people he'd pass on sidewalks or in basement shooting galleries. The first time he grabbed a woman's

purse on the street, knocking down this perfectly nice-look-
ing mom strolling a baby carriage down Fairlawn Avenue in
Hempstead, he ran into a nearby alley and cried.

He was still crying when the police found him and booked
him for petty theft and second-degree assault. In his mug shot,
he looks bewildered. He kept telling the booking officer that he'd
been a straight-A student in high school and a straight-arrow
patriot who'd only wanted to serve his country.

Tell it to the marines, the booking officer apparently replied,
trying to be funny.

Justin got probation for that first offense, thanks to an over-
loaded court system and some sympathy from the judge who
took Justin's military service and resultant PTSD into account.

Justin promised the judge he'd go to rehab and for a while
he kept his word. He dutifully showed up three times a week at a
drug rehab center in a local hospital and met twice weekly with
his probation officer.

The probation officer wrote the acronym *GAS* in the margin
of Justin's report.

Got a shot.

He was too optimistic.

It was a vicious cycle, Justin explained to the next booking
officer he encountered after being arrested for knocking over a
meth den.

Reliving his worst experiences in Afghanistan was supposed
to be therapeutic, he said, but then he felt like taking some meth
to forget those awful memories all over again. Did that make
sense?

This time the judge gave him actual jail time.

Justin spent six months in a medium-security lockup, where
his drug habit got moderately better but his PTSD grew worse.
Sometimes he'd scream out in the middle of the night and his
cellmate would have to hit him in order to get him to shut the
fuck up.

When he was released, he went back onto the streets.

He grew a long beard and was often seen muttering to himself. He lost some teeth. Sometimes he'd scream at people for no apparent reason, or go running down the block at full speed as if he were being chased by the Taliban again.

He'd sleep whatever place he could find. Park benches. Alleyways. LIRR stations. Then he found a place where no one could roust him. Where he could slip in at night and then slip out each morning.

It was a container factory.

There was a hole in the fence no one seemed eager to fix, and he was able to wiggle in and out undisturbed.

He found some flattened cardboard boxes that served as a kind of makeshift mattress in a crawl space beneath a hidden floor trap. Remember, he was a first-class sniffer good at finding things; just in case the factory decided to hire a night watchman, he figured he'd remain undetectable.

Justin would slip through the fence, enter the factory, open the floor trap, slither into the crawl space and close it. Then he'd fall asleep.

This was all in the report Joe wrote up for me, red-eyed, shaky, and slightly drunk, I think. A few weeks after that night he'd startled me at 2 a.m. when he came in out of the rain.

Joe wanted me to know who Justin Thompson was.

It was important to him.

CHAPTER THIRTY-FOUR

"Hey, kid."

Mathew called me at the office. He'd left messages a few times. Checking in on me and wanting to make sure I was okay. No need to call him back, he said. I hadn't.

"Hello, Mathew."

"Everything okay?" Mathew had resisted joining the crowd of haters. Good for him, even if we'd never been bosom buddies, Mathew and I—that'd been reserved solely for Jason. At least, up to the moment Mathew attempted to decapitate him with a golf club. Mathew was on his third wife, and third wives either tried hard to ingratiate themselves with their husband's social circle or demanded a clean sweep. She fit more into the latter category. We'd socialized at business events but not much else.

"It depends how you define *everything*," I said. "Me? I'm fine."

"Good to hear." Speaking of hearing, Mathew heard I'd inquired about the division of the business. He was sorry about the delay—these things took a crazy amount of time. All that financial untangling was, trust him, an accountant's worst nightmare. He was calling to see if he could be of any help. If I had any questions for him.

Yes. Why did you try to kill my husband on a golf course?

"Not at the moment."

"You sure about that? If you do, I'm here, kid." Mathew was older than me, but not that much older. It was meant to be a term of endearment, I supposed, but maybe it was more a term about hierarchy. I was being relegated to the kids' table, and I didn't particularly like it.

"One question actually?"

"Shoot."

"How was the business doing?"

A slight pause.

"The business was doing fine. *Is* doing fine. Why are you asking?"

"Purely out of self-interest."

"Ha. Appreciate your honesty. Nothing to worry about, kid."

"I'm not worried. I'm curious."

"Of course you are. The business is good. Equity more than solid. Jason's carry should be prodigious. Am I losing you?"

"A little."

"Which part?"

"The part after *of course you are.*"

"Okay. I'll slow down. The carry is Jason's percentage of the corpus. Reinvested and compounded. Clearer now?"

"*Corpus?*"

"The fund's total investment."

"Sorry. It sounded uncomfortably like corpse."

"Never thought about that. You're right." Pause. "I miss the son of a bitch, you know."

"Join the club."

"It seems surreal. Not having him around anymore. Hard to believe, isn't it?"

I didn't answer him. What was there to say that hadn't already been said? Once while I was waiting in my gyno's office, I'd read an article about a tribe in the Amazon jungle that supposedly has no word for death. It makes sense. When it comes to death, there are no words.

"You know," Mathew said almost conspiratorially, "he loved you."

"Thank you. Not sure I needed to be reassured."

Mathew obviously disagreed with that.

Because of her.

"I didn't mean ... I just wanted you to know that I knew Jason as well you *can* know somebody, and I knew that he loved you."

"What else did you know?"

"Excuse me ... ?"

"I don't know. You said you knew him better than anybody. I'm curious if you knew what my husband was up to in his spare time."

I don't know what made me blurt that out. Mathew's use of clichés and his overall patronizing tone. He knew that Jason loved me. He might've also known he was cheating on me. I wouldn't get an answer—the man code is structured to survive even the death of one of its members.

"Caron ... I honestly had no knowledge of ..."

"Forget it, Mathew. I appreciate you calling."

"Oh, don't be silly. Honestly, my pleasure. Whatever you need."

I did have one more question for Mathew, but I'd need to rely on Joe to find the answer.

What were you doing the morning the house blew up?

I called my father that night.

"Hey, Dad."

"Hey, honey." His voice was thin and raspy. That's what emphysema does to you, or what a lifetime of smoking will do—give you emphysema. It had left him permanently attached to an oxygen tank like a scuba diver who can't leave the ocean. It's an apt analogy—my dad said the disease felt like trying to breathe underwater.

"How are you feeling?"

"Worse than okay. Better than death."

"Fair enough."

"How are you doing, honey?"

"About the same."

"It'll get easier. When your mom passed, it got easier. Took a while. That's all." My dad had never remarried. I think it was due to the impossibility of ever sharing his immeasurable pain with anyone else.

"Dad?"

"Yeah?"

"Can you tell me that story?"

"Which one?"

"The bee one."

My dad used to make up bedtime stories on demand. I used to do that a lot apparently—demand them. Like that sultan in *Arabian Nights* who forced Scheherazade to keep spinning tales on pain of death. My father had faced the pain of my incessant whining, but according to my mother, he hadn't minded. This was B.D.—Before Daniel Died, when I was still a little girl who insisted on acting like one. The bee was my favorite.

"Seriously, honey?"

"Seriously."

"Can't sleep?"

"Yeah."

"Why not?"

"Seeing ghosts."

"That's what you used to me tell me when you were little and wanted a story."

"I know. It always worked."

"Okay. Let me see if remember it …"

"Thanks, Dad."

"Okay, so there was this little bee …"

"Right."

"And he learned the terrible truth about being a bee."

"Which was?"

"That after he stung someone for the first time, he'd die."

"I think you used to say that he'd go to bee heaven."

"You're older now. I think you can handle it."

"Sure."

"So he asked everyone in the forest, if he was going to die right after stinging someone, what was the point of even living?"

"Fair question."

"He asked the wise owl, who thought long and hard, but he didn't know. He asked the giraffe and the lion and the bear. No one knew."

"And then ... ?"

"And then he asked this gangly bird walking by."

"Right."

"And the bird wouldn't answer him."

"Stupid bird."

"Yes. Stupid bird. Because when the bee asked this bird again and the bird still refused to answer him, the bee got mad."

"How mad?"

"Really, really mad. Mad enough to want to hurt the bird."

"That's mad."

"He asked the bird one more time. 'If I'm going to die the first time I sting someone, then why am I even alive?'"

"But the bird still ignored him."

"I thought I was telling the story."

"Sorry, Dad."

"Yes. The bird *still* ignored the bee."

"Stupid bird."

"Exactly. Because the bee got so mad, well, he *stung* the bird."

"And ... ?"

"Suddenly the bird's feathers sprung out from its body in every color of the rainbow. See, this bird ... it was a *peacock*. And it was the most beautiful thing the bee had ever seen."

"But ... ?"

"But ... well, the bee died."

"Stupid bee."

"I don't know. Was the bee stupid? It died in the awesome presence of beauty. In the service of it, you might say."

"Thanks, Dad."

"Sleepy now?"

"I think so."

"No more ghosts?"

"Manageable ones."

"Okay, then. Good night, honey."

I'd lied.

Some ghosts remain unmanageable. The ones that hide under your bed and crouch behind your curtains. The ones that lurk in a closet.

Federations Candy Store. King Kullen. Dunkin' Donuts.

We'd pass them on the way to church. Me and Daniel. One, two, three. I used them as fodder for my list of weekly sins. *I ate candy without asking, Father. I stuffed my face with doughnuts, Father.* Gluttony was one of the seven deadly sins, wasn't it? Granted, pretty low on the list, but perfectly bona fide. It'd do.

Daniel was a resolute walker. Meaning he didn't meander or dawdle. He didn't stop to smell the doughnuts. He was kid on a mission, an altar boy in good standing. He didn't so much hold my hand on the way to church as tow me there.

I wasn't in any particular hurry—I didn't want to go to church—wasn't it enough having to go on Sundays? Danny had weekly altar practice, so my parents had him tote me along on Wednesday afternoons when I wouldn't have to wait in line for confession—off-peak hours for sinners.

On this afternoon there was someone new standing with Father McCrary. *Meet our new curate,* Father McCrary said. *Curate* sounded like *cure,* I thought. As if the man was there to heal the sick like Jesus had. Blind people, lepers, cripples—those malformed souls populating all those Bible stories they fed us on Sunday mornings.

Hello, the curate said. He was much younger than Father McCrary, if still incalculably old to me. In his twenties I'd guess now. He had blond hair and pockmarked cheeks. Maybe he'd needed to be cured of something himself, then joined the church to help other diseased people.

A curate wasn't a curer of disease, of course. He was like an *assistant priest*, Daniel explained to me on the way home. He was cool, Daniel said. He'd talked to him about comics. Batman versus Superman, who would Daniel pick in a fight? Daniel had picked Superman, because he could really fly while Batman had to rely on his Batarang and Batrope. Superman could outmaneuver Batman by flying up and over him, Daniel figured. The curate said Daniel was very smart.

A few weeks after that—maybe more than a few weeks; do kids really keep time?—Daniel suddenly turned into an un-resolute walker. I wouldn't have noticed this except for the fact that I found myself pulling *Danny's* hand on the way to church, and the sensation was so unexpected and completely novel that I stopped and asked him if he was sick.

A little, he said. Yes.

Should we go back home? I asked.

We can't, he said. I have practice.

We continued. Past Federations Candy Store, King Kullen, and Dunkin' Donuts.

Past the front door of Our Lady of Sorrows Church, where the curate was there to greet us, all smiles for Daniel.

Daniel didn't smile back.

Did I notice this then, or did I remember this later, or did I just make it up?

I was aware of *something*. A small chill rippled through me just inside the door of the church, the way I'd shiver every time

I walked into the confessional to face my inquisitor and off-load my dubious catalogue of sins.

Daniel went off with the curate. For altar boy practice. The curate placing his arm around Daniel the way Danny's baseball coach did after he made an error—a bad throw to first base, or letting a ball trickle between his legs. Daniel seemed to slump.

I went off to the confessional.

I took my brother's Mad *magazines without telling him*, I confessed. This was true, but probably not a real sin. *Anything else?* Father McCrary asked me.

I said a curse word, I told him. This was untrue. My father would say *shimmy, shimmy, coco-pop* in lieu of uttering any curse words inside the home. My mom had grown tired of him swearing in front of us kids and became determined to train him. *You got a shimmy, shimmy, coco-pop F on your English test*, he'd rail at Danny. Sometimes Danny would break into giggles instead of apologizing.

I was supposed to wait after confession. Till Danny was done with altar boy practice, which I imagined involved carrying goblets of wine and holding the bowl of Communion wafers. *You can be a waiter when you grow up*, my dad used to joke with him when he wasn't yelling at him about a failing test grade.

This day I was tired of waiting. I had homework to do. I didn't get Fs on English tests, partly because I was *gifted*, according to my mother, who'd seen my IQ score, and partly because it was the only way I could outdo Danny and thereby siphon off some of my father's affection. I don't think I was fully aware of this second reason till much later, when I began doing the things Danny used to do with my dad, all those activities I'd been ostracized from on the basis of being a girl. When I'd begun my own form of gender-bending. *Teach me that uppercut, Dad. Great throw by the catcher, Dad.*

I went looking for Danny.

He was somewhere in the back. The *inner sanctum*, Danny used to call it, which sounded highly mysterious and seemingly off-limits.

I walked down a hallway past black-and-white photos of previous priests, all of whom followed me the entire way down the hall, maintaining accusatory expressions befitting their earthly duties of carrying our numerous sins on their backs.

There was a door at the end of the hall.

Plain wood with no nameplate. Just a door.

I heard a sound from the other side of this door. A *cat* mewling? My friend Patty had a cat that mewled every single time she put it in its cage—a sound different from *meowing*, which was basically a cat hello.

This sounded more like crying. Like *I don't want to be here. Let me out. Now.*

I knocked lightly, but nobody answered.

Just the mewling cat.

CHAPTER THIRTY-FIVE

If you've ever seen a ring walk, you'll understand what I'm talking about.

In the years A.D., sitting on my father's knee watching Iron Mike or Roberto Durán strut down the aisle, it constituted my favorite part of a boxing match. The preening, the showboating, the bobbing and weaving to some unheard internal beat, the way they'd consume the adulation of the crowd or shrug off its hostility. They were both flaunting their invincibility and psyching themselves up to believe in it. It was pure theater and pure hubris.

That's what I imagined every single time I entered a courtroom on the first day of a murder trial. That I was entering the ring.

I didn't have an entourage—those handlers and managers and flunkies whose job is to massage muscles, egos, and flagging confidence. I had Jennifer. I had sheer will and empirically fortified balls. I had my boxes.

I was known for my boxes. Their sheer number and size. (Confession—they weren't always filled.) So why did I lug them behind me—up the elevator, across the marble floor to courtroom 6, down the center aisle, and all the way to the defense table?

Think of them as munitions boxes being lugged into battle in plain sight of the enemy.

They were meant to intimidate.

To declare that my client hadn't only brought in a big gun to defend him, but that she was loaded with ammunition. Expect an all-out shelling. A battle no less brutal than the storming of Omaha Beach. Prepare for casualties.

It was the way I rolled those boxes behind me that also made a statement of sorts—six of them held together with one of those industrial-strength elastic bands—a strut that owed something to Muhammad Ali.

It said, *I am the greatest*. It declared, *You can't beat me*.

I don't know if it had its desired effect on Jordan Sizemore.

He was known for his preternatural meticulousness, so I would be countering with blatant pugnaciousness.

Bang gloves and may the best liar win.

I won't bore you with the jury selection—needless to say, we won some, we lost some, we declared a truce on the rest, and it was more or less the best we could hope for. Given the pretrial publicity, everyone was asked if they could be impartial since everyone had heard about the case. Everyone dutifully lied and said sure. I was optimistic about jurors 12, 22, 39, and 41. Pessimistic about jurors 5, 14, 38, and 52. The other four? Would it be overkill to use another sports analogy courtesy of my dad? He taught me that every baseball team is going to win sixty games and lose sixty games. It's those other forty games that mean dancing through the confetti or waiting till next year.

Those four jurors might very well mean the same to Neil Shipman.

Eileen smiled and nodded at me. Jordan just nodded. He was wearing pinstripes—more akin to a business meeting than a murder trial, but maybe not. Maybe he was saying *I mean business*.

I'd gone for a medium-length skirt suit with a conservative blouse and black pumps—not necessarily appropriate attire for rolling around in the mud, but it'd do.

Eileen had gone black pants suit again. She was sitting shoulder to shoulder with Jordan—and for just a second I wondered about that, their careless inattention to each other's personal space. Was there something going on between them? Eileen had once confided to me over fairly potent margaritas that her marriage was on shaky ground. Jordan's marriage was supposedly rock-solid, which meant, of course, it wasn't.

"Finally," Neil whispered to me.

Every day he'd come to the courthouse in an orange prison jumpsuit and emerge from the office they offered the defense in neatly pressed Calvin Klein, Ermenegildo Zegna, or Canali. Still, there was something off about the picture. There's an expression I'd heard Jason use about floundering companies attempting to go public—*putting lipstick on a pig*. Okay, probably too strong a term in Neil's case, but the elegant darkness of his suits seemed to exacerbate the sallow prison pastiness of his face. He'd also put on weight—he looked like an athlete who'd descended even further down that hill and was quickly approaching bottom.

It didn't help that he was a sweater. Understandable, given the fact that he was facing life in prison, but not the look you want to give a jury. I put a tissue box on the table, which caused its own quandary. Better to let the sweat roll down his forehead, or blot it up and thereby bring attention to the fact that he was sweating, well, like a *pig*? We ended up with a compromise solution—Neil used the tissues for preemptive strikes before his sweating became too noticeable.

He'd already figuratively sweated through some pretrial haggling out of view of the jury—who looked like children being sent off to their rooms so the adults could talk.

My motion in limine had been denied, as Neil had snarkily predicted it would be.

Wait for the judge to shoot it down like he does all your fucking motions...

I wasn't surprised. Judges normally allowed in this particular kind of hearsay—especially judges known to be partial to prosecutors, like Judge Moronis. The witnesses who'd heard Neil threatening his wife's life would be allowed to testify—with the exception of Dan Hess, who'd been belly up to the bar with Neil in Cittanuova at 1 in the morning. The bar was the deciding factor here—Joe had gotten Dan to admit he'd had a few by the time Neil talked about offing his wife. Maybe more than a few. He must've reported that back to Eileen and Jordan—how he'd let that slip to the defense team's investigator. They knew he'd be easy pickings for me on the stand and had quickly cut him from the witness list.

A bigger battle transpired over allowing the domestic assault allegations into testimony.

The prosecution argued the usual, or to be accurate, Eileen did. It seemed Jordan was going to let her take the wheel whenever they went down any road having to do with victimization. Particularly and most noticeably against women. She trotted out stats about domestic abusers turned domestic murderers. The propensity for abusers to start with beatdowns that inevitably ended with bodies. There was a pattern here—not just with abusers in general but with Neil in particular—of ever-more-violent abuse. His explosions of rage ending in an explosion big enough to take down a house with his ex-wife sitting in it. *It shows an escalating pattern, Your Honor,* she stated, one that inexorably went from point A to the point of no return, and included a restraining order in between.

Sometimes you could overcome these arguments.

I tried.

Logic went as follows: just because someone was alleged to have physically abused their wife doesn't mean they'd murdered her. Can anyone forget the juror from the O.J. case—virtual namesake of the judge—Brenda Moran, who famously called the domestic abuse evidence a "waste of time"? This was a *murder* trial, she sneered after the verdict, not a *domestic abuse* one. Some judges tended to agree with that line of thinking. It was a little like looking at modern art. The prosecution was painting a picture and either you saw a pattern in it or you didn't.

I argued *didn't*. The domestic abuse allegations were just that. They'd never been adjudicated in a court of law. Neil had never been charged with domestic battery—just had it hung around his neck during divorce proceedings and the five minutes it took a judge to issue a restraining order.

It wasn't just a leap to go from those allegations to cold-blooded murder—it was a jump worthy of Evel Knievel. Yes, I actually referenced the name of that famous showboat, betting that Moronis was old enough to have sat wide-eyed on the couch when Evel jumped the Snake River Canyon in his X-1 rocket.

I liked painting pictures too.

The judge didn't rule on this one right away, unlike the bail hearing, when he hadn't even bothered to give the proceedings any thought. He understood the damning impact this kind of testimony can have on a jury; he'd just spent half a day witnessing our all-out exhortations to sway him to our respective sides.

His decision came the next day.

"I have given this a considerable amount of thought—and while this testimony from the state can be viewed as potentially prejudicial, it nonetheless speaks to a pattern of escalating abuse. The jury is entitled to be made aware of it, to place what the defendant is accused of in a context of reported and documented behavior. The defense, of course, is entitled to question any and all of that. The court will allow it."

I was 0 for 2. Neil reached for the tissue box as the jury filed into the courtroom like a pent-up team finally taking the field. I knew their demeanor would change over time—by week four they'd appear more like a chain gang readying for another day of hard labor.

Good opening statements are like movie trailers without the buttered popcorn. A condensed teaser of what you're going to be sitting through for however long it takes—filled with accusations, revelations, and in this case, an explosion worthy of a Hollywood action blockbuster. There was one notable difference, of course. Unlike the trailer for, say, a murder mystery, the prosecution was going to let you in on who did it.

After all, he was sitting right there to my left in a brown Canali suit, dabbing at his forehead with a limp tissue.

Sizemore had placed two photos front and center on separate easels.

That was exactly his point, of course.

He was saying *I'm putting* them *front and center: Emma Shipman. Jason Mooney.*

I could see a few members of the jury shift their attention from the photos to the defense table—pretty standard reaction in a murder trial whenever victims are referenced. What wasn't standard was who the jury was peeking at. Here's a clue—it wasn't the defendant.

That's his wife, they were thinking. *Jason Mooney's wife.* Instead of sitting somewhere in the gallery to see that justice was served, she was sitting at the defense table to see that it wasn't. Or maybe they were thinking something else—that they might be wrong, that it was just possible the sweating defendant didn't do it.

They'd plucked Jason's picture from Facebook, I thought. Normally the prosecution would've contacted me and asked for a photo. Only normal didn't apply here—they'd had to forage from social media. Or who knows—maybe they'd turned to Brenda.

I was trying to place the photo. Summer, I thought. Jason looked tan and rested. And then I saw it—the barest edge of someone's shoulder clothed in white linen. My shoulder. It was the portrait of a marriage and they'd cut the widow right out of it.

Emma was looking past the camera in her photo—as if it had caught her unawares. *Soulful* would be the best way to describe her expression. She looked even more like that English actress.

This movie trailer would have its movie star.

I suddenly realized I hadn't taken a breath—I'd been unconsciously holding it in. I knew I'd be representing the person accused of murdering Jason and Emma—I hadn't considered the fact that I'd be facing Jason and Emma. There they were, staring straight at me, as if questioning what on earth I was doing there.

"Ladies and gentlemen of the jury," Sizemore began, "I'd like to introduce you to the two people at the very heart of this case. Emma Shipman and Jason Mooney. You're going to hear a lot during this trial—a lot of evidence, both physical evidence and evidence through witness testimony. You're going to hear dates and timelines and cell phone data and DNA analysis and explosion analysis. You're going to hear scientific testimony from experts and witness testimony from friends and relations and business associates. You're going to hear exactly what happened the morning of April seventh at 10:45 when these two people were brutally killed by that man sitting at the table over there." He pointed in our direction, just in case the jury didn't know which table he was referring to. "And you're going to hear all that just from our side—the side tasked with finding *justice* for Emma Shipman and Jason Mooney. From that table over there, I imagine you'll hear more—most of it simply meant to confuse you. To send you down dead-end roads and garden paths and rabbit holes—anywhere and everywhere except where the evidence points. To Neil Shipman, who snuck into the home he was furious about losing to finally take care of the wife he was furious about losing—and the man he was furious his wife was with. Who the evidence will show—DNA evidence, and there's no stronger evidence than that—cut the gas line in that house he was furious about losing in order to *kill* Emma Shipman and Jason Mooney. Tragically, he succeeded. Here's the truth. You're not going to remember all of it. It's just too much. Too vast. Too detailed. Too intricate. Too horrible. But that's okay. Really, it's fine. You won't remember *everything* you're going to hear in this courtroom, but it will be okay as long as you remember *them*. Emma Shipman and Jason Mooney. They can't speak for themselves—Neil Shipman took care of that—so we will speak for them. And we will speak from the heart and we will speak from the soul and we will speak with facts and evidence and truth, and we will not stop speaking until you find this defendant guilty of the most heinous and horrifying of crimes. Emma Shipman and Jason Mooney—they deserve no less, so we will *give* no less. And in the end, I firmly believe that you'll give no less as well."

Okay. Give it points for eloquence. Even if it seemed a bit too eloquent for Jordan Sizemore, known more as a technician than for his soaring oratory. *Eileen DeBorgia*. Who'd minored in creative writing at Hofstra and was partial to Dylan Thomas, whose book of poetry I'd once seen her clutching on a park bench during a court recess.

The jury was doing what Jordan had asked them to. Staring at the photos of Emma and Jason. Offering them what amounted to a moment of silence. In show business they say you're never supposed to follow animals or children. In murder trials, it's poetic opening statements from the prosecution.

A lunch recess would've been nice.

It wasn't going to happen. Jordan hadn't only been eloquent—he'd been brief. Give him points for that too. A famous lawyer once said he would've written a shorter opening statement but it would've taken more time.

My turn.

CHAPTER THIRTY-SIX

Joe had been traversing the East End with nothing to show for it.

Looking for camera footage that existed anywhere within a twenty-five-mile radius of the house that might place Neil Shipman anywhere else on the morning of the explosion. That meant checking stores, farm stands, and estates—and that meant dealing with proprietors, homeowners, and estate managers who would rather be doing anything other than talking with the investigator for the defense.

The general consensus was that Neil Shipman had done it. Blown up two people.

Joe improvised. He began introducing himself simply as an investigator looking for information about the crime without revealing which side he was actually investigating for—a sin of omission but not of outright deception.

He was still coming up empty.

There were security cameras here and there—but the few he'd managed to gain access to showed no signs of a black Jaguar with a MONYGUY license plate—the car caught crawling by Emma's home at 10:30 that morning.

Joe had visited with four of the friends set to testify—one had outright refused, and another met with Joe simply to tell him to fuck off. Dan Hess had been the most loquacious of the bunch, but then Dan was a borderline alcoholic who'd met Joe over drinks and soon found himself off the witness list. The other two stuck to their stories, and Joe turned up nothing that would count as disqualifying. One had a pot arrest on his record, but it was when he was eighteen, and for a grand total of three joints. In a state that had recently legalized the stuff, no one was going to care that a teenage Paul Denucious had smoked it.

In addition to the four friends who would testify that Neil threatened to kill Emma, two of Emma's friends were prepared to testify they'd seen black-and-blue marks on her—and more importantly, heard exactly who'd put them there. From Emma herself.

Neither one of those friends would talk to Joe.

Then there were three partygoers who were there the night Neil was dragged kicking and screaming from the party he hadn't been invited to. Ready to testify they'd seen him snatch Emma by the arm and attempt to kidnap her (*I just wanted to take her someplace quiet to talk*, Neil sheepishly confessed), and then, after being asked to leave and refusing, being hog-tackled and heave-hoed through the estate gates like a drunk though the swinging doors of an Old West saloon.

One of the men who'd done the actual heave-hoeing was on the witness list as well, who when he wasn't doing security at Hamptons soirees was writing speeding tickets as a member of the Ffuck. This being the Hamptons as opposed to, say, the South Bronx, that would make him a more or less unimpeachable witness.

Neil's DNA had come back on the sprinkler pipes (though not on the boiler), so we could make a case that the reason it was on the gas line was the same reason it was on the sprinkler system—Neil simply liked to fix things. They would make the case that there was no reason for his DNA to be on that particular *part* of the gas line unless he happened to be slicing it in two. It wasn't located near any of the rubber connective fittings where someone who was fixing a gas line might be expected to work.

I put all this on Post-its that I stuck on a movable whiteboard that Jennifer wheeled into my office. I liked to stare at them until they imprinted themselves on my consciousness and became retrievable like the papers stuffed into those folders I filled my boxes with. The boxes I rolled into the courtroom and into battle.

One Post-it said, *Suspects.* So far, there was empty whiteboard below it.

Jefrey was surprised when he heard me on the other end of the phone.

"I owe you money or something?" he asked.

"Nope. All paid up."

"Good. Because when they said *restitution* I didn't know they really meant extortion."

"It's better than your cellmate asking you for it." I wasn't kidding. Unless my embezzler had been fortunate enough to make it to a minimum-security lockup, he would've been a prime candidate for shakedowns.

"What do you want?"

"Your set of skills. "

'. "I don't have money—but I do have a very particular set of skills—skills I've acquired over a very long career ...'" Jefrey said, effecting an accent that sounded like a cross between County Cork and the South Shore of Long Island.

"Excuse me ... ?"

"Liam Neeson. Don't tell me you've never heard that line before?"

"What line ... ?"

"Jesus. Never mind."

"Let's hypothetically say you actually were what they accused you of being," I said.

"What's that mean?"

"It means, let's for a moment say you were a master embezzler, extremely proficient in white-collar fraud involving missing monies."

"Let me get this straight. You called me up to insult me?"

"No. I called you up to ask a favor of you. I thought the fact that I hung the jury and kept you out of jail might make you say yes."

"What favor?"

"I want you to look at some financial records."

"What kind of financial records?"

"A hedge fund."

"What hedge fund?"

"The one whose books I want you to look at."

"Thanks for clearing that up. What exactly am I looking for?"

"I have no idea. Something tells me you'll know when you find it."

"I'm kind of busy."

"So am I. That's why I was asking you for a favor."

"Are you going to pay me for this?"

"Excuse me…?"

"You know, money. I told you. This restitution is killing me."

"No. I'm not going to pay you."

"Even a little?"

"Tell you what, if you ever embezzle anything again, I'll waive the consultation fee."

He sighed. "Okay. Whatever. Send it."

CHAPTER THIRTY-SEVEN

"Ladies and gentlemen of the jury. *Rush to judgment*," I began.

"I'm sure most of you are familiar with that particular term. But just in case you're not familiar with it, I'm going to define it for you. Because it's the only reason we're sitting in this courtroom today. *Rush to judgment*—it's when investigating officers—in this case from the Suffolk County Police Department and the district attorney's office, rush to accuse and arrest somebody for a crime without fully investigating whether anyone else might have done it. When they focus on the easiest and nearest suspect and close down any and all further investigation of the actual *crime* itself. When they pick who they want to lock away for that crime simply because, well ... it's *convenient*, and *then* look for the evidence that will help them do it. Think about that for a minute. Instead of doing what you're supposed to do when two people lose their lives—which is gather evidence and go wherever it leads you—they decide to do it backward. Charge the ex-husband in two seconds flat—lock him up for months on end—and then see what they can find in order to pin it on him. Neil Shipman might've not been the best husband—by that criterion half this courtroom might be in trouble. I'll even go one step further—he might not have even been the best *ex*-husband. But to use an apt expression—there's no crime in that. I'll repeat that. *There is no crime in that.* But that's what they're charging my client with. A crime. A most monstrous crime. Only here's the problem. My client didn't do it. He. Did. Not. Do. It."

My professor in trial law had taught a lesson called "The Power of the Pause." His point? That in a profession that emphasized the power of speech, there was often a greater power in absolute silence. Or to borrow a line from the glorious Alison Krauss—"you say it best when you say nothing at all." Pausing puts a period on statements you need to resonate with a jury— the audio equivalent of sticking a landing.

I'd taken my first pause now.

Right after telling the jury that Neil didn't do it.

"Now…you're going to hear allegations against my client. The kind of allegations that often rear their ugly heads during ugly divorces. That my client caused physical harm to his ex-wife, Emma Shipman. Here's the problem with that. He *didn't*. He never raised a hand against Emma Shipman. He was never charged with physical abuse against Emma Shipman. Never arrested for physical abuse against Emma Shipman. In fact, the only person who ever *accused* my client of physical abuse against Emma Shipman in any court of law was Emma Shipman's *divorce attorney*. The attorney trying to increase my client's monthly support payments to Emma Shipman and get her awarded the house my client had paid dearly for. In other words, we can safely say that whatever came out of Emma Shipman's divorce attorney's mouth had a distinctly ulterior motive. You're going to hear other things from them. That my client was seen on security camera footage passing that particular house on the morning of the tragedy. Here's the thing about that. And it's important to hear what I just said again. He was seen on security camera footage passing the house that morning. *Passing.* Driving west down Sycamore Lane—*passing* the house—and then *continuing* west down Sycamore Lane. Why was he going west? Because that's the way to his office in Southampton. That's right—he was on his way to work. Here's what the prosecution won't tell you but I will. There is *no* security camera footage of my client ever stopping that car. Of my client ever entering that house. Of my client ever entering that basement. None. Zero. Zilch. And you'll also hear about some DNA evidence. About my client's DNA being found on that gas line in the basement. Here's something else the prosecution won't tell you but I will. My client's DNA was also found on the sprinkler system in that basement. Because my client liked to go down and fix things in that basement. In fact, my client's DNA is probably all over that basement. Why? Because it was *his* basement.

"If you came to my house and swabbed the things in my house, guess what? You'd find my DNA over every single inch of it.

"And there's one more thing you won't hear from the prosecution but you will from me. What you might have heard from them if the police and DA's office had actually done their job instead of closing any and all further investigation. If they'd actually followed the evidence and investigated other suspects. But we *have* followed the evidence and we *have* investigated other suspects. And you will hear all about one of these suspects in this courtroom. And when you hear about this suspect, you will undoubtedly remember what I started this opening statement with. The term I used. It won't need any further definition from me. *Rush to judgment.* Because in the future, when you look up *rush to judgment* in the dictionary, you might very well see this case printed right next to it.

"Oh, and there is one last thing worth saying that might or might not have occurred to you. If I thought for one minute that my client was guilty, I wouldn't have set one foot in this courtroom to defend him."

"OBJECTION!"

I'd been steeling myself for that objection. Expecting it. Preparing for it. Still, its shrillness unnerved me. The way Jordan shot up out of his chair, knocking over his cup of coffee in the process, brown liquid staining the folder he'd primly set up in front him and beginning to drip, drip, drip off the table. The way Judge Moronis turned a furious shade of red, slammed his gavel down on the table with a resounding smack, and boomed: "Meeting in my chambers. Now."

A flashback is necessary here.

A meeting we'd had in chambers way back at the arraignment.

Judges' chambers are more or less their offices. Which you means you'll find the same things in a judge's office as you would in any other person's office. A photo of Judge Moronis with his wife and kids. A dated one, since he had all his hair back then and it appeared his kids hadn't yet reached teenage-hood. The last I'd heard, his older son was a corporate lawyer now. A couple of chicken-scratch drawings—courtesy of his grandkids, one of whom had written *Luve You Grandpa* in red crayon complete with a misshapen heart.

There was a pair of worn brown slippers sitting by a partially opened closet where you could make out a few pressed shirts dangling on hangers.

The judge had taken off his robe. It was a signal that we weren't in front of the jury or the press. The tone was decidedly casual.

"I thought we should have a little pretrial get-together," Judge Moronis said. He'd settled into one of his executive leather chairs—Jordan and Eileen, Jennifer and me. That was a signal too. That instead of claiming the seat behind his massive desk, he'd deigned to join us in our impromptu little coffee klatch.

"I'm referring to the peculiar nature of this trial," he added. "Or perhaps I should say, the peculiar nature of the defendant's representation." He was staring at me.

"Your Honor …" I began.

"Are you suggesting the circumstances aren't peculiar?" he cut me off.

"I'd prefer to term the circumstances *unusual.*"

"Whichever term you'd prefer, it is what it is. We have the wife of one of the alleged victims representing the alleged perpetrator. I've been a judge for twenty-eight years and I have no problem admitting this is a first for me. On that basis, I feel confidently justified in calling the circumstances *peculiar.*"

"As you wish, Judge."

"Fine. Glad we got that out of the way. What we haven't gotten out of the way is how we address that particular fact, or more accurately, don't. As it pertains to the jury, I mean."

"'Judge … ?"

"We need some ground rules, Counsel. Let's refer to it as a kind of strict compartmentalization. You're here as the defendant's lawyer. Not as the victim's widow. And never—and I mean *never*—the twain shall meet. You will make your arguments as a lawyer and only as a lawyer. Your personal relationship to one of the victims will not ever be referenced, spoken of, or introduced into this courtroom."

"I hate to be the bearer of bad tidings," I said, "but my personal relationship to one of the victims has already been referenced, spoken of, and introduced to the general public. Which no doubt will include the jury. You can read all about it on page one of today's *Newsday.* Unfortunately it's made a lot of page ones over the last month."

"Yes. I'm aware of that, Counsel. But what a jury knows or doesn't know is their business. What we tell them inside my courtroom is mine. And in my courtroom we will tell them nothing about your relationship to Jason Mooney. The cat might be out of the bag, but it's not going to be allowed to wander into courtroom 6. Am I being obtuse?"

Up to this point, neither one of the prosecutors had said boo. Which wasn't surprising since Judge Moronis was saying it for them. It was like listening to the school dean berate a fellow student for cheating. You keep quiet and silently celebrate their misfortune.

"Not at all, Your Honor."

"Good. Because if you disobey my ruling, I can guarantee our next meeting in my chambers won't be nearly as pleasant."

He was right.

The next meeting was here and it wasn't pleasant at all.

Judge Moronis hadn't taken his robe off this time. He was handing down a sentence and wanted to retain the trappings of absolute authority. He hadn't lost the floridness in his face either.

"*What did I tell you, Counsel?*"

"Judge...?"

"Are you honestly going to stand there and pretend you have no idea what I'm talking about? That you have no clue why our esteemed prosecutor over here yelled *objection*?"

The esteemed prosecutor was as silent as last time. Once again there was no particular reason for him to add to the chorus of condemnation. The judge would be taking me out to the woodshed all by himself.

"Judge, if you think I somehow defied your ruling in any way, then I'm—"

"If I *think*? If I think? Did I not tell you in these very chambers that there will be no— absolutely no—mention of your relationship to one of the victims. No reference, no allusion, no *anything*. Did I not say that if you defied my ruling, the consequences would be swift and unsparing? Did I not tell you that?"

"Judge, I would like to—"

"Yes or no, Counsel. Yes or *no*? Surely you're familiar with yes-and-no questions and how to answer them?"

"Yes, Your Honor."

"So if you're aware that I warned you in no uncertain terms to never bring that relationship into my courtroom, can you tell me why you defied that ruling and did precisely *that*?"

"But I didn't, Your Honor."

"Didn't *what?*"

"I didn't bring that relationship into the courtroom. We can ask the stenographer to come in if that would help, Your Honor. I'm fairly sure all I said was that if I felt my client was guilty I would have never set foot into this courtroom to defend him."

I was defining the battle as one of semantics—that I'd never actually stated I was the wife of Jason Mooney. That was my defense. That was my gamble. I would sneak it into the end of my opening statement, then prepare for the resulting firestorm and hope to make it out of there alive. I'd gone into courtrooms with worse arguments.

Jordan had had enough.

"Your Honor, she was clearly banking on what she knows the jury knows. She didn't have to say *As Jason Mooney's wife you know I would never set foot into that courtroom if I thought my client was guilty*, because as she herself mentioned in these chambers, the jury *knows* she's Jason Mooney's wife. She left out the words it was entirely unnecessary for her to say while saying exactly what you warned her not to."

The judge waved him off—he wasn't in need of a tag-team partner today.

"Counsel…" He ducked his head and took a deep breath—counting to ten either because I'd managed to outrage him even more than I had with my original statement to the jury, attempting to wiggle out of it with word twisting worthy of a certain ex-president (*I did not have sex with that woman—I had* oral *sex*), or because he was actually considering my argument in appropriately Solomon-like fashion.

"Counsel," he repeated, "while I appreciate the chutzpah of your contention that you didn't defy my ruling, that is *precisely* what you did. This isn't a debate tournament and you're not the debate team captain hoping to get points for tortuous semantic wizardry—it's a *courtroom* where I lay down the rules and you're expected to follow them. Instead you willfully decided to ignore them. You knew exactly what you were doing, and you went ahead and did it. I will tell the jury to disregard your last statement—I will strike said statement from the record—and if you ever, and I mean *ever*, disobey my ruling again, I will cite you for contempt of court and I will have you removed as counsel. Am I being clear?"

"Yes, Your Honor."

That's the thing about saying something to a jury.

It might get stricken.

It can't be un-remembered.

CHAPTER THIRTY-EIGHT

What I remember.

I remember the way you'd claim my hand like it was your property. I remember liking that.

I remember the way we'd both laugh at Adam Sandler—even in that dead-serious too-cool-for-school heist drama where he got his head blown off in the end.

I remember watching you sleep for the first time and whispering I love you, hoping you could and couldn't hear it. Hoping both things.

I remember that moment during sex when the physical and emotional first crossed wires, so that coming was both a release and a revelation.

I remember eating canned peaches sitting up in bed and spilling some of that sickly sweet syrup all over me and how you licked it up. Yum.

I remember the way your side of the bed felt after you left to take a shower. As warm as beach sand on a late afternoon.

I remember lying in a hammock together and picking out shapes in the clouds like I used to do when I was seven. An elephant. A mountain. A monster.

I remember the feeling in my stomach when I fully realized you were gone.

Chapter 7 in *Beyond Betrayal*: "Write down all the good things you remember about the person who betrayed you—because even those who take our trust shouldn't be allowed to take our memories."

Done.

CHAPTER THIRTY-NINE

Presenting a case is like presenting a story.

Once upon a time in a place called the Hamptons there was an explosion.

What kind of explosion?

Very loud, said the neighbor on the stand under gentle questioning by Jordan Sizemore. *Like a thunderclap. But it was sunny out, so there went that theory. It had to be some kind of explosion.*

So what did the neighbor do?

I called 911.

And what happened then?

We were dispatched out to Sycamore Lane, said the fire chief of the all-volunteer East Hampton Fire Department.

We got a call that there might be an explosion out on Sycamore Lane, said the police chief of the East Hampton Police Department, which was non-volunteer and so thought of the fire department as amateurs.

We were told to go to an address on Sycamore Lane, said the head of the very professional Suffolk County Bomb Squad Unit, which was based in Riverhead and so a good forty minutes away.

And what did they find when they all got there?

The house was demolished, said the firefighter who got there first. *I mean it was more or less gone.*

I thought the fireman looked familiar. Then I remembered— the one who'd showed up at my house one night to fight a non-existent fire.

Did they look in the ruins to see if anyone was hurt or killed? Jordan asked him.

In that situation, you're talking about a possible bomb explosion and protocol dictates we wait for the bomb squad unit. At that point, we don't know if it was a bomb or gas explosion, we don't know if there's another bomb waiting to go off, or what the hell's going on ... sorry ... excuse my French.

Quite all right, Judge Moronis interjected. *I admire your skill in foreign languages.*

What did the police do when they got there?

We called for an ambulance in case there were casualties. We cordoned off the area.

Did they think there were casualties?

Yes.

Why did they think that?

There were two vehicles parked in front of the house. Well, what was left of the house.

Can you describe those vehicles?

A red Corvette and a blue Mercedes.

But you couldn't see any casualties?

We couldn't enter the home yet ... what was left of this home ... we had to wait for the bomb squad unit to get there.

What did the bomb squad unit do when they got there?

We donned our EOD suits and got out the robot, said the head of the bomb squad unit.

Robot? What robot?

Sorry. Bomb disposal robot. It enables us to explore a bomb site that hasn't been cleared without having to put team members in harm's way.

So this bomb disposal robot has a camera ... it can poke around and see what's what?

Yes, sir.

Did you activate this bomb disposal robot?

No, sir.

Why not?

We pretty immediately smelled the gas. When we approached the foundation of the house.

And that told you what?

That told us this was almost certainly a gas explosion. The debris field was consistent with that as well.

Debris field?

A bomb would have left a crater. A bomb explosion generally causes debris to rise and then collapse downward into the hole. It was clear this explosion went outward. That's more consistent with a gas explosion.

Okay. What did you do then?

Once we'd determined it was a gas explosion, we could safely explore the premises for possible victims.

And did you find any victims?

Yes, sir.

Can you tell us what you found? I know this is difficult for you.

We found two deceased victims in the rubble, sir.

How did you know they were deceased?

We checked for vitals. It appeared they'd both been killed on impact.

I offered my first objection. *This is pure supposition, Your Honor. The time of death is set by the medical examiner, not the bomb squad.* It was an admittedly trivial point, since the time of death had no particular bearing on my defense. I just wanted the prosecution and jury to know I was paying attention.

Objection sustained, said Judge Moronis.

These victims? Can you describe them?

A man and a woman.

Where were these victims found?

Where…?

Were you able to determine what part of the house they'd been in when the gas explosion happened?

Yes. It appears they were in the living room. Near the fireplace.

Sorry, and again I know this must be difficult for you, can you describe the bodies as you found them?

Describe them…?

Well, what were the victims wearing?

I'd been wondering if Jordan was going to go there—let the jury know, that is, any juror who hadn't read a single paper, scanned a single online article, or listened to a single newscast in the last month, that the victims were found naked. Two naked bodies. He was taking a calculated risk, willing to risk victim shaming for the benefit of letting the jury see what Neil saw—what they'd no doubt claim he saw after parking his car and sneaking back to the house. His ex-wife and her lover naked together before a fireplace. They'd contend that the sight of them together *inflamed* him even further—sorry for the unavoidable pun—and even if he hadn't intended to kill them when he first peered through that back window, he became determined to murder them after catching them in the act.

They were unclothed.

They were naked? It couldn't be that their clothes, I don't know, blew off in the blast?

No, sir. We would have seen remnants. Particles. Something.

Okay, understood. What was the condition of the victims' bodies?

They'd been somewhat, well…flattened, sir. From the blast and the rubble. It's not unnatural with gas explosions.

This is what I pictured. Wile E. Coyote being flattened by the Roadrunner driving a steam roller. Not my husband lying in the morgue. It was easier.

What did you do then?

We closed off the gas line. Both victims were body-bagged by the EMTs.

We checked for flammables, said the volunteer fireman.

We continued to secure the area, said the policeman. *We searched the cars and through the rubble. We called in the fire investigator.*

Before the ME took the stand, and then Fire Investigator Frank DeMarco—who glanced at me on the way to the witness box with a look I'd grown tiresomely accustomed to from friends and acquaintances that could generously be termed as puzzled and less generously termed as abrasive—before that, I asked one question on cross to the fireman, police, and bomb squad witnesses.

Did you see the defendant when you arrived at the house?

No, said the fireman.

No, said the policeman.

No, said the bomb squad unit leader.

Thank you. I have nothing further for this witness.

The ME was there to testify as to exact cause of death. The cause of death would seem pretty obvious when two bodies are found in a house that looks like Dresden after the Allies firebombed it, but you never know. Maybe they'd both suffered simultaneous heart attacks at the height of passion just before the house went up, and all murder charges would need to be taken off the table.

No.

There were extensive injuries to both victims consistent with a gas explosion that each in their own right could've proven lethal, said the ME.

Can you take us through those injuries?

Their initial injuries were from the primary blast wave. The external pressure on the chest becomes greater than the internal pressure, and the chest wall moves inward, putting pressure on the lungs—in effect bursting them open. Both victims showed extensive damage to the lungs. The inability to breathe would've been enough in itself to cause death. They both suffered ruptured eardrums as well, though those injuries would not on their own have proven lethal. The lung and ear injuries were the direct and primary effects of the gas explosion. Then we have what we term indirect effects of the explosion. That is, there was also extensive damage caused by high-pressure fragments. There were shards of glass embedded in both victims. In the case of Jason Mooney, a fragment of glass had severed his carotid artery—which, had he still been alive at the time, would've immediately proven fatal. The glass fragments in Emma Shipman hadn't severed any arteries, but her head had been severely impacted by a section of roof. She had a crushed skull and extensive brain damage. Again, if she'd somehow survived the initial blast wave, the head injury alone would've almost certainly proven fatal.

The judge had ordered me to employ strict compartmentalization during the trial, but only as it pertained to the jury—that I should address them as the defense lawyer and not as the victim's wife. I was attempting a kind of compartmentalization now, but as it pertained to me—with about as much success. I was listening to the ME list the litany of injuries in a emotionless monotone, and trying to process it much the same way—as mere words on the ME's death notice, as opposed to serrated daggers aimed at my heart. I found myself digging my nails into the top of my thigh under the table and out of the jury's view. That night I would find the nail marks still embedded in my skin.

Can you determine which of these injuries you described were the actual cause of death?

As I stated, each injury on its own could've been the reason for their deaths, and given the almost instantaneous nature of these injuries—that they all took place with seconds of each other, it's impossible with certainty to say which one was the determining factor. Suffice it to say that the gas explosion unequivocally caused the death of these two individuals, and that their injuries collectively proved fatal.

Jordan dismissed the witness. I deferred from cross. What caused their death wasn't in dispute. Who caused it was.

Frank DeMarco trooped up to the stand, but not before throwing me that look that stated, *I can't believe what you're fucking doing.* Frank had helped me out on that arson case before he'd begun cashing checks from the state—he'd testified that the manner of arson committed at my client's container warehouse was consistent with methods used by the people who'd been squeezing my client for protection money. Frank had also been the one who'd called me late at night to tell me Jason had been murdered. Frank was a friend. Emphasis on *was.*

Can you tell the jury what you do, Mr. DeMarco?

He could.

I'm head of the fire investigation unit for the Suffolk PD.

And does that include investigating explosions?

Right. Our job is to try and determine the cause of fires and explosions and whatnot—especially where the cause isn't immediately self-evident.

Self-evident?

Someone says they fell asleep smoking in bed and woke up to see the place on fire. Someone put fireplace ash in a paper bag and left it against the side of the house and then saw it ignite. Those are more or less self-evident, but even then we're still required to investigate and sign off on the cause.

How much experience have you had investigating these kind of things? Fires and explosions?

More than I'd care to admit.

At the risk of your vanity, the judge said, *we need an actual number.*

The crowd tittered.

That's enough, the judge said, but the way late-night talk show hosts quiet their opening applause.

I've been a fire investigator for thirty-two years, Frank said.

Long time. Have you received any awards or commendations during that time?

I have. I received the National Fire Investigator of the Year Award in 2011.

You must be very proud.

Not really. I deserved it in 2010 too.

More laughter. Frank enjoyed performing as well. Maybe when they both retired—Frank and the judge—they'd take their act on the road. I was almost ready to interrupt the lovefest between Jordan and Frank and say the defense is willing to concede Frank's sterling résumé and we could all move on. But then I wasn't willing to concede it.

Can you tell us what you thought arriving on the premises of 4178 Sycamore Lane that morning?

Thought...?

Yes. What were your initial thoughts regarding the cause of the explosion?

It seemed like a gas explosion. I could still smell it in the air. The debris field was prototypical for a gas explosion. The bomb squad unit felt pretty sure about that as well.

And did your investigation confirm that?

It did. I poked around in the basement. What you do is follow the line—the gas line—follow it from the heater out. That's what I did. We were lucky—the basement had remained pretty intact.

And what did you find?

It'd been sliced.

Sliced? Can you elaborate on that?

The gas line had been sliced. Cut. That's what had caused the gas buildup and the resultant explosion.

Sliced? It couldn't have just worn out, or separated by itself?

No. Sometimes you get leaks around the fittings, and yes, sometimes lines are so old they begin to fray. Or sometimes it happens inadvertently—the gardener sticks a shovel where he shouldn't. That kind of thing. All those breaks in the gas line look different from this one. Those are tears or cracks or rips. This was sliced—neatly sliced, like with a knife.

So someone had intentionally done this? Cut the line in two?

Yes.

Objection, I said. *This is supposition on the part of the witness.*

I'll rephrase the question, Your Honor, said Jordan, not even waiting for the *sustained.*

In your professional opinion, backed up by thirty-two years as a fire investigator, including one National Fire Investigator of the Year Award—would you say that someone would've had to slice that gas line on purpose?

In my professional opinion, yes. There's no way it happened on its own.

What would someone cutting the gas line expect would happen?

Objection. Me again. *How can this witness possibly answer what was going on in the mind of a supposed perpetrator?*

I'll sustain.

I'll say this for Judge Moronis. He wasn't letting his recent anger at me get in the way of ruling for me, at least here and there.

I'll rephrase the question, Jordan said. What happens when someone slices a gas line?

The gas seeps out a fairly steady rate, then rises due to the methane. Eventually it would've filled the entire house.

How long would that have taken?

Around fifteen to twenty minutes. Given the dimensions of this house.

And what would that do the occupants of the house?

If they didn't notice in time, it would've caused them to fall unconscious and then, sorry to say, most likely expire.

And that would've taken around fifteen to twenty minutes, you say? Long enough for whoever sliced that line to safely leave the house first?

Yes.

But the occupants of this house didn't fall unconscious. Something else happened here.

Yes. The other problem with gas is that any little thing can set it off. Cause it to explode. That's what happened here.

What happened exactly?

According to our investigation, the fireplace acted as the accelerant. The match that set the whole thing off.

So one of the deceased lit a fire in the home's fireplace. Jason Mooney or Emma Shipman?

It would seem so, yes.

And then?

Boom.

It's what Frank had said to me on the phone that night. Boom. That's the way the world ends. Not with a whimper but with a boom. My world.

Thank you. I have no further questions for this witness.

I did.

Hello, Mr. DeMarco.

Hello.

Have you ever been wrong before?

Excuse me?

In thirty-two years of investigating fires and explosions, have you ever been wrong?

He stared. He was calculating that if he said *no*, he'd be lying, and he knew I knew he'd be lying, since one of those times he'd been wrong was when he was cashing my checks. On the other hand, if he said *yes*, he'd be impeaching his own credentials. He decided to split the baby.

Everyone gets it wrong sometime. Not this time.

I didn't ask you about this time. I asked if you've ever gotten it wrong. If you've ever done an investigation, said this or that happened—it was arson or it wasn't arson—and then were proven to have been mistaken. Yes or no?

Like I said, everyone gets it wrong sometimes.

So that's yes?

Yes.

Those other times you got things wrong, when you signed off reports, testified on the stand, you must've been pretty certain too. Some other defense lawyer or prosecutor for the state probably asked you the very same question I just did and you probably gave the very same answer. *Sure, I've been wrong sometime, but not this time.* Then, well, you were.

Objection, Jordan said. *She's putting words in the witness's mouth.*

Sustained, said the judge.

Okay. Did you ever say on the stand that you were sure, absolutely positive, that this time there was no doubt as to the veracity of your conclusion. But then that conclusion, your conclusion, turned out to be false?

I don't remember.

You don't remember?

I don't remember if on the few times I may have been erroneous in my conclusions, I testified to certainty to those conclusions.

It's possible, though, right?

I suppose.

What if I have an expert on fires and explosions like you who's ready to take the stand and say—with certainty say—that the gas line separated naturally. From simple stress.

I'd say he was dead wrong.

I did have an expert. Just less an expert than Frank. Someone whose business wasn't investigating fires and explosions as much as going around the country testifying about investigating fires and explosions. What we in the business of trial law respectfully call a mercenary but sometimes disrespectfully call a whore. Which is what the prosecution would certainly call him as well—given the hefty fee he received each time he testified.

Well then, I'd suppose we'd have a kind of he said, he said situation, wouldn't we?

Excuse me?

We'd have two expert witnesses testifying to two different conclusions as to what happened to that gas line, one of whom—yourself—has already admitted giving testimony that turned out to be patently false.

Objection. If the defense counsel is asking this witness a question, I can't discern it.

If the esteemed prosecutor will allow me, I promise I'm getting to it.

Overruled, Judge Moronis said. *Proceed, Counsel.*

If I have an expert witness ready to testify with certainty that the gas line separated on its own—which would mean there was no crime at all here, but just an unfortunate and tragic accident—a conclusion completely counter to yours—and given that both conclusions can't be right and you've already admitted to being wrong *sometimes,* can you admit to the possibility that you're wrong *this* time?

The gas line was sliced, Frank said. *Someone cut it.*

I have to ask for a yes-or-no answer here.

Can you repeat the question? said Frank, who knew what the question was but had quickly developed a clear distaste for the questioner.

Is it within the realm of possibility that you've gotten it wrong here, just like you got it wrong on those other cases you were so certain about?

No. It's not.

No? It's not within the realm of possibility? Not even a fraction of a chance? Not even half of a percent? Not even a little, bitty bit?

Objection. Jordan again. *She's badgering the witness. He's already answered the question. He said no.*

Sustained.

That's all I have for this witness.

Frank left the stand, if not bleeding and battered, then slightly bruised, like that banana you can't quite decide whether to throw out. I'd done about as much damage as could be expected, introducing what shouldn't be a novel notion but with most juries still is—that expert witnesses can be wrong. That the science of explosion investigation is an inexact one. Certainty was best left to priests and prophets.

Moronis looked tired. He glanced at the wall clock like a schoolboy praying for the bell to ring. There were still forty-five minutes of perfectly good court time, but maybe he had a late tee time or a visit with his grandkids or maybe he just needed a nap.

Neil looked kind of haggard himself. He'd paused his preemptive tissue strikes somewhere during Frank's testimony and he looked like he'd just exited a steam room. Southampton Village Dry Cleaners would be hard-pressed to eradicate the spreading stains under each arm of his gray Calvin Klein suit.

The jury looked beleaguered as well. That pretrial adrenaline had slowly dissipated, giving way to a dawning realization that this was going to take a while.

Today they'd be getting a reprieve.

Court is adjourned, Moronis intoned.

I heard one of the jurors mutter, *Amen.*

CHAPTER FORTY

Jefrey was in a rare mood.

Maybe it was spring fever. He seemed "jumpy as a puppet on a string," although not "gay in a melancholy way." In fourth grade, I'd summoned up the courage to stand before the entire fourth grade and belt out "It Might As Well Be Spring." While the acned kid who did yo-yo tricks garnered full-throated applause, my audience response would best be termed *tepid*.

My embezzler was performing for an audience of one.

"Ready for the show, ladies and gents?" he asked slyly.

We'd met at the only place in the Hamptons that might be called a diner. Tucked away at the corner of the Stop & Shop parking lot, behind the row of sparsely patronized designer shops, it had five booths and an actual counter with stools.

We'd settled in a booth at the back, where he asked the waitress if she could put truffles in his omelet.

She said no, possibly because she didn't know what truffles were. Still, it's a fair bet they weren't on the menu.

He ordered a cheddar cheese and broccoli omelet instead, with toast, orange juice, and coffee, but only after making sure I was paying.

"My accountant told me we have to tighten our belts, and I said fine, send me some belts."

He complained about his wife *nudging* him about money. That she didn't understand he wasn't exactly at the top of everyone's hiring list at the moment. That headhunters weren't exactly breaking down the doors to represent him. And that *restitution* he was ordered to pay by the court—loan sharks were more forgiving.

"Look at the bright side. You're not locked up with one—a loan shark."

Jefrey stared glumly at me. His mood had shifted. He'd been all chipper just a minute ago because it probably felt like he'd been let out a different kind of jail, where he had to dodge his wife's harangues about money instead of beatdowns by the Aryan Brotherhood. Which made getting out of his house the closest thing to a prison break. But him talking about money had *reminded* him about money and how he didn't have as much of it anymore.

"I knew if anyone could find something, you could," I said. Stroking his ego felt almost as dirty as stroking a different part of him, but I wanted to get him happy and talkative again.

"Who says I found something?" he asked.

"I don't know. I got a feeling when you started patting yourself on the back."

"Ha. Okay. Maybe I have."

"Are you going to let me in on it?"

"Are you going to pay me?"

"I thought we went over that already."

"That was before I found what I found. No paying, no talking."

"You're seriously going to shake me down?"

"I wouldn't put it that way. I'm just asking for an honest day's pay."

"Given our relationship, you might want to drop the *honest* part."

"Ha. Sticks and stones."

"Fine. How much for your honest day's work?"

"I don't know. I figure I should charge what you do. Fair is fair. What was it again … five hundred an hour?"

"Expensive day."

"Who said it only took me a day? It was complicated."

"Okay. How about you tell me how much you want?" It wasn't my money. It would go on Neil's bill—along with Joe Rawlings, the DNA lab, the fire investigator, and all the other things that go into a first-rate criminal defense these days. I'd add it to the file I'd labeled T&L. *Total Liability*, I'd told Jennifer.

"Twenty-five grand."

"Sorry, I didn't realize you'd made this your life's mission. No."

"Twenty grand."

"When you start being serious, let me know."

"Ten grand. Come on. *Ten lousy grand.* You know how many hours I spent on this?"

"No. But I'm pretty sure it wasn't ten grand's worth. Seventy-five hundred."

He hesitated, peering at me like a poker player trying to discern if I was bluffing or not.

"Okay."

"Deal. I'm listening."

"Uh … can I get the check first?"

"Seriously?"

"How do I know you're saying yes now but you won't say no later?"

"I don't have my checkbook on me."

"Really?"

"Yes. Really. I don't usually go around paying off my clients. The way it usually works is they pay me. Or don't you remember?"

"*Ex*-client."

"For now."

"Thanks for your faith in me. Really touching."

"Sorry. Given that you're shaking down the legal counsel who kept you out of jail, my faith in the probative values of restitution—at least in your case—is just a bit shaky now."

"Who's *shaking down* anybody? I told you. You hired me for a job."

"I asked you for a favor."

"It turned into a job."

"Let's agree to disagree. Can I get the results of all your hard labor now?"

"Sure." The glint was back in his eye. "Ready ... ?"

"I was ready ten minutes ago."

"Okay. I really had to do some digging here. But you know what they say ... if you dig deep enough ..."

"You reach China?"

"More like Chinatown." He leaned forward across the table. "There are several ways hedge funds can pull off a little hanky-panky, okay?"

"That's what this one is doing? Pulling off a little hanky-panky?"

"I'm getting there. Let's connect the dots first. Most hedge funds funnel their trades through another entity, understand? The entity that actually does the day-to-day trading. Follow me?"

"So far."

"Great. This one uses the same blueprint. Carramoore Trading LTD—fully listed, no SEC investigations far as I can tell. Seems all aboveboard." He was smiling at me, but it was the kind of smile that says *I haven't gotten to the good part yet.*

"So?"

"So. It's all aboveboard until you check under the *hull.* Then not so much." He took a long sip of coffee and smacked his lips. He seemed determined to drag this out—his moment in the sun. Or maybe he was simply in no hurry to get back to his wife, even if he'd be walking into the house seventy-five hundred dollars richer.

"I wondered who owns Carramoore Trading LTD," he continued. "So I dug around a little. *More* than a little. Took me *hours.*" He emphasized *hours,* I think, to prove to me that his

seventy-five hundred had been honestly earned. "And guess what I found?"

"I can't possibly."

"MichHoldings."

"*MichHoldings? So ... ?*"

"So who owns MichHoldings?"

"You got me. Who?"

"By any chance do you happen to know anybody named Michelle?"

I flipped my mental Rolodex. Michelle Bamberger—classmate at Buchanan High, best breasts in senior class, worst morals; Michelle Lanjours—president of Defense Lawyers Association, married to a woman who resembled Ted Cruz; Michelle Sams—one half of a couple Jason and I had sometimes socialized with, the more interesting half. Then I got it. Of course.

"Michelle Gorman."

"Bingo."

"Mathew's wife."

"The very same."

"They were trading through an entity that Mathew's wife owns. Is that illegal?"

"Borderline illegal, certainly unethical. Because they make a commission on every trade whether the trades do well or not. Which means there's incentive to just keep trading. Like back and forth. Every time they trade—*ca-ching!* Follow? Also I wouldn't exactly say Mathew's *wife* owns Carramoore. In fact, if you told her she owns a trading company she'd probably ask what you've been smoking."

"Mathew owns it. Mathew and Jason?"

"Mathew certainly. Who knows about Jason?"

"You're saying Mathew could've kept that from Jason? His partner?"

"What? Partners all love each other? Ever hear of Martin and Lewis? The Captain & Tennille?"

"Don't tell me. The Captain & Tennille broke up?"

"More like *blew up*. Look, I don't know what I don't know. But I do know what I do know."

"Care to run that by me again?"

"I said there are *several* ways for hedge funds to commit a little hanky-panky, didn't I? Here's one more. Hire your uncle Ralph to be your auditor."

"They hired someone's uncle?"

"Figure of speech. I don't know if the auditor is Mathew's uncle or cousin or idiot nephew. Here's what I do know. Fancy hedge funds like your late husband's—they hire auditors whose offices are in buildings where they make you sign in in the lobby and offer you an Evian when you sit down. I checked out where your husband's auditor's office is—over a Spanish deli in Riverhead. A one-person shop and no one's ever heard of this person."

"Meaning?"

"It's a sham."

"Okay. All this... the trading entity... the sham auditor... it could have been kept from my *husband*?"

"Do you know how their business was split? I'm talking workwise. You know, what the division of labor looked like. Hedge funds usually have a seller and a trader. You know, a glad-hander who sucks up the money and a brain who puts it to work. Was Jason the glad-hander or the brain?"

I pictured Jason making the rounds at a party. Any party. The easy chitchat, the handy jokes, the ready smile. The answer to Jefrey's question was obvious.

"Could Jason have found out? If he didn't know about it, I mean... that Mathew was cheating investors... maybe cheating him?"

"Sure. If he made a phone call or two. That's the hard part—thinking you need to make that call. It's just a failure of imagination."

Imagining that your lifelong partner and best friend was taking you to the cleaners. That's what he meant.

Now I was picturing something else.

Jason and Mathew on the tenth green at 6 a.m. with Mathew about to swing a golf club at my husband's head. About a *lie*, Mathew told the landscaper. Maybe the one Mathew had been telling Jason for years. Or not telling him.

"Thanks," I said. "You have this in writing somewhere?"

"No. All up here." He pointed to his head. "Thinking of putting me on the stand?"

I never told Jefrey why I'd asked him for this little favor. I hadn't needed to—he read the papers like everyone else.

"Not sure you'd be the most credible witness. But thanks anyway." I'd have to find a white-collar forensics guy, but now at least I could tell him what to look for.

"You sure? I'm pretty persuasive."

"Agreed. You persuaded me out of seventy-five hundred dollars." I got up to leave. "You can leave the tip."

CHAPTER FORTY-ONE

I went to a bar.

Not the Dove-Tail Inn's. A place in Sag Harbor where you can order Hungarian goulash served by a Romanian bartender.

I'd been mostly DoorDashing it lately, when I wasn't boiling endless pots of limp spaghetti. I was beginning to feel as if I were quarantined again, ordered into my own personal lockdown. I needed the white noise of other people.

There was a couple at the bar exhibiting all the signs of a first date. She was hanging on his every word even though he seemed to be talking about local zoning ordinances. She kept flipping her hair as if performing some exotic mating ritual.

Wasn't it Thursday, and wasn't Thursday night considered date night?

The kind of date night exclusive to the unattached, as opposed to the marital sort.

You know. Those nights when married couples put aside their day-to-day mundanities and attempt to recapture the ardor of their relationship's beginnings—those first few months when hearts hammer, pulses quicken, and libidos surge and you spend an inordinate amount of time in front of your bedroom mirror trying on different looks—all of them meant to seduce. My college roommate Kim used to say she was looking for a man who'd make her *seat* wet but not her eyes. Eventually it's the eyes' turn. When bills and children and screaming matches and letdowns and regrets and recriminations have begun to do their insidious damage like spreading cracks in a home's foundation. Without constant re-cementing, those houses are sure to topple.

Jason and I had begun having date nights.

Yes, we actually called them that. *Tonight's date night*, we'd slyly whisper.

Ours weren't solely with each other.

A table for three, garçon. Garçon is French, like *ménage* and *trois*. These tables were strictly metaphorical. We silently acknowledged the illicitness of our arrangement by sneaking into each other's homes on a more or less rotating basis, agreeing to an unspoken contract. We would operate under the cover of darkness. We wouldn't kiss and tell.

Our date nights were once or twice a month.

Jason had gone through a brief flirtation with cocaine in his twenties, he'd once confessed to me. A flirtation, not an addiction, he insisted, accomplished by limiting his snorting to one day a week and no more. Which made it acceptably recreational as opposed to criminally addictive.

I'm not sure I could say the same about our get-togethers, which seemed to fall somewhere between recreational and addictive. The principle was the same, I think. If we kept it to twice every month or so, how awful could it be? How guilt inducing? How shameful, really?

Enormously.

The first time she came to our home, another line was crossed.

Before we'd sprawled across other people's beds—the Dove-Tail Inn's and Emma's. Other people's beds were foreign territory and therefore existed in a realm where untoward depravities could conceivably take place. When in Rome you do as the Romans do. Think Caligula.

Our bed was different. It had heretofore been sacrosanct. It was, after all, the marriage bed. Back in my Sunday school days, they'd alluded to it as something holy—where a man and woman joined by God did God's work, which was to be fruitful and multiply. It was off-limits to interlopers.

Only there the interloper was.

I mentioned that looking at her in the Dove-Tail Inn was a little like staring at a mirror image—gazing at her naked body and seeing mine. I was being prideful—one of the seven deadly sins I'd been taught back in Urbana, situated just below adultery and ahead of gluttony, meaning every time we got together I was committing a double exacta of sins. Emma's body was far more perfect than mine. Maybe because I was a working lawyer with stress fractures who couldn't do five-mile runs anymore and she was a nonworking ex-wife who could Peloton to her heart's content. I got to study that body in detail—like taking a seat in the Met and drinking in the Renoir nude that takes up half a wall on the third floor. Renoir liked his women fleshy—times and tastes have changed. Emma was lithe—more like a Degas ballerina. With a ballerina's sinewy muscle, tone, and grace. I could admire her body objectively, at least until the moment I entered the painting myself. Speaking of paintings: once lying in a guilty afterglow, I had an odd flashback to a *Twilight Zone* episode I'd seen as a kid—a Nazi war criminal on the run sought daily refuge at a museum where he'd try to will himself into a painting of a peaceful country glen. On the night his pursuers were close behind him—the Mossad I guess—he broke into the dark museum, stood before the painting, and finally accomplished his goal; when his pursuers entered the room he was nowhere to be seen, though they could hear a soft, almost imperceptible wailing. The camera focused on the space where the country painting hung. The museum had shifted things around during the night and a different painting hung there now: a crucifixion—look closely and you could see the Nazi writhing in perpetual agony.

I related that story to Emma.

"Are you saying you're destined for eternal damnation? Because of ... *this*?"

"It's crossed my mind."

"You don't have to be ashamed," she said. "It's just sex."

"Father McClary would disagree." If he was still alive, he would. He'd been old even then—at least to an eight-year-old girl in a crinoline Communion dress. Older than the curate.

Emma was wrong, of course. It wasn't just sex.

Emma found a kind of solace in Jason and me. Just like she did in her house on Sycamore Lane, which she'd begun referring to as her *fortress*, only lacking a moat and drawbridge. We were a safe haven too.

Let's have another heart-to-heart, she'd whisper after Jason dozed off.

It was about her heart, mostly. She'd tell me things about Neil.

A Prince Charming at first. He'd love-bombed her, had worn out his Black Amex card on red roses and champagne. She didn't much like champagne, but it was the thought that counted. She'd worried about herself back then—that she contained an aimless streak that caused her to drift instead of paddle, and that one day she'd find herself all washed up on some lonely shore. You'd see them at Pierre's in Bridgehampton—women in their early fifties still barhopping with a series of aging Peter Pans. Neil had swept her up in this raging current where all she had to do was let go. There was something comforting about her loss of will, about purposely handing it over to someone else.

He was almost gentle at first. Insistent sometimes, sure, occasionally full of over-the-top bravado, but with her, gentle. The sex was better than good and there was a kind of surrender in that too. Then it changed, of course.

Mostly when she began asserting herself. When being swept away began to feel more like being caught in a riptide that was slowly carrying her out to sea. When it felt like drowning. She began uttering the word *no*, or *I don't think so.* Not about sex— well, sometimes about sex, but mostly about more prosaic things, what he wanted to do on a particular weekend or what his point of view was on some current event, a political candidate, something as simple as the latest Netflix show. If she didn't agree with him, if she offered an alternate opinion, he'd turn increasingly angry, then worse than angry. *The Hulk*, she'd thought the first time it happened. That comic book personification of male rage— except that when Bruce Banner became the Hulk he turned his rage against supervillains, and Neil seemed intent on turning it against her.

A pattern defined itself—the usual pattern with these things, she learned after a while. A blow-up, followed by an apology and a sincere promise to never, ever do it again, followed by the next blow-up.

Lying in bed, Emma whispered the kinds of stories usually annotated by journalists in war-torn nations. The kinds of atrocities that made me reflexively hold her tighter. That's when I could sense it—her need for safety. If you were trying to remain safe, I thought, two protectors were better than one.

My heart was part of these heart-to-hearts. I'd read that when they examined an astronaut who'd spent a solid year in the space station, they discovered his heart had shrunk. Up in space and not subject to the earthbound laws of gravity, it had lost twenty-five percent of its mass. We were lost in space and unbound by earthly conventions as well—only my heart had done the opposite. It had expanded.

You don't have to worry about him anymore, I'd whispered to her one night after she'd revealed something especially hard to listen to.

We'll protect you. I promise.

"Drink?"

A man had sat down beside me. It was date night and he was without one.

"No, thank you," I said. Then: "Sure. Thanks."

"What's your name?" he asked me.

"Emma," I replied.

"Well, nice to meet you, Emma."

"You might want to wait a bit before deciding that."

"What are you telling me? You're not nice?"

"Not particularly."

"I don't believe you. I was taught girls are made of sugar and spice and everything nice."

"And what...you're made of snips and snails and puppy dogs' tails?"

"Ha. Got me there."

"You haven't told me *your* name." The owner of a small home generator business—I'd decided that's how he paid the rent. He wasn't exactly a laborer, but I didn't see him owning a closetful of white-collar shirts. He evidently didn't read the news; then he likely would've known my name.

"Andy" he introduced himself. "You a local?"

"Not to a local."

"Second house, huh?"

"It gets offended when I call it that."

"Hey, you're funny. Anybody ever tell you that?"

"My brother." When I used to inhale the Cheez Whiz right out of the can, then squeeze my cheeks to make it shoot out like yellow Silly String.

"Well, tell your brother he's right on."

"I can't."

"Why not?"

"He's dead."

"Oh geez. I'm sorry. I walked right into that, didn't I."

"Don't worry about it. It was a long time ago."

"Still. I'm sorry."

"Do you install home generators?"

"*Huh?* No. Why?"

"I was thinking of installing one. I thought that's maybe what you did."

"I'm an accountant. CPA."

"Oh."

"Need someone to do your taxes?"

"No. I need someone to do me."

"*What... what did you say? Are you ... umm ... ?*"

"Flirting with you? Yes. I think so. "

"Well now ...". He leaned into me. I could smell some kind of aftershave—not Creed Aventus. Old Spice.

"Hi there," I said.

"You want to um ... go someplace quieter?" he whispered.

"What do you have in mind?"

"Well, how's my house?"

"No. I don't think so."

"Well, where, then? Yours?"

"No."

"Okay, I'm stumped."

"Your car."

"My car? Don't get it. You mean you want to ... ?"

"Yes."

"Well ... ha. Okay. I mean it's been a while since I ... you know."

"Me too."

He owned a Subaru hatchback. I told him to drive it out to the Sag Harbor pier and he parked at the very end. Moonlight made the bay look like rippling silver foil. He reached over and sloppily kissed me, then slipped his hands inside my coat and began fishing.

Later, when he came, he moaned, *Emma, oh, Emma ... Emma ...*

I smiled.

CHAPTER FORTY-TWO

"How would you say the day went?" *Newsday*'s ace and only crime reporter, Chris Policano, asked me on the steps of the Riverhead courthouse a few minutes after we'd adjourned. He was being intentionally sardonic.

"I think we successfully countered their DNA testimony."

"I wasn't talking about the DNA testimony."

I knew what he was talking about. I knew what tomorrow's headline would be too. Tonight's headline, in the rushed online version.

"It's a long trial," I answered.

The state's DNA expert had looked the part.

Nerdy and earnest, with a face I was tempted to call empathic. An empathy that apparently extended all the way to Neil. He'd revealed the touch DNA he found on the gas line almost apologetically, as if it personally pained him to have to implicate the defendant in the crime.

"Was there a match with the DNA you lifted from the severed gas line?" Jordan asked him.

I objected. "It hasn't been established that anyone actually *severed* the gas line, Your Honor—least of all my client. I will put an expert witness on later who will testify that gas line separated from simple stress."

"Sustained."

"I'll rephrase the question. Was there a DNA match found where the gas line was—in the opinion of our expert fire and explosives investigator—purposely *severed*?"

"Yes."

"And whose DNA did it match?"

He nodded toward our table.

"Sorry, we need you to state the actual name for the record. Are you pointing to the defendant?"

"Yes," he said. "Neil Shipman."

"Neil Shipman," Jordan repeated for emphasis. "And what are the odds that this DNA you found—precisely where the gas line in the opinion of our expert witness was purposely cut in two—that it could belong to anyone else?"

"I would put it at one in one billion."

"One in one billion. So what you're saying is for all intents and purposes it's impossible that anyone else besides Neil Shipman could've left that DNA?"

"For all intents and purposes, yes."

The jury seemed to turn their heads to stare at Neil all at once—the way a flock of birds will change direction en masse.

I wasn't going to challenge their expert's testimony—that it wasn't Neil's DNA he'd found on the gas line. Our argument was that Neil's DNA logically belonged on that gas line for a completely non-nefarious reason, a position that would later become clear when I put Len Dawson on the stand. For now, I just wanted to muddy the waters.

"Did you test other areas of the basement?" I began my cross.

"Other areas?"

"Yes. Anything else besides the gas line?"

"No. We were trying to determine if the perpetrator had left any DNA."

"Your Honor, for the record, it has not been established that there even *was* a perpetrator. Given that this witness is an expert in DNA and not an explosives investigator, I would ask this witness to refrain from using that term."

"Sustained." He turned to the witness. "You will not refer to a *perpetrator.*"

"How should I refer to this...person who left their DNA, then?"

"How about *possible* perpetrator? That work for you?"

He nodded.

"We were simply trying to determine if a possible perpetrator had left any DNA."

"Do you ever fix things around your house?"

"*What?*"

"I'm asking if you ever fix things around your home. You know, a leaky faucet, a garden hose, a light bulb?"

"Well, sure. Of course. Now and then."

"If you tested those things for DNA, what would you find?"

"Excuse me...?"

"If you tested that light bulb for DNA, would you find any?"

"Probably."

"Great. And whose DNA would you be likely to find on it?"

"Mine."

"Yours. You'd be likely to find your DNA on that light bulb because, well, you're the one who'd fixed it, correct?"

"Yes."

"So if Neil Shipman went down to *his* basement, to fix *his* gas line, wouldn't you be more than likely to find *his* DNA?"

"I suppose."

"And if Neil Shipman went down to his basement to fix his sprinkler system, you'd be more than likely to find his DNA on that too, correct?"

"Possibly."

"Possibly? It just so happens our DNA expert will later testify that's exactly what he found on the sprinkler system. Neil Shipman's DNA. Does that surprise you?"

"No."

"Why doesn't that surprise you?"

"Well, because, well, I guess because it was his basement—at one time, anyway."

"Right. It was Neil Shipman's basement. So finding his DNA all over what was his basement wouldn't be at all surprising. In fact, it would pretty much be expected?"

"Objection. Counsel is putting words in the witness's mouth."

"I'll rephrase. Would you expect to find Neil Shipman's DNA in what used to be Neil Shipman's basement?"

"Probably."

"Only probably?"

"It would depend on several factors. When the DNA was left there, on what surfaces, in what environmental conditions."

"Fine. How about on that gas line in this particular basement? How long would DNA be able to last on that?"

"Well... given that the basement was enclosed and pretty much protected from the elements, I would say quite a while."

"Quite a while. More than long enough to still be there even months after Neil Shipman had left the home?"

"Very possibly."

"Very possibly. Very, *very* possibly?"

"I guess so. Sure."

"Thank you."

The prosecution had been prepared for this, of course.

Next up. A worker from Grant Heating. I thought I recognized him—I was half sure he'd serviced our temperamental boiler a few winters ago.

"Can you state your name and occupation for the jury, please?"

"Leon Spassky. I work for Grant Heating."

"And what do you do for Grant Heating?"

"I fix boilers, heaters, gas lines. You name it."

"And how long have you been doing that job?"

"Oh... thirty years, I guess."

"Long time. Would you say you're an expert in fixing gas lines?"

"I don't get any complaints."

"Is that a yes, then?"

"Why not. Yes."

"Well, as an expert, what are some of the problems home-owners might expect to have with their gas lines?"

"Well, there are leaks, of course—around the valves and con-nectors and sometimes rips in the line. And there can be block-ages. Mostly from contaminants building up by the access point. You can develop valve issues with contaminants as well. Those are pretty much the basic things to look out for."

"So other than *rips* you say can develop in the line itself—and our expert witness has testified that the damage done to this particular gas line was by purposeful cutting—other than that, all the other problems you mentioned occur by the connectors, valves, or access points. Is that correct?"

"Yes."

"Your Honor, I'd like to enter Exhibit D-2, if I may. This is the schematic drawing of the gas line at 4178 Sycamore Lane."

"Any objection, Counsel?" Moronis asked me.

"No, Your Honor."

Jordan handed the drawing to the witness.

"As I just stated for the jury, this is the schematic drawing of the gas line in the Sycamore Lane house. The valves, connectors, and access point are clearly marked, are they not?"

"Yes."

"We also clearly marked where our expert witness says the gas line was sliced. Do you see that as well?"

"Yes."

"Can you tell the jury how far that particular section of line is from the nearest valve, connector, or access point?"

"Oh ... I'd say maybe twenty feet."

"*Twenty-three* feet, to be exact. Twenty-three feet from the areas of the gas line, which, according to your own expert testi-mony, are the only places problems actually arise. Yes?"

"Yes."

"Okay. So is there any reason you can think of why someone would attempt to *fix* a gas line in that particular section
of the line? Why he'd actually place his hands around the gas
line there? Twenty-three feet away from any valve, connector, or
access point?"

"I can't think of any."

"You can't think of any?"

"No."

"Right. I can't think of any either."

On cross, I asked Spassky if he was an expert in fixing
kitchen mixers.

"Excuse me … ?"

"Are you an expert in fixing kitchen mixers? You know, those
contraptions with blades that people use to mix dough for cakes
and breads?"

"No, I'm not," Leon said, looking confused.

"Yeah. Neither am I. So, Mr. Spassky, if I asked you to fix my
kitchen mixer because I certainly don't how to, where would you
start looking?"

"Looking?"

"Yes. What part of the mixer would you start with—start
tinkering with, and maybe even *place* your hands around?"

He could tell where this was going now; he shifted uncomfortably in his chair.

"I don't know."

"Right. You don't know. Very honest of you. You don't know
because you're an expert in fixing gas lines but not in fixing
kitchen mixers. Correct?"

"Right. I mean, yes."

"So it's entirely possible, then, that if I asked you to fix my
kitchen mixer, you might start with the wrong part, correct? You
might, say, look at the blades instead of the motor or the plug or
some other place where the problem actually was. Right?"

"I suppose."

"And if some DNA expert looked at those blades later, he would most assuredly find your DNA on them. Wouldn't you say?"

"I don't know. I'm not an expert in DNA."

"Right. Just like you're not an expert in kitchen mixers. And just like Neil Shipman is not an expert in gas lines."

"Objection," Jordan stated, but half-heartedly. "Counsel isn't posing a question."

"I'll rephrase. If someone's not an expert in fixing gas lines, isn't it possible—in your expert opinion—they might begin working in the wrong area? If, let's say, they thought they smelled gas one day and decided to go down to the basement and check it out. Isn't it possible they wouldn't know that most leaks happen by connectors and valves and what have you—and start looking on the line itself? Just like if I asked you to fix that kitchen mixer and you checked out the blades instead of the motor?"

"I'm sorry ... not sure what you're asking me."

"You testified that you couldn't think of a reason why anyone would try and fix a gas line twenty-three feet away from the connectors and valves. I'm asking you if someone didn't *know* that most leaks happen in connectors and valves, isn't it possible they might start working in the wrong area of the line?"

He hesitated.

"I don't know. It's possible."

"Yes, quite right. It's possible." I'd gotten him to admit that there might be a logical reason that Neil's DNA was on that line. This was where I should've said *I have no further questions for this witness.*

Right there.

"One more question, Mr. Spassky. In your professional opinion, could the cut in the gas line have been caused from simple *wear and tear ...*?"

Spassky blinked. Coughed into his hand. Looked up at me.

"Not in a million years," he said.

A soft gasp from the jury, followed by spontaneous murmuring from press row, followed by the judge slamming his gavel down and demanding quiet in the court.

The cardinal sin of criminal defense: never, ever, ask a question you don't know the answer to. I'd gone and asked it. The jury had already heard DeMarco state that the gas line had been purposely cut. Now Spassky had confirmed it for them.

I launched into damage control.

"You were called as an expert how to *fix* gas lines. You're not an expert on how to *break* them, correct?" I was purposely ignoring the fact that I'd gone and asked him a question about precisely that topic—how the gas line had been cut.

"I know when a gas line's been sliced," he said.

"That's not what I just asked you," I said. "I asked you if you're an expert on whether a gas line has been purposely damaged or not."

"If you want to fix them, you have to know what you're fixing."

I kept flailing away, trying to undermine his testimony and limit the damage that had been entirely self-inflicted. I mostly failed.

"I have no further questions for this witness," I said, cognizant of the futility that had crept into my voice.

It was several questions too late.

Jordan refrained from a re-direct.

No need.

"Guess you'd like that one back," Jennifer said when we left court.

"Et tu, Brute...?" I'd already had to dodge Chris Policano's questions about today's amateurish blunder. I wasn't in the mood to hear the same from my assistant.

"Just not like you," she said.

"Even the greatest had slipups now and then."

"The *greatest* . . . ? Who's that exactly? Clarence Darrow? Dick 'Racehorse' Haynes? Johnnie Cochran?"

"Muhammad Ali."

Jennifer had been a bit sulky lately. Prone to passive-aggressiveness, or, to be more accurate, aggressive-passivity.

When I asked her for a yellow legal pad the other day, she'd dutifully handed it to me, but dropped it several inches short so I had to reach for it. When I asked if she'd mind bringing me a coffee, it came ten minutes later and was lukewarm. When she questioned why our T&L expenses were so high, I joked they were actually *Travel and Leisure* and she about-faced without so much as a smile. When we got into my Audi and I asked her to fasten her seat belt, not out of concern for her safety but to stop the maddening seat-belt warning that was slowly burrowing into my brain, she took her sweet time.

"What?" I asked her.

"Nothing."

"He's a client. Our job is to defend him. Not marry him."

"Thank God for that."

Jennifer was on Brenda's side in this. She couldn't understand why I'd taken the case. She didn't like being around Neil—a clear occupational hazard given that she had to sit right next to him five days a week.

"It's not like we've had a roster of people up for sainthood up till now, have we?" I said.

"None of them murdered your husband." She blushed. "Sorry." She really did look sorry. "I'll strike that from the record. He makes me uncomfortable, all right?"

"How?"

"How? You're a woman. You know how. The way he leers at me. How's that?"

I hadn't noticed Neil leering. But then, I hadn't been exactly looking for it.

"You want me to talk to him? *No leering.*"

"No. I know I shouldn't even be bringing this up."

"That's okay. You didn't. I did."

"You're absolutely right about our clients—we've had worse. Forget it."

"I'll talk to him."

"I said forget it."

"Sure. Only if you can."

CHAPTER FORTY-THREE

"EXPLOSION LAWYER IMPLODES."
I had to hand it to Chris. All in all, a pretty clever headline. In the online version, he referred to my error as something more commonly seen from junior lawyers on their first court case, not twenty-year veterans charging five hundred dollars an hour.

Fair enough.

I scanned a few other mostly disparaging articles, then turned on my Spotify in an effort to drown out the universal chorus of condemnation.

"Wonderwall" by Oasis.

A memory came flitting back. Jason and I once fought about that song. One of the first clues something was rotten in Denmark: the arguments about nothing.

The song had come on the car radio. *I remember the year it came out,* I said. *Nineteen ninety-three. I was thirteen and wore retainers.*

Nineteen ninety-four, said Jason.

No. Nineteen ninety-three. I'm positive.

You might be positive. But you're wrong.

I'm not wrong. But does it really matter?

I'd use the word positive *about something when you're actually positive about it.*

I am positive.

Yes. Positively wrong.

How about we drop it?

We didn't drop it.

It escalated. Veered into old grudges and unatoned slights, ending up with, of all things, a comment I'd made to his mother in Boca Raton. Something about me asking her if they ever *dredged* the pool in her senior-living community. Fine. I'd meant to say *cleaned*. Blame it on the ever-present layer of suntan oil, body cremes, and other unidentified strata floating on its slightly scummy surface. Jason blamed me. For grievously offending his mother and her choice of senior community.

It was unintentional, I said.

It was snide.

It was four years ago. Haven't we passed the statute of limitations?

Apparently not.

Another time we fought about where I moved his keys.

I'm not joking.

As I was half watching something on TV, he suddenly loomed in front of me like a cop with a newly issued warrant.

Where are they? he demanded.

Where are what?

My keys.

I give up. Where are they?

I'm not joking. I left them on the hall table. Now they're not there.

I didn't touch them.

So the keys decided to get up on their own and take a stroll somewhere.

If you say so.

You moved them.

I would've first had to notice them to move them. I didn't.

They're not there. I put them right on that table.

Yes, I got it. The keys aren't there. I didn't move them.

You're always moving things.

At that moment I felt like moving myself to another room. Anywhere I wasn't being grilled about Jason's fucking keys. I tried laughing it off.

Have you considered the possibility we have a poltergeist?

No, he hadn't considered that possibility. Jason scowled and strode off in search of his elusive keys. FYI—they turned out to be in a pair of sweatpants he'd stuffed in our upstairs hamper.

Another clue: long conversational pauses more common to bad dates.

After *how was your day—fine—how was yours—fine*, conversation would wither on the vine, the silence pressing down like something physical. We'd fill it with snippets of dreaded small talk.

Did you see gas is up to $3.95 a gallon?

I think the Blue Parrot is going out of business.

Strawberries are in season. I'll pick some up tomorrow.

I was ready to ask for the check and insist on going Dutch. I was also tempted to ask Jason something else: *What's wrong here?*

I was too afraid of what his answer would be.

Last but not least: Jason's eyes.

What about them?

People close their eyes during sleep. Sometimes when they're scrounging for a memory. Or if they're tasting something wicked good—the cherry cheesecake at the East Hampton's Palm, to use a prime example.

Sometimes people close their eyes when kissing.

Not Jason.

He was an eyes-wide-open kisser.

Not anymore.

He began closing his eyes when he'd kiss me in bed. Eyes crunched shut.

As if he were seeing someone else.

I thought I knew who.

CHAPTER FORTY-FOUR

It looked like they'd slowed the footage down.

The one from the security camera positioned on the red-brick wall of 4178 Sycamore Lane.

They hadn't, assured the man from Key Security, the company that had installed it along with a second camera they'd positioned over the front door of the house. Hank Larson effected the look of a proud parent showing off his progeny—practically beaming as he told the jury that the camera had a 24.95 frame rate with military-grade night vision, meaning it captured everything day or night in real time. The time clock at the bottom of the frame seemed to confirm that. It hit *10:30 a.m. April 7* just as Neil's matte-black Jaguar slunk past.

This was important to Jordan Sizemore—that the film hadn't been slowed down.

Why was that? Because it meant Neil had slowed down—deliberately decelerated as he passed his ex-house with his ex-wife sitting in it, throwing doubt on our contention that what the camera captured that morning had been just another one of Neil's morning commutes.

Morning commuters listen to the Springsteen Channel or Jeff from Wantagh screaming about the Mets or they chat on their Bluetooth while driving to work, and they manage do all of those things without taking their foot off the gas pedal.

Neil wasn't driving, Jordan was intimating. He was stalking.

Scoping out the would-be murder scene.

The jurors seemed intently focused—following the car from right to left like a movie audience holding their breath before the inevitable carnage. They knew what was coming—there was the alleged murderer passing the house mere minutes before it would blow sky-high with two people in it. All that was missing was an appropriate soundtrack—pulsating music rising in pace and volume along with their collective heartbeats.

Instead they had Hank Larson.

Hank and Jordan.

"So. Mr. Larson, if the camera is recording in real time, that would mean the car was going what... about five miles an hour, tops?"

"Sounds about right," Hank said.

"And can you tell us what the driver of the car, Neil Shipman, is doing in this camera footage?"

"He appears to be looking out the driver's-side window."

"Which means he would've been looking directly at the house, correct?"

"It would appear so."

I objected.

"It's impossible to tell with certainty what Neil was looking at, Your Honor. He could've been looking at a deer or a tulip or a red-tailed chipmunk."

"Overruled. The witness said he *appears* to be looking at the house."

Jordan wasn't done.

Larson wasn't on the stand just to talk about the two security cameras. He was there to confirm the absence of a third one, specifically the absence of any camera situated *behind* the house.

"So the security cameras were set up to see people approaching the house, correct?" Jordan inquired.

"Yes. The one on the front wall could see anyone coming from the street. And the camera over the front door captured anyone coming from the car park. Each camera was equipped with a wide-angle lens so they could cover an area of over 180 degrees."

"But there wasn't a camera facing the back of the house?"

"No."

"So if someone, the defendant, for instance, approached the house from the back, there wouldn't have been any camera set up to capture that? There would be no record of that?"

"Correct."

"Thank you, Mr. Larson. I'm done with the witness."

My cross was short but pointed. I ran the same footage, this time focusing solely on the last section, where the rear of Neil's Jaguar disappeared screen left.

"Mr. Larson, what happens in these last ten frames?"

"What *happens*...?"

"Yes. You spent an awful lot of time focusing on the first eighty-seven frames, didn't you? How the car slowed down to...what did you estimate? Five miles an hour? And what Mr. Shipman appeared to be looking at? I'm asking you what happens in these last ten frames?"

"Well...the car leaves."

"Right. The car leaves. And when it leaves the frame is the car *still* going five miles an hour?"

"Well, that's hard to say..."

"It seemed pretty easy for you say how fast it was going before. I'm asking you how fast it appears to be going here at the end? Just as it's leaving the frame?"

"I don't know...faster, I guess."

"You guess?"

I replayed those last ten frames. Once. Twice. Three times. You could see the car lurch, as if the Jaguar had suddenly gone from prowling to attacking.

"Wouldn't you say, Mr. Larson, that the car appears to be picking up quite a bit of speed as it leaves the frame—as it continues on its way down Sycamore Lane?"

"Again, I can't say exactly how fast the car was going. But yes, it seems to be going faster."

"Does that seem unusual to you? A man driving past his old house—the one he lived in for years—and briefly slowing down before picking up speed again and continuing on his way to work?"

"*Unusual...?*"

"Out of the ordinary? Strange? Inexplicable?"

"I guess not."

"Right. It doesn't seem strange to me either. In fact, I think what *would* be strange is someone passing the house they used to live in—the one filled with all kinds of memories they'd built up over years, and *not* slowing down to take a look. Wouldn't you agree?"

"I don't know."

"You used to live at 476 Myrtle Avenue in Wantagh, Mr. Larson, didn't you? Sorry, I took the liberty of doing a little research."

"Four seventy-six? Sounds right. I mean...it was fifteen years ago."

"Sixteen years ago, to be exact."

"Right, okay. Sixteen."

"Have you ever passed that house in the last sixteen years?"

"Objection, Your Honor." Jordan. "Immaterial. Whether Mr. Larson has ever passed the house he used to live in has absolutely no bearing on this case."

"The state used the witness to comment on the defendant's behavior while driving by his old house. The intimation being that the defendant's behavior was odd and evidenced some sinister intent on his part. I'm entitled to ask this same witness whether that behavior was in fact odd or not."

"I'll allow. Overruled."

"So, Mr. Larson, have you ever driven by your old house in the sixteen years since you moved?"

"Yes."

"Yes. And when you passed it, did you slow down to take a look at it for old time's sake, or did you just zoom on by?"

"I might have slowed down a little."

"You might've, or you did?"

"I probably did."

"Right. So if I asked you again whether it would be unusual if someone slowed down going past their old house, what would you answer?"

"No. It wouldn't be unusual."

"Agreed. It *wouldn't* be unusual if someone slowed down to take a look at their previous home they'd lived in for years. Thank you, Mr. Larson. No further questions."

CHAPTER FORTY-FIVE

'd cleaned out Jason's clothes and sent them off to Goodwill.

I'd rifled through Jason's half of our downstairs bureau and carted three boxes of mostly junk out to the trash cans.

I'd made a clean sweep of the basement, where I found an old baseball card collection, his broken tennis racket, a few discarded golf bags, and other useless residue of a life.

I hadn't cleaned out his upstairs study.

I'd left it alone.

I'm not sure why. Okay, I'm lying.

It involved opening a door to a place I didn't belong. A place I wasn't supposed to enter.

A door is a door is a door is a door, isn't it?

It is.

Unless it's *that* door.

The door I opened expecting to find a mewling cat.

I found Daniel.

I was looking for my brother because I was tired of waiting for him to finish altar practice and I wanted to go home and finish my schoolwork, so I'd walked down the back hall and knocked on the door. When no one answered, I'd opened it.

Opened the door.

When you tell a jury to disregard something they've heard, they can't unhear it.

When you tell yourself to forget something you saw, you can't unsee it.

I know this. I've tried.

Where are Danny's clothes? I thought. What was *Danny doing on the floor?* Why was he making *that sound*, as if he were trying not to *cry* but was? He must be crying because he was *freezing* because he didn't have any clothes on. Why was the curate allowing Danny to *freeze?* Why had he taken Danny's *clothes?* Why was he just standing there and *doing nothing?* Wait, the curate *was* doing something. What? Something with Danny. Something *to* Danny.

Danny looked up at me. I will see that look always. I will see it forever.

Horrified. Embarrassed. *Pleading.* It's the pleading I mostly remember, though.

It's the pleading that remained unanswered.

The curate turned around and stared at me. His face resembled theirs—the faces of the priests who'd watched me walk down the hallway, accusing me of something I hadn't done yet but still might. The curate raised his hand to his face. He put his finger to his lips.

Shhhh…

Tell no one.

Yes, understood. Yes.

No one.

Not my mother or father or even Father McCrary, who was standing at the other end of the hall when Danny and I emerged, both of us probably looking like shell-shocked survivors of some cataclysmic event, Danny's cheeks still with tear tracks like dried-up streambeds, and what did Father McCrary do? What did he do when he saw a crying boy and his stupefied and already guilt-ridden sister emerging from the back office where the curate had been conducting *altar practice?*

He turned away. He walked away.

Like I would.

Turn away and walk away. I didn't go to my mother when we got home and say *Don't send Danny to church anymore.*

Something happened there. Something bad. I didn't know what sex was—does any eight-year-old?—but I knew what crying was. I knew what *pleading* was. I didn't say to my mother *Stop inviting Father McCrary over to Sunday dinners. Over to our house.* Father McCrary and *the curate,* who accompanied him to Sunday dinners now, who requested that Daniel show him his room—all of us sitting at the table waiting for my mom's baked apple pie, and the curate saying how much he'd love to see Danny's room, and Danny turning white and saying he didn't want to, but my father saying *Don't be rude, Daniel, show the curate your room.* And me sitting there saying nothing, nothing at all, not a peep, even though my stomach was being tied in knots and if my mom had offered me a piece of the apple pie right then I would've thrown it up. *Tell,* I thought. *Say something. Speak.* It was like that game Danny and I played where we'd see who could hold their breath the longest, and I'd wait until I was ready to burst. I was holding something in now, something monstrous, and I felt as if I might die. Right there at the dining room table.

The curate and Danny didn't come back for fifteen minutes.

I turned away.

I walked away.

Until the morning I walked into Danny's bedroom and opened a different door and found him hanging by Aunt Josephine's striped tie.

A door is a door is a door is a door.

But there are the doors you're never supposed to walk through.

Ever.

The day I snuck into my husband's study I had to will myself through it.

After all, I snuck, not entered.

He never locked it. When you're a kid you plaster *Keep Out* signs across your bedroom door, but in adulthood *No Trespassing* signs aren't necessary. Boundaries are silently agreed on and generally respected.

I'd been in there a few times before, once to see if the orchid I'd bought him had succumbed to neglect, and once because I thought Jason was actually in there working. These were brief forays that may have lasted a total of two minutes.

This was different.

I knew Jason was at work and unlikely to show. I'd been at work myself but told Jennifer I was heading out to do an errand. I was. The errand being to surreptitiously enter my husband's study and poke around for ... *what?*

Anything.

The study had a large bay window that faced the backyard. I could hear the muffled sound of a mower—it was Freddy's day to do the lawn. For one panicked moment, I thought about closing the blinds, afraid Freddy would spot me and barge into the house to demand an explanation.

It was ludicrous, of course.

That's what suspicion will do to you—manufacture threats that don't actually exist.

But that would ignore the one that did.

My husband had a large mahogany desk—an old-fashioned writer's kind—with more drawers than necessary and a swivel chair that faced a large Apple desktop. He'd left it on.

I purposely ignored it. At first I did. It was like spotting an open shower door in the co-ed bathroom we'd all shared in college, where I'd instinctually avert my eyes out of equal parts respect and embarrassment.

I went for the drawers. No respect for them, apparently. No embarrassment either. The first drawer had reams of paper with Jason and Mathew's hedge fund's logo printed at the top. Financial stuff and clearly of no help to me. In the very back of the drawer were pennies, paper clips, two rubber bands, and an old photo.

Jason and me on our honeymoon in Italy.

I wasn't what I was looking for. It was the exact opposite of what I was looking for. I felt a sudden sharp stab of guilt. For being in this room. For rifling through his drawers.

We were standing on a cliff somewhere on the Amalfi Coast. I remembered. We'd asked a local to snap our picture—he'd suggested a backdrop of the topaz-blue Naples Bay. We were smiling—but not the kind you affect for the camera. The kind that shows up on its own and that you couldn't hide if you tried.

We'd spent that afternoon trattoria hopping.

A glass of Chianti here. A glass of Barolo there. Some bread and oil and freshly caught calamari to soak up the alcohol. The locals were fond of navigating the twisting coast roads at Formula 1 speeds, so it was prudent to drive at least half-sober.

I gently slipped the photo back inside.

The second drawer had a few old golf scorecards. A round of eighty-two. A round of seventy-nine. A newspaper clipping about Jason and Mathew's thriving hedge fund. A broken pen, an empty Rolex watch case, two iPhone chargers. An anniversary card I'd bought Jason several years ago. *Yay, We Still Like Each Other!* it proclaimed on the cover over a stick-figure drawing of a man and wife. On the inside: *You're supposed to give tin for your tenth anniversary, but I went slightly more upscale.* It had accompanied the Rolex I'd bought him. I'd received pearls in return.

I hadn't been looking for the anniversary card just like I hadn't been looking for the honeymoon photo—these signposts of a marriage. I'd been expecting to find the remnants of one.

When I finished scouring the last drawer—an old *National Geographic* and two *Golf Digests*, I turned my attention back to the softly glowing computer screen.

I'd mentally pushed it to the side as off-limits—a decision I'd tabled till later, after I was done reconnoitering the innards of his desk.

Now that screen was beckoning me.

I didn't know if his computer locked automatically. If I'd need a password, and if I did need one, if I'd actually make myself sit there and come up with the virtual plethora of possibilities: birth date, name of first pet, last four digits of social security number, first street address—the kind of answers online banks demand when you're locked out of your account. More often than not, I failed at these security questions, having long forgotten what my first pet's name was—*Fluffy* or was it *Muffy?*—and who knew if I'd had a car whose license plate began with *JK, NK,* or *FU?*

As it turned out, I needn't have worried if Jason locked his computer. When I touched a key—I picked *J* for Jason—a pristine desktop screen suddenly appeared out of the glow, like a soft morning mist blown away by the sun.

There were his various files and apps, lined up as neatly as his suits. It was a fair bet Jason didn't have 10,338 emails still sitting in his Gmail account. His fastidiousness wouldn't have allowed it.

But maybe he wasn't as fastidious about every email.

He wasn't.

There was an email he'd received just last night. Brief, simple, and devastating.

10 a.m. Thursday. Dove-Tail Inn, it said. Signed: *XXXX.*

It was three days before Jason would be murdered.

CHAPTER FORTY-SIX

The girlfriends were on the stand.

There to attest to the fact that they'd seen black-and-blue marks on Emma—and to tell the jury exactly who Emma said put them there. I'd argued *hearsay* back at the prelim. It's not like I'd be allowed to question Emma about what she did or didn't say. She was dead.

Judge Moronis had listened. Judge Moronis had ruled.

Their testimony would be allowed.

First up: Charlene Mitchell.

Emma had mentioned her to me. A friend from the fashion world, back when Emma was busy planning fashion weeks and wearing haute couture. Charlene had interned at *Vogue*—the fashion equivalent of boot camp. She was tough and funny, Emma said.

On the stand she exhibited only one of those attributes.

When she described the marks she'd seen on Emma, her tone was biting. She maintained an expression of grave concern throughout—the kind they probably teach doctors in medical school.

"She had *black-and-blue marks* across her upper arms."

Would you say they were slight marks, or deep ones? Eileen asked.

"*Deep.* I mean, really dark. *Purple* almost. She looked like she'd been hit by a bus."

I objected. Charlene wasn't a doctor—certainly not an expert in what the human body would look like after colliding with a bus.

I was overruled.

Did you ask Emma about those black-and-blue marks? Eileen asked.

"Yes, of course. I asked her if she'd banged into something. If she'd fallen down, had an accident, something like that."

And what did Emma say?

"She told me *Neil* had done it."

Neil Shipman—Eileen repeated his name for emphasis—she told you Mr. Shipman had caused those severe black-and-blue marks on her arms?

"Yes."

Did you ask her *how* Neil Shipman caused those marks?

"She said he'd attacked her. Shoved her up against a wall and gone berserk."

Were you concerned at all on hearing that?

"Of course I was concerned. I mean Emma was my *friend*. I told her that was unacceptable. That she needed to get out of there."

And what did your friend Emma say to that?

"She said she was already seeing a divorce lawyer. It was in the works."

So, would you say Emma was scared of her husband?

"Objection," I interjected. "Witness can't testify as to the mental state of the deceased. How would she know whether Ms. Shipman was feeling scared or not?"

"Sustained."

Did Emma Shipman ever say she was scared of her husband?

"She *alluded* to it."

How did Emma allude to it?

"She said she could tell when Neil was going to explode. She'd leave. Go to another room, lock the door, sometimes she'd leave the house and go for a drive—over to a friend's house, anywhere."

So Emma told you she could sense when Neil Shipman was ready to explode in rage again—maybe get violent with her again—and so she'd take shelter, get away from him."

Another objection. "Counsel is putting words in the witness's mouth. Nowhere in Ms. Mitchell's statement did I hear her use the words *take shelter* or that Neil was going to 'get violent' again."

"Sustained."

I'll rephrase the question. Emma told you she could sense when Neil was ready to explode. And she would leave. Go somewhere Neil Shipman wasn't. Correct?

"Yes."

Why would she do that?

"Why do you think? Because she was afraid of him. Of Neil hurting her."

I was resembling a popinjay—up on my feet to hurl another objection. Emma said she'd sometimes get up and leave the house—she hadn't said why.

Sustained.

It didn't matter.

The jury could still put two and two together. Neil was violent. Emma had run from him.

On cross, I asked her if Emma had ever lied to her.

"What?"

It's a simple question. Did Emma, during all the years of your friendship, ever lie to you?

"No."

No? Not once? Never? She never gave you an excuse why she couldn't, let's say, make some dinner with you, and then you found out—guess what—she'd lied. The excuse she'd given you wasn't true?

"Not that I recall."

So in all the years you two were friends, she never lied about being unable to meet you for a dinner. Okay, fine. What about something more important than meeting you for a dinner?

"I said no. Not that I recall."

So if I asked you about someone Emma began dating back before she met Neil Shipman, a man you yourself once dated—if I asked you if Emma ever lied about dating that person, and if you had to find about it from someone else—what would you say to that?

Charlene turned a slight shade of red, as I silently thanked Joe for digging up that someone else—a woman named Toni who'd been on the outs with Charlene for years and had been all too eager to unload on her.

"I don't remember. If she told me or not."

Really? You don't remember if Emma told you she was dating an ex-boyfriend of yours? A man named Sam Fontana? Wouldn't you remember if your best friend told you she was dating someone you used to care very deeply about? Isn't that the kind of thing that would, I don't know, tend to stick in your mind?

"I told you. I don't remember."

I can put someone on the stand who'll testify that you were very upset about Emma lying to you about Sam Fontana. Who'll testify, in fact, that you two had a big falling-out about it back then. You and Emma. So...you still don't remember if Emma lied to you about dating your ex-boyfriend?

Eileen objected: Emma possibly lying about who she once dated was immaterial.

I'm trying to establish the veracity of Emma's claims to this witness, I told the judge.

Overruled.

I re-posed the question—asked Charlene again if she still wasn't able to recall her friend Emma lying about dating her ex-boyfriend.

"I don't know," Charlene said softly. "Maybe. Possibly."

Possibly. So *maybe* you remember. Fine. Now that we've established Emma lied to you then, can we agree it's possible she could have lied to you on other occasions?

"No."

No? Did you know Emma was seeking an order of protection against her husband at the same time she was fighting for possession of the house at 4178 Sycamore Lane and trying to get the court to increase her support payments?

"I wasn't sure what she was doing exactly as far as her divorce went. The *details*. I only knew what she told me."

Of course. You only knew what she told you. Makes sense. Friends don't tell each other everything. But she did manage to tell you about those black-and-blue marks and who purportedly put them there, right? She made a point of telling you that?

"I *asked* her. And yes, she answered me. Her husband put them there. *Him.*"

Right. We know what Emma told you. Because you, of course, just told us. We also know because you were actually *listed* in a court document filed by her divorce lawyer when he was fighting for those increased support payments and the house on Sycamore Lane. Were you aware you were listed in that court document?

Charlene stared at me the way she must've stared at Emma when she'd discovered her BFF was dating Sam Fontana.

"No. But I wouldn't have minded if I was aware."

Of course. Why would you? And who knows—maybe it just slipped Emma's mind. But now that you know Emma told you Neil had caused those black-and-blue marks on her arms, then promptly listed you as a possible witness in a proceeding where she was trying to get more money out of Neil Shipman—something, by the way, she *neglected* to tell you—do you think it's possible that Emma, well, made it up? That, at the very least, she had a possible ulterior motive for telling you Neil had hurt her? Isn't it possible Emma could've concocted the story about Neil shoving her against a wall because she intended to use your possible testimony as ammunition to get the judge to agree to what she wanted?

"*No.* Never."

Emma had lied to you before, hadn't she? When she was seeing your ex-boyfriend behind your back? Why couldn't she have
been lying about what Neil supposedly did to her?

"Because she wasn't lying. Because she had *marks* on her
arms. I saw them."

Marks that could've been caused by a minor fall or banging
into something. You said so yourself—according to your own
testimony, you asked Emma if she'd fallen down—if she might
have had an accident?

"She didn't have an accident. The only accident was marrying him."

I asked the judge to strike that from the record. The judge
agreed, cautioning Ms. Mitchell to simply answer the question and refrain from sharing her personal opinions about the
defendant.

She looked unchastened.

"She *told* me Neil had done it. I believed her."

Yes, I said. That's what friends are for. I have no further
questions.

CHAPTER FORTY-SEVEN

B ack before the invention of Waze, I'd sometimes pick roads
I'd never driven down before. I would purposely turn left
instead of right. Turn north instead of south. Simply for the challenge of it. The goal being to see if I could deliberately make a
wrong turn and still find my way home.

I'd chosen a road here. I was halfway home.

Did I know another turn was coming?

Not on this particular Saturday night. After all, Saturday
night is the loneliest night of the week. So the song goes.

I could second that.

On work nights, I worked. Often to exhaustion, waking up
surrounded by wrinkled sheets of paper, like homeless men who
feather their park benches with discarded newspaper. Like the
homeless ex-vet Justin Allen Thompson might have done on
freezing November nights before he discovered a hidden room in
a container factory. I tried not to dwell on Justin Allen Thompson.
I mostly succeeded.

Saturday wasn't a work night.

On Saturday nights, I mourned.

Jason and I once took an olfactory tour. No, not a *factory*
tour of the kind politicians are always taking in election years. A
smelling tour. It was given by a seventyish but still spry Catalonian
who lived near the French border and had suffered a rare disease
that briefly stole his sense of smell. This was all pre-COVID. He'd
needed to slowly train his brain to recover it. He'd discovered

that smell was directly hotwired to his emotions and had decided to let other people in on the secret.

I could second that as well—the emotive power of smell. Scent had once brought me to my knees clinging to an old suit of Jason's. It had left me prostrate across our apartment bed.

The tour consisted of tramping around the Cap de Creus, a rocky headland above a rocky sea. And smelling things. No, smelling is too casual a word for what Ernesto had us doing. Jason and I and a couple from Wichita on their honeymoon who kept asking us to take their picture. We *inhaled*. Sprigs of wild rosemary. Of purple lavender. Of vitex—whose leaves local monks liked to swirl into their tea—for the fragrance, Ernesto said—or maybe for their aphrodisiacal properties—men being men, even when the men are monks. The new bride had playfully shoved a handful at her husband.

This house was like an olfactory tour.

In certain nooks and crannies, I could still smell my betrayer.

My housekeeper, Gabby, came once a week to scrub, scrape, and scour, but the smell lingered.

It made the loneliest night of the week lonelier.

I was trying to remember the seven stages of grief. Shock. Denial. Bargaining, sure. Anger, of course. The stage I was refusing to leave, even as cued music was frantically trying to usher me off, stage left.

I was stuck on what the other three stages of grief were—should I Google them or should I not?—when my cell rang.

It was the judge's female clerk, telling me Judge Moronis wanted a meeting tomorrow.

Yes, she knew tomorrow was Sunday. Yes, she knew that was an inconvenience. Sorry, it was important.

As I drove to the empty courthouse the next morning, I tried to recall if I'd ever had a judge's chamber meeting on a Sunday. Yes, once. A prosecutor had suddenly died of a heart attack, and the judge needed to talk about an adjournment to get the new prosecutor up to speed.

An empty courthouse is like an empty theater. If you've ever walked into one of those, you'll understand. It's nearly unrecognizable without its players. My footsteps—normally drowned out by the crush of lawyers and litigants—echoed ominously across the marble floors. I'd forsworn my usual Sunday footwear—a pair of banged-up Converse, for some impressive three-inch heels.

Click. Clack. Click.

When I opened the chamber door, I half expected to find no one there.

No such luck.

Jordan and Eileen were calmly sitting there with identical expressions on their faces. Cat-that-ate-the-canary expressions. If they opened their mouths, yellow feathers would surely come drifting out. They were dressed as if they'd been on their way elsewhere. A golf course in Justin's case. A stroll through Amagansett Square in Eileen's. Maybe the judge's clerk had been unable to locate them last night and they'd been lassoed in this morning. Or maybe they hadn't needed to dress up since they weren't the ones about to be put on the defensive.

That onus would be squarely on the defense counsel.

Moronis was dressed casually as well. A pair of chinos and a blue washed-out polo shirt. Without his robe, without even a tie and button-down shirt, he looked like a retired insurance agent on his way to a Sunday barbecue.

"Counsel." He motioned me to a chair. "Care for some coffee? I made it myself, so I can't vouch for its quality."

I noticed two half-drunk cups sitting by Justin and Eileen. They'd obviously been there a while, which meant they'd been asked to come earlier. Why?

"If we're here to read the Sunday comics, can we start with *Mutt and Jeff*?" I said. No off days for wiseacres.

No one smiled.

"There's been a new development," Moronis said.

"Great. Want to let me in on it?" I was annoyed at having to show up on a Sunday. At Jordan and Eileen having been invited to show up first. At the expressions on their faces. At the two dead canaries.

"We've come into some new evidence," Jordan said.

"We're midtrial," I reminded him. This new evidence wasn't going to be any help to my client. That much was obvious.

"It's *video footage*," the judge said, "involving your client."

"Doing what?"

"Entering the back door of 4178 Sycamore Lane at 10:33 on the morning of April seventh," Jordan said.

You're never supposed to look surprised in front of a judge.

Indignant.

Chagrined.

Outraged.

They're all fine.

"Bullshit. There was no camera in the back of the house. Your own witness testified to that, or did I mishear?"

"Right. There was no camera in the back of the house. No one said anything about up in the air."

"Up in the ...? What are you talking about?"

"A drone," Jordan said. "I'm talking about a drone."

The judge slurped his coffee. Loudly.

"Some filmmaker was apparently out there shooting drone footage that morning. Well ... a wannabe filmmaker, correct?" He looked toward Jordan for confirmation.

"Tim Latham," Jordan said. "An NYU film student doing a school project. He was sending his drone over the neighborhood. It just so happened to pass over the backyard of that house at 10:33 on the morning of April seventh and captured your client walking in the back door. How do we know it was that morning? The footage is time-stamped— day and minute."

I tried to gather myself, but it was like trying to gather a pile of pickup sticks in that game Daniel and I used to play as kids.

"This is *outrageous*, Your Honor." Yes. I'd decided on *outrage*. "Evidence needs to be entered in a timely manner. *Before* trial. This is completely unacceptable. The prosecution could've gotten this months ago."

"As a point of fact, we couldn't have gotten this months ago," Jordan stated calmly. "The kid hadn't even looked at it. The project was apparently nixed. When he read about the trial, he thought the footage might've been taken on the same day as the murder. He decided to look. Maybe he'd captured the actual explosion. He hadn't. He'd captured something more important. A man entering the house from the back. He immediately contacted us. I'm sorry."

It wasn't a professional *sorry*. It's tone was decidedly empathetic. Not *Sorry we're pointing a smoking gun at your head. At your* client's *head*. Here in the judge's chamber on a Sunday morning, Jordan was defying the judge's admonition about compartmentalization and saying *I'm sorry your client killed your husband*.

It knocked me off-kilter—this simple, if unasked-for, kindness. It took me a minute to answer as a furious and blindsided defense attorney and not as the furious and blindsided widow. It was becoming hard to keep them apart.

I recited the book chapter and verse. The one that states evidence needs to be gathered before trial and shared with the defense, that the defense shouldn't be forced to suffer for the prosecution's mistakes about the timely collection of said evidence, that there are rights of due process, all the while reminding the judge of the prejudicial impact late evidence introduced into trial can have on a jury. Call it the buckshot approach—hoping I'd wear Moronis down with the sheer onslaught of objections.

"Okay," Moronis said, looking more irritated than weary. "I expect you'll want a formal hearing on this, then?"

Which meant something else.

He'd already decided he was going to rule against me.

After all, it's not every day someone hands you the Zapruder film. No, better than what Zapruder had captured—it was as if the prosecution had been handed footage of the grassy knoll itself.

"Yes," I said.

There was someone I needed to visit.

CHAPTER FORTY-EIGHT

Joe insisted on coming to the lockup with me. On one condition, I said.

"You can't murder him."

"How about I just beat the shit out of him."

"You'd lose your license."

"I don't care."

"I do. I'd lose mine."

"Wait a minute—are you seriously telling me you're staying with this cocksucker? You're not *withdrawing*? You're going to keep representing this murdering piece of shit?"

"I haven't decided."

"You hate your husband that much?"

"No. I hate being asked if I hate my husband."

"Tell me why."

"Why what?"

"Why you're not asking to recuse yourself as counsel."

"I told you. I owe you a ..."

"A paycheck, got it," he interrupted me. "Tell you what ... fuck the paycheck. I'd prefer an explanation."

"Sorry. You don't get to choose."

"Sure I do. It's called the free enterprise system."

"You're going to quit on me, Joe?"

"This hits a little too close to home. You know ... yours."

"Right. Not yours."

"I don't know if anyone's told you this, but you're supposed to give a shit when someone murders your husband." He shook his head. "I'd really love to know what's going on inside that god-damn head of yours."

"I'm trying to figure out what I'm going to do when they show that videotape to the jury. That's what's going on inside this goddamn head of mine."

"Good luck. Maybe you can try the evil-twin theory."

"He's an only child."

"Then you're fucked. And so's he."

"Sorry, but you're not supposed to be happy about that."

"Sue me."

"I think there are laws about betting against your own team."

"I'm not betting. I'm rooting. And I'm not sure I'm still on the team."

For the moment, Joe remained. When Neil entered the room where *Moronis sucks dick* was still prominently carved into the lone wooden table, Joe glared at him.

"Who's he?" Neil asked.

"Neil … Joe. Joe … Neil. I thought you should see who your thousand a dollars a day is going to."

Joe kept glaring.

"You have a problem?" Neil asked him.

"No. You do."

"Okay," I said, "there's another reason Joe's here. I thought he might be of some help if you decide to lie to my face again."

"*Huh* … ? Who's *lied* to you? I've told you everything."

"With one little exception."

"*What* exception?"

"The part where you said you kept driving down Sycamore Lane that morning. Where you said you never entered the house. You know, those forty-five minutes you couldn't seem to account for."

"I have no idea what you're talking about …"

"Exactly my reaction when I got ambushed in the judge's chamber."

"Ambushed? I'm not following you. Who ambushed you … the judge?"

"More the prosecution."

"What the fuck are you talking about?"

"They have a video of you entering the house at 10:33 that morning," Joe said, emphasizing each word as if he were talking to a foreigner with a limited knowledge of English. He'd been itching to hammer the proverbial nail into Neil's coffin, so he'd made sure to take his time.

"Video … what the fuck … *what* video … ?"

"The one taken by a drone. You know those little things that buzz around in the air. Some of them have cameras."

"I don't know what the hell you're talking about."

"You said that already. You don't know what a drone is? Or the fact that this one captured you walking into the back door of the house twelve minutes before it blew the fuck up?"

"It wasn't me."

"It was you," I said. "I saw it. Unless you have an identical twin. And I believe we've been through your family history already."

Neil slumped. He turned white.

Then red.

Then a combination of both, the colors of an overturned strawberry parfait that's just gone *splat*.

"I saw his car parked there," he offered softly. "I … I just wanted to know who it was."

"Jason's car?"

"The red Corvette. I'd seen it there before."

"And … ?"

"I told you. I wanted to know who it was."

"So you were just curious."

"Yeah."

"And just a little pissed. That too."

"I told you. I was curious."

"You also told me you kept driving down Sycamore Lane that morning. You didn't. Where'd you park the car?"

"In the brush. Down a side road."

"In the brush. So no security cameras could see it."

"So she couldn't see it."

"And then overcome with curiosity, you walked in the back entrance. Where there was no security camera either."

"I didn't want to disturb them."

"How considerate of you. What were you going in there to do...make coffee?"

"I didn't want them to hear me, okay? But I heard *them*. In the living room. *Fucking...*"

I felt a twinge in the center of my chest. *Where your heart is*, a doctor told me when I was seven. Not on the left side where they make you place your hand during the Pledge of Allegiance. Right in the center of your chest.

"That must've made you pretty upset. Your ex-wife having sex a few feet away from you. It flipped a switch, didn't it?"

"Switch...?" he repeated dully, as if unfamiliar with the term.

"Yeah. Switch. The one inside of you. The one the prosecutor will be talking about in court. The one that sent you down into that basement."

"I didn't go into the basement."

"What did you do? Invite them to have that coffee with you?"

"I left."

For a moment, no one said anything.

Then Joe laughed.

"The fuck you did. You went into the house because you wanted to know who your ex-wife was fucking. You caught them in the act. It sent you over the edge. You walked downstairs and you cut the gas line."

"I didn't."

"Bullshit."

"I don't have to sit and take crap from you. I'm paying you *money*."

"Stuff it up your ass. You may need to. I heard they're always low on toilet paper in here."

"I didn't *do* it. I didn't kill them. I didn't, swear to God. Sure, okay, fine, maybe I wanted to. Who wouldn't? Maybe I wanted to beat his fucking brains in. That's why I left. Why I made myself walk out of there. I was afraid that's what I would do."

"Funny," I said. "You've never exhibited much self-restraint before. Four cops had to launch you out of that backyard party. And there's all those love taps you gave your wife. You didn't show much self-control there, did you?"

"I told you. Her lawyer made that up."

"Right. She must have beaten herself up. You walked into that house—saw them having sex—and you went downstairs and you cut the gas line."

"I didn't. I swear. I wouldn't lie to you."

"Just like you didn't lie to me before."

"If I told you I'd gone into that house, what would you have thought?"

"What I'm thinking now. That you killed them. That you sliced that gas line."

"I didn't kill *anyone*."

Someone knocked on the door. Tony on a coffee run. Joe told him thanks but no thanks, we were busy. Tony's footsteps retreated down the hall.

"I need you to believe me," Neil pleaded.

"You need the jury to believe you," I said. "Good luck."

"Wait a minute." He squinted at me. "What is this...? Are you *quitting* on me?"

The power of the pause.

Joe had turned to stare at me with an expression bordering on hopeful. Not Neil. He looked like someone who'd just realized all hope is gone. I hadn't realized this room had a wall clock. All the times I'd been stuck in this room for hours on end but had remained blindly unaware of it. I could hear each tick of its second hand. Like a countdown.

Tick… tick… tick…

"I think we're done here," I said.

CHAPTER FORTY-NINE

N THE SUPERIOR COURT OF SUFFOLK COUNTY.
STATE OF NEW YORK

v.

NEIL SHIPMAN

DEFENDANT.

NOTICE OF SUBSTITUTION OF COUNSEL.

PLEASE SUBSTITUTE (NAME OF COUNSEL) AS COUNSEL FOR NEIL SHIPMAN IN THIS CASE.

ALL FURTHER PLEADINGS, ORDERS, AND NOTICES SHOULD BE SENT TO SUBSTITUTE COUNSEL.

CHAPTER FIFTY

I t's easier getting on a case than getting off one.

It's messy, and judges don't like messy. For one thing, it means a long delay to give new counsel half a chance to succeed. For another, it opens up new opportunities for appeal. Then there's the personal angle. Some judges take a counsel asking to withdraw as a personal affront, as if they're being publicly jilted. Then there are other judges who can't wait to be rid of you.

It all depends.

You need to supply a reason, of course.

That your client lied to you isn't a particularly strong one.

Clients lie all the time. Especially guilty clients.

If they, for example, crept into a house to cut a gas line in order to kill two people and thought it better not to let their lawyer in on it. A judge will likely consider that reasonable under the circumstances. Their general admonition in cases like that? Deal with it.

Of course, this case was a special case.

The peculiar nature of the defendant's representation, was the way Judge Moronis had phrased it back at the arraignment.

In other words, the defendant being represented by the wife of one of his victims.

That was a self-admitted first for Moronis.

The newspapers had noticed the peculiar nature of the defendant's representation too. That's why the case had already made nine front pages and counting.

Harry had been right, by the way. I'd been universally por-
trayed as someone carrying out a kind of twisted personal ven-
detta. Someone angry enough at the alleged victims to hold her
nose and represent their alleged killer. Even when the victim was
her own husband. Of course, the papers—*Newsday* in particular—tended to downplay the *alleged* part of the narrative. It was
too vague and wishy-washy. Newspapers trafficked in declarative
sentences these days. Suppositions were an anachronistic relic
from more innocent times.

Trial watchers on Reddit dissected every new piece of evidence and discussed it with one another. A lot of them ended
up dissecting me; I became accustomed to being torn apart by a
rabid legion of amateur vivisectors on a more or less daily basis.

Maybe this would quell the furor. At least as it pertained to
me.

Regardless. The peculiar nature of my representation gave
me a peculiar out.

I took full advantage.

It's one thing for a lawyer to catch their client in a lie. It's
another for that lie to mean the lawyer is suddenly representing the probable killer of their spouse. That has to be taken into
account. Respect must be paid.

All things being equal, Moronis probably wouldn't have
granted my motion to withdraw. The case was too far along.

Things were unequal in this case. Upside down and borderline incestuous.

Something else helped my motion to withdraw. Neil Shipman
agreeing to it. He could've fought the motion if he'd wanted to—
demanded I stay on as counsel. He didn't.

I think he really *did* need me to believe that he'd walked
out of that house the same way he'd walked into it. Innocent of
everything but violating an unfair restraining order. I'd refused
to give that to him.

Faced with a demonstrably legitimate reason to ask off the case and a surprisingly compliant client, Moronis ruled accordingly.

Withdrawal granted.

Chris Policano all but tripped over me as I made my way out of the courthouse after the judge's ruling.

"A heads-up would've been appreciated," he said.

"I know exactly how you feel."

"Care to elaborate?"

"Yes. But no." My motion to withdraw had spoken in generalities. Not: *I just discovered my client actually walked into the house that morning, so given that he murdered my husband I think I should probably stop representing him.* Just a vague allusion to him withholding critical information from me and an inability under the circumstances to continue representing my client in good faith. What that information *was* would become apparent once new counsel took over—when that counsel would be forced into an evidentiary hearing where Moronis would surely rule against him, and then later have to sit there while blown-up footage from a drone was played over and over again to a jury. Not to mention the press.

I was relieved I wouldn't be the one sitting there.

Case closed.

I shoved my boxes into storage. Asked Jennifer close out the T&L account. *What's* that *stand for again?* she asked me. *Total Loser,* I said.

I took another case a few weeks later—a couple charged with bilking the government out of millions in COVID relief. They'd created fictitious companies, filled out dozens of fraudulent loan applications, and spent the proceeds on cars, houses, and trips to the South of France. They made my embezzler look like a gross amateur.

What happened to Neil?

What you'd expect.

I managed to keep up with the case online. My new routine: finish my day's work on the fraud case, pour myself a glass of Johnnie, then click through the news.

Neil had hired a new defense lawyer. Not just any defense lawyer.

F.U. Recchia.

The *F* was for Frank. Rumor had it he'd made up a new middle name—Urtheil—just so he could carry that belligerent moniker into courtrooms. *F. U.* It fit. If I channeled Muhammad Ali striding into court, Frank channeled Jake LaMotta. No rope-a-dope for him—just charge, flail, and give no quarter. He'd made a name for himself defending some well-known mobsters and getting not a few of them off. He attended their weddings, showed up at their funerals, and defended them as legitimate businessmen being unfairly hounded for their Italian last names.

It was a good choice on Neil's part—a Hail Mary of course, but still. And F.U.? He was inheriting a dead-bang loser, but a loaded dead-bang loser. When he lost, no one would blame him, and he'd get to add another Bentley to his reputed estimable car collection.

The judge had called a monthlong break. Enough time for F.U. to familiarize himself with the basic hopelessness of the case and probably watch the drone footage a few dozen times.

He called me after seeing it for the first time.

"*Pussy*," he addressed me, but, believe it or not, affectionately.

"Retreat is the better part of valor," I answered. "I learned that from my dad—he did a lot of retreating in Vietnam."

"Yeah. We lost that one, didn't we?"

"You're going to lose this one."

"I have not yet begun to fight."

"John Paul Jones?"

"Vinny the Chin Gigante."

"Why'd they call him that?"

"Because *Vincent* sounds like a sissy."

"I was referring to the *Chin*."

"I know. Who knows? It worked."

"He died in prison, didn't he."

"Does it matter where you die? You're dead."

"How can I help you, Frank?"

"Tell me Shipman has a twin brother."

"Sorry. Tried that one. He doesn't."

"Maybe they were separated at birth."

"Maybe you want to take a plea."

"Me? Nah. It doesn't fit my brand."

"Oh, right. F.U."

"F.U. too. You mind telling me why, by the way?"

"Why what?"

"You took the case. I've heard of women scorned, but you just don't strike me that way."

"How do I strike you?"

"Let's say you don't seem like the emotional type."

"What's wrong with a little emotion?"

"A little? Nothing. Representing your husband's killer would take more than a little."

"How can I help you, Frank?"

"Your investigator. I might want to borrow him."

"Good luck. He's not feeling very partial to your client."

"He's partial to money, isn't he?"

"Generally. Not in this case."

"He took yours, didn't he?"

"Until he took a look at that video."

"Yeah. Fucking drones. You can't even take a piss without someone filming it."

"Sure you can. Do it in a bathroom."

"I prefer pissing on someone's leg. Some prosecutors, generally."

"Jordan's no lightweight."

"Sure he is. Or else he'd be sitting where I am."

"Feel free to call Joe. As long as you understand he'll feel free to hang up on you."

"I'm pretty persuasive."

"He's pretty stubborn."

Before we said goodbye, Frank asked me if I'd like to have a drink with him.

"I believe you're married. For the fourth time."

"So…?"

"F.U."

Frank went full throttle at the evidentiary hearing—all conducted out of the jury's view. "F.U. TO THE PROSECUTION" blared the next day's *Newsday* headline.

Frank accused the prosecution of misconduct, malfeasance, and general ineptitude, then ran out of things to accuse them of. None of it worked. However late the evidence was, and Moronis admitted that it was very, *very* late in his ruling several days later, its direct and crucial bearing on the case couldn't be overlooked.

The video footage was allowed into testimony.

It did to Neil's case what Neil did to 4178 Sycamore Lane.

Blew it up.

A still photo from the video took up three-quarters of *Newsday*'s front page. It was taken just before Neil entered the back door. He'd looked up—toward the upstairs bedroom windows perhaps—maybe he'd been wondering if that's where they were. Emma and her lover. It allowed the drone to clearly capture Neil's face. As if the kid—Tim Latham—had asked Neil if he wouldn't mind stopping and posing for him.

"KILLER SHOT," blared *Newsday*, another headline that more or less wrote itself.

When the kid took the stand, F.U. intimated the footage could've been faked. He inquired if Tim ever used Photoshop or other like computer programs. Sometimes, Tim said. These programs are able to seamlessly alter video footage, aren't they? F.U. asked. They can, Tim said. You can even place one video image into another, correct? Sure, the kid reluctantly agreed. F.U. pounced: So how do we know that wasn't done *here*?

As soon as he'd recognized what the drone captured, he'd gone to the authorities, the kid replied. The footage was exactly as he'd shot it.

The jury didn't need to take his word for it.

Jordan called a video expert from the FBI, who confirmed Tim's assertion with the usual expressionless FBI certitude. (Despite the FBI having been exposed for numerous transgressions over the years—domestic spying, virtual blackmailing, and an ingrained racist culture—jurors still acted like Efrem Zimbalist Jr. was up there every time one of them took the stand.)

The trial didn't end there, though it might've.

Jordan trotted out the four friends who swore Neil had threatened to kill Emma. Normally their testimony would've preceded the video footage because good prosecutors like to build up to their stunning climax. The footage was so damning in this case, Jordan was unable to resist showing it to the jury posthaste. It was the right call, but it made the rest of the trial feel distinctly postcoital.

Still, F.U. did a fairly good job undermining the friends' testimony, even if didn't matter anymore.

The most problematic of the bunch was Alex Saunders.

The friend Neil vented to on the fifteenth hole of a golf course. *We'll see how much she wants the house when I blow it the fuck up*—Alex dutifully recited the line verbatim for the jury.

Did Saunders think Neil was seriously threatening to blow up his house? F.U. asked him on cross.

All I know is he was pissed. About losing the house. He wouldn't shut up about it. How she didn't deserve it and how husbands always get screwed in a divorce. I had to listen to eighteen holes' worth of that.

F.U. asked if Saunders had gone to the police.

Well, no, he hadn't.

Why not? If he'd thought Neil was being serious, that he was actually telling Saunders he was planning on blowing up his house—wouldn't the witness have called the police to report it?

That stumped Saunders. Well, in truth, he hadn't thought Neil was being serious *then*, but after the house blew up, he thought, well, he probably had been. Neil said what he was going to do, and then he'd evidently gone and done it.

But at the time Neil said those words to him, F.U. bore in, Saunders hadn't picked up the phone and called the police—he'd picked up his golf clubs and played another three holes. Even grabbed a few Coronas on the nineteenth hole, hadn't he? At the time Neil said those words to him, Saunders believed they were just that. Words. Correct?

Well, yeah, guess so. At the time.

F.U. asked Saunders if he'd ever said he was going to kill someone.

Saunders couldn't be sure about that. Maybe he had.

And had Saunders looked *pissed* when he said it?

Well, again, he wasn't sure if he had said those words. But if he had, then yeah, he supposed he'd probably looked angry.

Just like Neil looked when he was talking about his ex-wife getting the house?

Yeah.

And had Saunders meant it when he said he was going to kill someone?

No.

So how could he sit there and testify that Neil meant it?

Saunders left the stand like a man who'd spent too long at sea and was now searching for his legs.

Sure. F.U. did an admirable job carving Saunders up. It was way too little and way too late. The jury had just seen Neil Shipman entering the back of a house that blew up less than fifteen minutes later with his ex-wife sitting inside it. His ex-wife and her lover.

Jason.

When F.U. finally got around to putting on his case, he was forced to put on Neil.

Normally you don't put murder defendants on the stand. It isn't required and it almost always blows up in your face. The video had changed the calculation. The jury needed to hear from the person they'd seen entering the murder house. They needed to hear an explanation for Neil entering that house other than him wanting to kill his ex-wife and her new lover.

Neil tried his best.

He told the jury pretty much what he'd told Joe and me back in the lockup. That he'd seen the red Corvette, then had to know whom it belonged to. Was just extremely curious to know whom his ex-wife was sleeping with. Yes, he knew he should have kept on driving down Sycamore Lane. He wasn't supposed to enter her house—there was an active restraining order against him. He was wrong to walk in there—he admitted that. But it was just to know whom his ex-wife was hooking up with. He'd heard them in there ... having sex. And then ... well, he'd left.

Why did you leave? F.U. asked him.

Because he was afraid of what he might do. He wanted to leave before he did something he'd regret. That's why.

And what did Neil do once he'd left the house?

He'd continued on his way to work.

Why hadn't Neil simply told the police that?

Because he knew it would've made him look guilty. Like he'd actually killed them. Yes, he was wrong there too. No two ways about it. He shouldn't have lied to the police. He should've told them the truth. But he'd been scared.

F.U. asked him point-blank. Did Neil kill his ex-wife, Emma Shipman, and Jason Mooney? Did he cut that gas line?

No, Neil replied.

The papers dutifully reported Neil's response, but also dutifully reported that Neil resembled a leaking fire hydrant. He was sweating that profusely.

Then it was Jordan's turn.

Why had Neil hidden his car on that side road? he asked. Why had he picked the back entrance, where he knew there was no security camera? If he was simply curious, why didn't he just knock on the front door and announce himself?

Neil had a restraining order against him, he attempted to explain. He wasn't supposed to be there.

Speaking of that restraining order, did Neil care to remind the court why it was there in the first place? Wasn't it because Emma Shipman was literally afraid for her life?

No, Neil sputtered, he'd never hurt her.

We already heard testimony that that's *exactly* what Neil had done. About the black-and-blue marks all over Emma Shipman's body. About Emma confessing to her best friend that they'd been put there by Neil.

It wasn't true, Neil insisted.

So Emma was lying and her best friend was lying and the four friends who testified that Neil threatened to kill Emma Shipman were lying, but Neil Shipman, who already had a restraining order against him for violent behavior against Emma Shipman and who'd lied about entering that house the morning of the murder—he was telling the truth.

Yes, Neil stated.

Jordan threw the jury a can-you-believe-this look.

Then he launched into the DNA evidence.

He asked Neil if he knew how long the gas line was.

Neil didn't know.

Jordan told him. Forty-five feet. Then he asked Neil if he thought it was unusual that Neil's DNA was found in precisely the spot where the line was sliced. In those itty-bitty eight inches. What a remarkable coincidence that was, wasn't it?

Neil stated he'd gone down to look at the gas line when he thought he smelled something.

So why hadn't Neil looked by the connectors? Where someone might reasonably expect a gas line might leak? Why would he go to a section of the gas line twenty-three feet away from any connectors or valves? The very place where the police discovered the line had been neatly sliced.

Neil didn't know that much about gas lines. He hadn't known where to look.

But Neil knew exactly where to *cut*, didn't he?

No, Neil insisted.

Jordan asked Neil what about the sex he'd witnessed.

He hadn't witnessed it, Neil said. He'd *heard* it.

So Neil—who was supposedly dying of curiosity about whom his ex-wife was sleeping with, had decided to not even bother taking a peek? Wasn't that the whole supposed reason Neil had given the jury for walking into the house? To see who it was? Then after catching them in the act, he'd decided to just walk out—did Neil really expect the jury to believe that?

Yes. He'd been afraid of what he might do.

Jordan agreed that Neil had reason to be afraid of what he might do. Because he'd gone and done it. It didn't involve walking out of the house, though. It involved walking down into the basement. And slicing that gas line.

No, Neil insisted.

Seeing them have sex—because Jordan asserted that's exactly what Neil had done, actually *seen* them—had set him off. Made him crazy with jealousy. Sent him into a rage. And that rage had sent him down into that basement. Where he'd cut the gas line, knowing the gas would kill them. One way or another, the gas would finally get rid of the ex-wife who was stealing the house from him and sleeping with someone else, and, added bonus—it would get rid of the person she was sleeping with. And then, and only then, did Neil actually leave the house. Not because he was afraid of what he might do. Because he was afraid of what he'd done. Of being found out. Of being arrested. *Wasn't that so?*

Neil sputtered and denied and sweated.

The cross-examination went on for an entire day and a half. About three tissue boxes' worth.

The defense rested.

Jordan gave a brief closing argument, calmly emphasizing the two linchpins of the state's case—the motive and the video. He started by showing images of before and after—first Neil entering the back door, then pictures of a house in splinters. Three minutes and forty seconds without saying a single word, according to a reporter who'd timed it; it was intentional—Jordan was saying *this* is a case where the evidence speaks for itself. He reminded the jury that when prosecutors lay out a murder case—that so and so entered a house at such and such a time and did such and such a thing—they seldom have a video showing the defendant actually *doing* it. Entering the house just minutes before the murder—cutting a gas line around fifteen minutes before the house would explode—which according to the prosecutor's experts allowed the gas to permeate the house and for the house to become dangerously combustible—only awaiting the fateful match that finally would set it off, with the defendant safely away. A defendant who'd made sure to hide his car, and, if it weren't for an NYU film school student flying his drone over the neighborhood that morning, hide his entrance into the home. Motive. Intent. Evidence. It was all there, Justin intoned. There was a picture of him featured in every online article wearing the same pin-striped suit he'd begun the trial with— entirely calculated, I knew; he wanted to remind the jury of what he'd told them on the first day. He reiterated it here—that they wouldn't need to remember everything. They'd just need to remember Emma Shipman and Jason Mooney. To do right by them. Jordan had every confidence they would.

Frank gave it the full F.U.

The prosecutor had mentioned three things in his little speech, he began—so and so entering a house at such and such a time and doing such and such a thing. He said they had a video showing exactly that. But no such video exists. How could F.U. say that? Because there was no video of the defendant doing that third part—*such and such a thing*. Walking into a basement and slicing a gas line. Committing murder. And guess what, ladies and gentlemen of the jury. The bedrock of our criminal justice system is *innocent until proven guilty*. *Proven*. And the only thing that video proved was that Neil had entered the house. How many ex-husbands seeing a stranger's car in the front yard of their home *wouldn't* be tempted to go into that home and discover whom their wife was sleeping with? Some sure, but *others*? *Most*? Neil simply did what many others would have done. Sure, like Neil stated on the stand, he knows he should've kept driving down Sycamore Lane. He knows he did the wrong thing by entering that house. But then? Neil did the right thing. He walked out. He left. He didn't want to do something he'd regret. And he continued on his way to work—where, as others have testified here, he went through a normal workday. He didn't run. He didn't hide. He didn't buy a plane ticket to Mexico. He went about his normal life. Not the actions of a guilty man, were they? Of a man who'd entered a house and killed two people—including the ex-wife he loved. He reminded the jury they'd put their own gas line expert on the stand who'd testified the line could've split from simple wear and tear. (Recchia had borrowed my mercenary, whom Justin got to admit spent most of his time flying from one trial to another for fees that would make a Hamptonite gag.) Reasonable doubt, ladies and gentlemen, Recchia intoned. And in this case the reasonable doubt was entirely reasonable. Neil Shipman was innocent of this crime. The jury must acquit.

They came back in less than five hours.

Enough time to take a vote and request the drone footage in case it hadn't been damning enough the first time they'd watched it. Then they took another vote. The final one.

Guilty of the first-degree murder of Emma Shipman.

Guilty of the first-degree murder of Jason Mooney.

It was no surprise to anyone who'd even been half following the trial.

Afterward, F.U. rose to laudably indignant heights and gave reporters the usual my-client-is-innocent dissertation, assuring them he was already gearing up for an appeal. I'm sure he was— it'd be hard to resist all those dollar signs.

On the day of the verdict, when I turned on News 12, where a solemn-looking reporter stood on the courtroom steps to reveal the jury's decision, I poured myself a Johnnie Black to silently toast them.

I sipped it slowly, savoring each drop.

I nearly licked the glass clean.

Three months later, I was knee-deep in pretrial motions when Jennifer came into the office and told me Neil had gotten two life sentences without the possibility of parole. To be served concurrently, a small but insignificant kindness from Moronis, since even one life sentence for Neil was a death sentence.

"How do you feel?" Jennifer asked me.

"Really tired," I said. "Can you get me a coffee?"

It came piping hot.

CHAPTER FIFTY-ONE

Summer in the Hamptons.

No parking spots.

Two-hour waits to get into Cittanuova. Two-week waits to get into Nick & Toni's.

Jammed BodyPump classes at Sag Harbor Gym.

Bumper-to-bumper traffic on Montauk Highway.

Empty deli sections in Schiavoni's by 2 p.m.

It made you long for September.

My COVID fraud trial was two weeks away. It would've been seriously cutting into my pool time if I was someone given to lounging in pools. Caron Keough Mooney: obsessive workaholic at your service. On the subject of my name, I was seriously considering reverting back to my maiden one. *Mooney* seemed like a useless appendage—like our tailbones, remnants of when we had actual tails. We can walk away with them tucked between our legs, but only in the metaphorical sense. Introducing myself as *Mooney* was leading to too many lifted brows, unsavory stares, and outright smirks.

I was currently servicing my high-flying couple—who should have high-flown to Madagascar or any other country without an extradition treaty. Their fraud had been stunning in its magnitude, the actual figure they'd accrued by copiously lying to the US government staggering.

I took a break from reading depositions on a day when you might expect I would've kept going. Cloudy, with intermittent rain and a strong wind whipping in from the ocean. The kind of day on which I suffered no self-recriminations for being an obsessive workaholic. I felt like getting some air.

I drove down Scuttle Hole Road, past mansions set far back from the road as if showing you the actual distance between their lives and yours. Yes, I'm using *yours* in the pejorative sense. Feel free to lump me in with the rest of the nouveau riche.

The weeping willows were in full cascade, as if burdened with unimaginable grief. They were in the right place for it.

I parked the car in a mostly empty lot.

Maybe that's why I'd picked today to put down my depositions and make my way down Scuttle Hole Road to here.

No one would be around.

I walked down the familiar path bordered by various-sized gravestones with *beloveds* chiseled across them. Beloved father. Beloved mother. Beloved son or daughter. No matter what these people had been in life, they were all beloved in death. And why not? Isn't death the time to put aside grudges and feuds and even hatreds?

Emma had her gravestone now. A fine pink marble slab consecrating a *beloved daughter*. That would be the final summation of Emma. *Blessed, beloved daughter.* Her mom was still alive, I remembered—she's the one who would've ordered the gravestone and designed the inscription.

Four or five small stones were resting on the top of the gravestone.

I scoured the ground, looking to add to the memorial, but the grass was scrupulously groomed, with no stones in sight. Maybe I could find some at the edge of the willows. When I looked toward the trees, I caught sight of someone, a flash of body half-hidden behind a gnarled trunk. I stepped back in surprise; the person disappeared. Flitted away, like deer do around here. *Now you see me, now you don't.* There are exceptions—some deer will stand their ground and stare defiantly back at you. Whoever had been hiding wasn't like that—defiant.

I felt a small shiver race down my back.

It added to my overall sense of unease. This wasn't the first time I'd felt someone / saw someone tailing me around lately.

I was strolling down Water Mill in search of a tropical smoothie on a recent afternoon when I felt someone's eyes boring directly into my back. Someone who'd been following the trial, I imagined—seeing my picture plastered across a front page or on some amateur website where the reader comments were tinged with acid. When I glanced behind me, nothing out of the ordinary. A normal block of people on a normal Tuesday afternoon doing normal afternoon things. Window-shopping, lolling on benches, waiting for the sole traffic light to change.

Then one night my house alarm went off. We'd never used to set it—Jason and I—it's not like we lived in a crime zone. I'd begun using it after the satellite trucks gathered at my front gates that first night, then routinely set it during the trial. Some of those online commenters liked to comment on what they wished would happen to me. In case you're wondering, it wasn't that I win the lottery. Most of their wishes involved various and imaginative forms of violence being done to my person.

Better to be safe.

I was drifting off to Trevor Noah—in that twilight state between sleep and wakefulness. The alarm jolted me—made me shoot up off the bed. Alarms are designed that way, of course, to be physically grating—their actual sound, I mean—the opposite of a church bell's joyous gonging, for example. An alarm's shriek is designed to well … *alarm* you.

Another grating sound joined it. My home phone was ringing.

"Mrs. Mooney?" a voice inquired.

"Yes."

"We're seeing that your alarm is going off." It was the security company, telling me they'd already dispatched a police car to my home. They asked if perhaps there was an intruder inside it.

"I don't know," I told them. "I don't hear anything,"
"I would sit tight until the police arrive," they advised.
Sit tight. Good idea. I drank the half glass of Johnnie I'd
brought upstairs with me in order to get even tighter.

When the police appeared by my front gate, I buzzed them
through, then went downstairs to open the front door for them.

"We have a report your alarm went off?"

"Yes," I said, thinking that was a blatant statement of the
obvious. The alarm was *still* going off. I'd taken their advice to
not move and hadn't bothered disabling it.

"Mind if we look around?" one of the policeman asked.

"I'd mind if you didn't."

"Okay if we turn it off?" he asked politely.

"Please do."

The house went quiet. The police went snooping.

They did a fifteen-minute search, upstairs and down, then
assured me there was no one in the house. They went to look
around the grounds. After ten minutes or so, one of them peeked
his head into the front door and asked me to step outside.

He led me to where his partner was standing—just outside
a back window where blue hydrangeas abutted the wall. In the
stark floodlights, the blue looked almost metallic.

"Any reason you would've been standing here?" the cop
asked.

"Not unless I was sleepwalking."

"Do you do a lot of sleepwalking?"

"I was joking."

The cop pointed to the ground. The sprinklers kept the
ground soggy in this section of the grounds—the hydrangeas
mostly blocked out the sun. There were two deep footprints there.

"Looks like he was standing here for a while."

"How do you know it's a he?"

"Size eleven, I'm guessing. You know any women with size
eleven shoes?"

"I had a client who played for the WNBA."

"Any reason she'd want to break into your grounds and peek through your back window?"

"None I can think of."

"Then odds are it's a man. Have you had any other break-ins lately?"

"No."

"Any strange incidents?"

"Incidents?"

"I don't know. Nasty emails. Threats."

"Plenty. I'm a defense lawyer."

"So...?"

"Sometimes people don't like who I'm defending."

"Did you report them?"

"No."

"Why not?"

"It'd be a full-time job. I already have one."

"I wouldn't just dismiss them as online crazies, ma'am."

"I'm not. That's why I have an alarm system."

"All right. Look, we searched the entire grounds. Whoever it was, left. Are you okay being alone here? Maybe you want to sleep at a friend's tonight."

I didn't tell him I could count them on one hand these days. My friends. There was Maggie, of course ... then I'd need to think awhile.

"Thank you. I'm fine."

"You sure?"

"Yes. I'll reset the alarm. Promise."

"Okay. Good night."

It wasn't a good night. I stayed up for most of it. I went online and looked at advertisements for dogs. German shepherds. Dobermans. Pit bulls. The kinds of dogs that dissuade intruders from intruding.

I needed to take my mind off things.

The next morning I drove to Sag Hardware and bought a bag of birdseed. Then drove ten minutes down Noyac Road to the Elizabeth A, Morton National Wildlife Refuge. You park in a small car lot and walk two hundred yards down a dirt path shaded by a canopy of trees. And then? You get to have nature literally eating out of your hand. Something about the birds here. Hold your palms out with birdseed and they readily alight on them and peck away. Plovers, flycatchers, nuthatches. For an hour or so you turn into a human birdfeeder. I used to come here with Jason—he grew up scoping out seabirds in Brooklyn's wetlands—a respite from running for his life from future clients of F.U. Recchia.

I find it soothing. If not quite being one with nature, being momentarily aligned with it. The birds feel light as, well, a feather, and yet strangely substantial. Their little clawed legs feel the way metal tweezers do when you pluck your eyebrows. Slightly painful, but in service of a greater good.

One of them—a nuthatch—had just alighted on my palm when it suddenly flew away. The other birds too—the ones arrayed over nearby low-slung branches waiting their turn. They scattered like blown leaves.

The sun dipped under a cloud. A chill permeated the air.

I looked around. The car park had been deserted today. I'd seen no one on the paths. But someone on the path was seeing me. Okay, sure, it was just a feeling, but an intense one. The birds had sensed something, hadn't they? Enough to forsake free birdseed and take flight.

I had the sudden urge to do the same.

I fast-walked back to the car lot. I thought I saw something flitting between the trees on either side of me, or was it simply dancing shadows caused by the half-clouded sun?

"*Hello.*" I stopped. "Is someone there?"

The soft rustling of leaves. The crack of a twig. The far-off gurgle of a stream.

I walked faster. The car lot was just around the bend. My car was still the only one sitting in it.

When I reached it, I didn't see the paper slipped into the windshield until I was back in the front seat buckling my seat belt. It was the way I was *meant* to see it. From inside the car. With the picture directly facing me.

It was taken before it had all gone wrong for him. When he was a fresh recruit perhaps, before Afghanistan and meth and madness.

Justin Allen Thompson.

My passenger door opened and he slid inside and sat there for a while just breathing.

"Hello, Joe," I said. "I didn't know you liked birds."

CHAPTER FIFTY-TWO

"Sometimes I really hate myself," Joe said.

"Any particular part of yourself?" I answered. "For me, it's my nose. Too thin."

"My godawful pessimism. That stupid thing I have where when something turns out the way I want it, I think someone must be playing some kind of trick on me."

"Oh. That."

"Yeah. That. Like this recent case of ours. I wanted you to dump the prick. I wanted the prick to get the death penalty if the death penalty hadn't been abolished but was totally okay with the next-best thing. That's what I wanted."

"Well. You got it."

"Exactly. But me being me, I started questioning why I got what I wanted. I mean, who am I? I don't think the Lord our Father is spending his time looking out for me. He's got better things to do with his time."

"You know what they say. He works in mysterious ways."

"So do you. Like, for instance, why did you take the case in the first place? It was a mystery to me. And I fucking hate mysteries."

"That's why I hire you. You're good at solving them."

"Too good."

He'd been drinking. I could smell the fumes wafting over from his side of the car.

"So me being pessimistic me," he continued, "me saying to myself, okay, you got exactly what you wanted, why aren't you celebrating, why aren't you throwing a goddamn party, what do I go and do?"

"I don't know. Tell me."

"Okay. I start looking at the video again."

"The video of Neil going into the house."

"No. I'd already looked at that a thousand and one times. No. The other video."

It was getting darker outside the car. A leaf skidded across the windshield.

"The other video?"

"Yeah. The one from the front-gate camera. The one that showed the prick's car slinking past the house at 10:30."

"Oh."

"And I'm watching and watching it. And you know how your eye sees things peripherally? I mean it's focused on the prick's car with that pretentious fucking license plate. What was it again? MONYGUY. Can you believe that asshole? I keep watching it slow down and slide past and the prick staring out the window."

Joe bent his head down and peered out the windshield. "It looks like rain."

"Probably so. You were saying."

"I kept looking at his car. Over and over. And then suddenly I started noticing *another* car. Like I said, it must be a kind of peripheral vision. The eye picks up on things. Then the brain has to play catch-up."

"Another car?"

"Yeah. About two cars after our hero left the frame. I don't even know why I played the tape that long. I mean, for what purpose?"

"Because you're Joe."

"Right. Because I'm Joe. And I can't leave well enough alone. I told you ... I hate myself sometimes."

"And this other car?"

"That's the thing. I remembered it. This other car. I did. Down to the license plate."

"From where?"

"A silver Lexus SUV. You remember it too, don't you? The silver Lexus SUV another camera picked up sliding into a container factory at 1 in the morning. The one they said belonged to our client but couldn't ever prove. You remember that car, right?"

"I remember."

"And I think to myself. What are the odds? I mean, what are the chances that in the space of one minute, one minute tops, first one car goes by belonging to a client of ours, and then right behind it, just two cars away, another car goes by that belongs to a *different* client of ours? I mean, I ask you, what are the odds of that ever happening?"

"Long."

"That's what I thought. Long. And then I thought about that client. And how once upon a time, we saved his miserable ass. And how grateful he was. How down-on-his-knees grateful. Not just because we got him off. Because we didn't tell—we kept a miserable secret for this miserable client for all these miserable years. And he said he'd do anything for us. For you. Anything at all. Remember him saying that?"

"Yes."

"Oh, Caron. My darling fucking Caron…" Joe put his head in his hands and wept. "What the fuck did you do?"

CHAPTER FIFTY-THREE

This was the moment it began with my future betrayer.

You've guessed by now, haven't you?

The book sitting on my bedside table is titled *Beyond Betrayal.* Let's title this particular moment Pre-Betrayal.

The moment my betrayer and I were lying breast to breast, in the middle of another heart-to-heart.

Emma and I.

Jason was dozing behind me. It had become routine. The two of us keyed up and restless after sex, Jason sleepy and satiated.

It feels like we're alone, she whispered. *Just the two of us.*

Yes, I whispered back.

And saying that, feeling that, the next step should've seemed obvious. Did you ever play the game Mother, May I? as a kid? In order to touch the person who was it, you needed to be granted permission to take a step forward. A *giant* step or a *baby* step. It was their choice.

That night in bed, it felt like a baby step. Hardly a step at all.

So let's… she whispered.

Let's… let's what? I asked, even though I knew what. Of course I did.

Be alone. Just the two of us… alone. She was staring wide-eyed at me—deep green with flecks of gold scattered like glitter. I could feel her moist breath against my lips—a scent both fragrant and bitter. Me—that's what she smelled of.

All right, I said. *Yes.*

I think I'd known we'd be together the first time I'd ended up facing her instead of my husband in a just-romped-on bed. It's natural, isn't it—you turn toward the source of heat.

It's date night, Jason and I would whisper to each other. But as I slipped on the La Perla underthings Jason had bought me for various Valentine's Days and anniversaries, I knew it wasn't Jason I was dressing for. As I shaved and creamed various body parts, I knew it wasn't him I was preparing them for.

It was date night, but my date wasn't Jason. He'd been relegated to wingman.

It's only sex, she'd said to me when I confessed to feeling guilty, but we both knew it wasn't. Not for her. Not for me.

When did it become, well ... love?

Somewhere, what started out as letting go turned into longing for. A mysterious alchemy resistant to any cool and impartial examination. I won't even attempt it.

I booked a room at the Dove-Tail Inn. It seemed safer than her house or mine.

Maybe it was just dirtier.

It felt different without Jason there. Freer. The only eyes on us were our own. We didn't have to share, so we gorged. We giggled like schoolgirls playing hooky. We moaned like porn stars—the ones I used to watch with Jason.

Afterward, we showered together, taking turns washing each other's hair.

That night in bed, I still smelled her.

Even when you push me away you still cling to me, she'd written in that email to me after a fight. The one I'd discovered after she was gone. The one that caused me to touch myself after reading it. What had we fought about? I remember—she'd stood me up. An afternoon dalliance that wasn't. Something had come up, she told me later.

And the threesomes? They petered out and stopped.

It was too weird. Too excruciating. I'd moved past the point of sharing her. The last time we were together—the three of us—I felt physically nauseous when Jason touched her. I wanted to smack his hand away—throw myself on top of her in order to protect her. Or was it to protect me?

I guess it's run its course, I casually remarked to Jason when he mentioned that it had been a while since we'd seen her.

I was on a different course now.

In the middle of one of those rom-com montages, you know, an infatuated couple strolling on a beach, laughing in a meadow, cavorting in the snow—except we were relegated to a ten-by-twelve bedroom and all our cavorting took place on a bed. I'm talking about that overall sense of giddiness, feeling like you're fourteen years old again and waiting for the phone to ring. About seeing my life separate into two parts: seeing Emma, and the anticipation of seeing Emma.

Sure, there was work. A new client who'd embezzled millions and was going to be a pain. And there was Jason, still Jason, whom I couldn't quite designate the injured party here. Why was that? Maybe because he'd previously been *part* of the party and had simply been shown the door when it was time for him to leave. I was thinking too legalistically—totting up the extenuating circumstances and pronouncing myself not guilty.

One night Jason noticed a bruise on my left breast.

He noticed it because when he reached for me as a clumsy prelude to fucking, I went *ouch*.

What's the matter? he asked. Then he saw what the matter was.

My nightgown had slipped down and revealed a purplish bruise extending over my entire nipple.

Emma had bitten down hard on it that afternoon —a moment that had teetered between pain and pleasure and so was both.

I covered myself and told Jason I'd been clumsy. I'd bumped into a dresser that afternoon.

You bumped your breast into a dresser?

There's a moment when two people know one of them is lying, but they let it lie. Because to confront the lie would be worse.

Jason turned over and went to sleep.

Maybe that was the first clue—his disinclination to confront. Maybe he'd already begun reversing things—both of them had. Turning your average threesome into a French bedroom farce. What if the *third* in a threesome decided to secretly sleep with each of the other two? To carry on separate affairs with lovers who are inextricably entwined? What if the hypotenuse in a lover's triangle went rogue?

I began picking up on other clues—the ones that proclaim your husband is otherwise engaged. The fights about nothing—something I'd said to his mother four years ago, where I had or hadn't moved his keys. The forced conversations, pregnant pauses, looks that drifted off into space. Sex became dutiful instead of playful, like another household chore being checked off the list. *Buy groceries. Clean bathroom. Have sex.* I know—wasn't it the same for me, going through the motions of matrimony? Perhaps I was simply better at it. I'm convinced women are the more natural deceivers—adept at covering up blemishes and imperfections from tweenhood on.

My own deception made me more acutely aware of his.

I started to wonder who. Started to obsess about it. Was it that secretary in his office with an excessive boob job and six-inch heels who never seemed to meet my eyes when I said hello? Or that wife of a friend who served on the board of his cancer foundation—always a touch too intimate with him at parties, where they always seemed to end up in some dark corner?

Emma didn't even make the suspect list at first.

Okay, I'm lying.

Emma was always on the list. I was simply hoping to pin it on someone else, fervently wishing it *was* his secretary or fellow board member or some woman I'd never set eyes on before. Anyone but her.

The reason I became so obsessed about who Jason was sleeping with was because I'd become so obsessed with Emma.

I said this was a hate story.

I know. You thought it was Jason I hated. My deceiving husband.

You were wrong.

The hate was reserved solely for my deceiving lover.

It was Emma's name I etched into the sand for those frigid winter waves to wash away.

It was memories of Emma I dutifully wrote down and recounted for you because according to Chapter 7 of *Beyond Betrayal*, those who take our trust shouldn't be able to take our memories.

It was the *E.S.*, not the *J.M.*, carved into that diamond bracelet that had sent me to my knees.

It was Emma I still smelled in certain nooks and corners of my house.

It was Emma I screamed to alone in my bedroom the night after two people died in a house explosion, even though one of those people was my husband of more than fifteen years.

Yes. I did know it all along. I feared it. I dreaded it. I refused to truly acknowledge it.

Until I searched Jason's emails that day in his office and was forced to.

10 a.m. Thursday. Dove-Tail Inn.

It was signed *XXXX*.

But it was sent by Emma.

CHAPTER FIFTY-FOUR

"They weren't supposed to be there."

The rain had come, first in a fine mist that coated the windshield like morning dew, then in a raging torrent that sent streams of water cascading down from the hood. The trees bent under its onslaught. An antlered stag scampered out of the brush, stared at us, then loped slowly through the car lot.

Joe was slumped over—from the alcohol or from the titanic burden of unwanted knowledge.

"They *were* there," he said.

"Yes. They were there. They were supposed to be somewhere else. At a hotel." I'd fainted to the office floor when I'd heard, honest I had, Joe. I'd sat through the entire funeral as if anesthetized.

"What did you say to your client, Caron? How did you put it? Called him out of the blue and said, hey, remember when you said you'd do anything for me? You know. On account of how we forgot to tell the prosecutors about that guy you burned to death? The one they never found because he was hidden under a trapdoor. But I did. I found him. You know, that little secret we kept to ourselves because you would have been up for murder two instead of arson and juries care more about bodies than buildings. That little solid we did you back then … I've come to collect on it. Is that what you said?"

"Something like that."

Alec Chiapolis had been surprised to hear from me. Not very happy about it. Our conversations were always about what wasn't said, stilted and weighed down by our mutual and unacknowledged guilt. I remembered his face when we'd told him about the buried body Joe had discovered in the charred remains. Like my father's face when the doctor entered the waiting room to tell us my mother had died. The operation to remove her tumor had been a success, they told us. Then it wasn't. My father's face had turned bloodless—it had all rushed to his heart.

Chiapolis never confessed to setting his container factory on fire. He didn't need to. That day, his face confessed to it.

Who do you go to when you want to commit arson?

An arsonist.

No one will be there, I told him. An empty house. I want you to burn it to the ground. You owe me. In the end, he must've improvised—figured a gas explosion would be just as effective as setting it on fire, and give him enough time to make it out of there alive.

"Didn't he notice the cars?" Joe asked. "Just asking. You tell him no one's supposed to be there but there are *two cars* parked out in front. That didn't make him think maybe you were wrong about that? Make him pack up and leave?"

"He didn't go through the front gate. Maybe he wasn't peeping like Neil did when he passed the house. Or he saw the cars there and thought people with houses that big have a car for every day of the week. I don't know."

"You haven't asked him? You aren't the least bit curious? You know—given he murdered your husband?"

"I thought it better if we didn't speak afterward. For obvious reasons."

Obvious to me. Not to Chiapolis. Not after he picked up the morning newspaper and read that he'd killed two people. He'd tried to contact me by normal means. Phone calls. Emails. Then when I didn't answer him, by abnormal means. Calling in a fire at my house and standing in full view of my front-gate camera with a sign in his hands. *FIRE.* Chasing me down an empty winter beach and trying to smash my car window in—making sure to leave another message before he left.

Why?

"And when he walked in the house? He didn't *hear* them? Like Neil did? Like Neil heard them in there?"

"Maybe they hadn't reached the groaning part yet. Maybe they were just staring into each other's eyes."

Joe was slumped further into his seat. He peeked sideways at me, as if afraid of what he might see—a stolid face with no expression—then turned back and stared through the windshield.

"You were that fucking angry."

"I was that fucking angry." I wasn't going to elaborate on who I was that fucking angry at. Not here. Not now. Not to Joe.

"To kill them."

"To burn her house down. They weren't going to die if they weren't there."

The house was her refuge. Her haven. An easy target for a love-spurned woman with payback on her mind. Revenge is supposed to be served cold, but I'd gone the other way. To a full-out conflagration, to a beach bonfire the Hamptons would never forget. Neither would Emma.

How could you do that me? How could destroy what we had? How?

"But they *were* there. Plans change. People say they're going to go someplace, then they don't. Things come up. People change their minds. For chrissakes, Caron, that didn't occur to you?"

"I wasn't my most rational self at the time."

"Rational enough to set it all up. To call Chiapolis. To send him out to that house."

"Yes."

"They must have just missed each other. Think about that. Neil and Chiapolis. Neil must've left just like he said he did—walked out of the house. Then Chiapolis walked in. It's a miracle they didn't bump into each other."

"You've stopped calling him the *prick*. Neil, I mean."

"He's serving a life sentence for something he didn't do. Makes him a little less prick-like in my eyes. Speaking of which. Does that bother you at all? Wait, don't answer. I know."

"Know what?"

There are some things Joe didn't know. The myriad things Emma had told me Neil had done to her. The brutal attacks. His coiled, emotional sadism. It made what I did to him easier. Not easy, no.

Easier.

"I took a look at your expense sheet. I asked Jennifer. Don't be mad at her—she was starting to seriously worry your roll call of embezzlers were starting to rub off on you. There were charges that made no sense. Unless you were paying someone off you didn't want her to know about. Then, sure, it made perfect sense."

"I didn't know you'd added *auditor* to your business card. It used to just say *investigator*."

"I have to admit. You were cute about it. *T&L*. Every time Jennifer asked you what it stood for, you gave her a different answer. What did you tell her? *Total Liability. Total Loser. Travel and Leisure*. Only they weren't the right answer. You managed to leave that one out."

"It must've slipped my mind."

"Not mine. T&L. *Tim Latham*. Cute."

"Oh, right. Tim."

"When did he come to you, Caron?"

"Before he went to them."

When I pictured the average NYU film student, I pictured someone intelligent and artistic with a budding social conscience. I obviously don't spend enough time on the internet. I haven't witnessed the moral rot therein. Tim Latham was narcissistic, scheming, and greedy. In other words, a real shit. He'd come to me first, he'd assured me. To sell me the drone footage. Or he threatened to take it to the authorities. He was sure I'd pay him, then bury it. I did pay him. One hundred thousand dollars. But not to bury it—to make sure he *would* take it to the authorities. He was surprised about that—couldn't figure out my angle. Doesn't everyone have one? Just doing the right thing, I told him. And making sure he did too.

"You made sure it got to Jordan," Joe said.

"As sure as I could be."

"To bury Neil. To slam that cell door shut. And leave you free and clear. That's why you took the case. You wanted to make sure Neil lost. "

"Free, yes. Clear, I don't know about that."

"Guilty conscience?"

"A holdover from childhood."

It's not easy presenting a sham defense. To look proficient enough to avoid an appeal for incompetent legal representation, but be deficient enough to lose. It wasn't an accident I'd asked that man from Grant Heating if the gas line could've separated on its own. It just appeared that way. Like a momentary stumble from the usually meticulously prepared Caron Mooney. *It's not like you*, Jennifer told me afterward. But it was like me. I was meticulously preparing Neil to lose. I knew what Spassky's answer would be; I knew it wouldn't be good for my client. I was a boxer taking a dive. I had to keep punching but not enough to send Sizemore to the canvas. It was a delicate dance. Let's call it a tango—a dance about death and betrayal. Then Tim Latham showed up on my doorstep with some drone footage and made everything easy.

"What are you going to do, Joe?"

"Cry."

"And after you stop crying?"

"Cry some more."

"And then ... ?"

"Not sure. It's like there's a cupboard I keep locked tight. In the cupboard is Justin Allen Thompson. And that kid I railroaded back on Long Island for his parents' death. The detective who lied to him—who told him his dad had woken up and fingered him—that was me. You know, the very same detective who had a side thing going with the dead man's business partner—the one who took off to California the next day. Think I forgot to mention that to you. Sorry. I told you—I keep the cupboard locked tight. IA made me their bitch boy after that—they knew, and they made me a fucking pariah. I'm getting sidetracked. This cupboard. The question is … is there room for more? Can I squeeze a few more in or can't I? Neil and Emma and Jason. And *you*. Can I squeeze you in? Will you all fit in there?"

"Sorry, Joe. I can't answer that for you."

"No. You can't."

"The rain's stopping," I said. A sliver of pale yellow was emerging through the slate-gray clouds like a crack in the darkness, promising the hint of something better on the other side.

"Time to go home," Joe said.

CHAPTER FIFTY-FIVE

This is a hate story.

And a love story. And a murder story.

And stories are meant to be told. Or they remain secrets.

I've told it.

Father McClary patiently listened to it. Every single part of it.

It was time to go home, Joe said, and so I did.

Back to Urbana, where I walked into Our Lady of Sorrows Church and found Father McCrary still there. Old as Methuselah but still getting around under his own power and willing to sit on the other side of the dark latticed screen from me.

A confession is not just an unburdening. It's a reconciliation between the sinner and the church they've wounded with their sins. It's a plea for forgiveness.

The unburdening took time. After all, there was so much to unburden.

I'd killed my husband. Jason Mooney. I'd loved him once and I'd married him on a sparkling spring Saturday where I said *I do*, even though I felt like saying *I must*. That's what it felt like—that if I didn't marry him on that particular day the world would be forever misaligned and my chance at happiness forever gone. That's how the magic happens sometimes. You agree to a lunch at a crappy Chinese restaurant to appease your friend and you find your husband. *My other half*, the expression goes, but in truth, he was my other two-thirds. Socially voracious as opposed to socially awkward. Optimistic to a fault as opposed to pessimistic on principle. When a friend of ours told Jason that her sixty-two-years-married parents had died on the same day, Jason remarked how touching that was, while I asked if it was a murder-suicide. Opposites attract, I'd tell people—just look at us, the alcoholic and the workaholic. I was kidding, of course. Jason didn't have a drinking problem—it's just when I pictured him, it was always with a drink held loosely in his right hand while chatting up some fellow partygoer. I was more likely to be found with an open iPhone in mine, scanning whatever depositions and motions couldn't wait till later.

Jason had bought me an electronic picture frame for one of our anniversaries, in which he'd downloaded every trip we'd ever taken. I'd look up and see the two of us staring out from a verandah in Taormina, a tree-lined boulevard in Paris, an endless beach in the Grenadines. We were generally smiling.

Until we stopped smiling.

Until Jason began chatting up a certain partygoer at Maggie's. *Emma…?* Jason had introduced her as I sauntered over to reclaim him. *Shipman*, she'd finished.

And then she'd claimed me.

I'd felt a jolt when I saw them together that day. I'd chalked it up to the frozen margarita but I was wrong. Something was *un*freezing in me that moment, even if I'd remained resolutely unaware of it. Let's call it my midwestern chill. What a rock-ribbed Illinois childhood shaped by endless church Sundays and one unfathomable Wednesday afternoon will do to you. And a dead brother you helped murder as surely as if you'd knotted Aunt Josephine's tie around his neck. The curate said tell no one, and I'd obeyed. I'd kept his unconscionable secret and ignored my brother's unendurable pain. There's a stone statue outside Our Lady of Sorrows Church I'd passed on the way in—had probably passed a million times as a kid. Mary wearing a shroud of grief for her dead son—that was her sorrow. I wore a shroud of guilt for Daniel—that was mine. I couldn't remove this shroud; I couldn't crawl out from underneath it. Perhaps I could've expiated it by joining the Innocence Project or one of the other myriad organizations dedicated to getting the wrongfully convicted out of jail. I'd gone the other way—I would save the guilty instead. I would unburden them of secrets and hold them tight—the way I'd held my own secret in for decades. We're not supposed to be judged by the sins of our fathers, but what if it's the sin of a father, a father and his curate, and I'd pay tribute to that instead?

My parents used to take me to a nature preserve outside Urbana that warned everyone to *stay on the path*. I'd obeyed that admonition as strictly as I'd obeyed the curate's. Who knew what would happen if you went off the path? Poisonous snakes might be lurking there, the kind God warned Adam and Eve about.

Jason and I went down a path together. Jason and I and Emma. We went down the path together and then we went down it separately. In the end, my fears turned out to be entirely justified.

There was a snake lurking there.

It's pathetic to fall so hard in your forties. In love. In lust. Does it matter what it is, when the only thing that matters is when you're seeing her? When and where and for how long? If love is a sickness, then mine turned terminal.

I'd murdered my brother, and then I'd murdered them.

They will be my cross to bear. All of them. Jason and Emma and Daniel, and Neil too, staring at a bare prison wall for the next forty years or so.

That expression—*cross to bear*—has become so ubiquitous, so casually thrown around, that it's almost lost its meaning. The stained-glass window in Our Lady of Sorrows Church is there to remind you: Jesus, hands bound, crown of thorns drawing blood, straining under the weight of a massive wooden cross he will carry all the way to Golgotha.

I will carry mine to Cedar Lawn.

I don't know what Joe will do. If he'll open up that cupboard and make room for four more ghosts, or if he'll drive down to the place he used to work in and unburden himself of them. Much like I'm doing here.

There's a difference, of course. Father McCrary can't tell.

Because he's a priest. And because he has his own grievous sins to atone for.

Before I left the confessional, I told him there was something else I needed to unburden.

I knew about my brother, Father. I knew what the curate was doing to him. In the back office. In the bedroom in our home when we all sat there eating dinner. I did nothing. I said nothing. And because I did that, I condemned him. I killed him. And the thing is, you knew what the curate was doing to my brother too. When we walked out of the back of the church that day and my brother was half-hysterical, you knew why. You knew what he had to be doing in my brother's room while you sat there waiting for another slice of my mom's apple pie. You knew and you let it happen. And then I had to sit and watch you give the eulogy at his funeral. Listen to you tell us God wanted another angel. Instead of telling us that the curate just wanted another altar boy. I wanted to stand up and scream stop. I didn't. I kept silent. I've kept silent all these years.

Silence greeted me from the other side of the latticed screen.

I told Father McCrary this would be my last confession.

Then I walked out.

Soon enough, I'll know what Joe's decided. One day I'll get an unexpected visit from Detective Solano at my office, or I won't.

I would like to say this is a redemption story.

There is no redemption, of course.

There is just this world and the choices we make in it.

Then we live with them.

ABOUT THE AUTHOR

"James Barry" is the pseudonym of a *New York Times* best-selling author of numerous crime novels and thrillers, several of which have been adapted into films.

Made in the USA
Monee, IL
20 February 2023

28307079R00204